THE CURIOUS CASE OF MARY ANN

by JENN THORSON

Waterhouse Press

PITTSBURGH, PENNSYLVANIA

Published by Waterhouse Press. Pittsburgh, Pennsylvania, U.S.A.

ISBN: 978-0-9838045-8-1

Cover design by Dave White.

Cover photography by Ben Yokitis.

Printed in the United States of America

To all the dreamers, gleeful weirdos and outsiders.
You matter.

Very soon the Rabbit noticed Alice, as she went hunting about, and called out to her in an angry tone, "Why, Mary Ann, what are you doing out here? Run home this moment, and fetch me a pair of gloves and a fan! Quick, now!" And Alice was so much frightened that she ran off at once in the direction it pointed to, without trying to explain the mistake it had made.

"He took me for his housemaid!" she said to herself as she ran. "How surprised he'll be when he finds out who I am!"

Lewis Carroll, *Alice in Wonderland* (1865)

Jabberwocky

'Twas brillig, and the slithy toves
Did gyre and gimble in the wabe;
All mimsy were the borogoves,
And the mome raths outgrabe.

"Beware the Jabberwock, my son!
The jaws that bite, the claws that catch!
Beware the Jubjub bird, and shun
The frumious Bandersnatch!"

He took his vorpal sword in hand:
Long time the manxome foe he sought—
So rested he by the Tumtum tree,
And stood awhile in thought.

And as in uffish thought he stood,
The Jabberwock, with eyes of flame,
Came whiffling through the tulgey wood,
And burbled as it came!

One, two! One, two! and through and through
The vorpal blade went snicker-snack!
He left it dead, and with its head
He went galumphing back.

"And hast thou slain the Jabberwock?
Come to my arms, my beamish boy!
O frabjous day! Callooh! Callay!"
He chortled in his joy.

'Twas brillig, and the slithy toves
Did gyre and gimble in the wabe;
All mimsy were the borogoves,
And the mome raths outgrabe.

Lewis Carroll, *Through the Looking-Glass,
and What Alice Found There* (1871)

ACKNOWLEDGMENTS

Wonderland and Looking-Glass Land, as created by Lewis Carroll, have always held a dear, rather obsessive place in my heart. The dream-like qualities, the whimsy, the juxtaposition of color and darkness, humor and harshness, truth and madness have captivated my imagination since childhood and the concepts have grown along with me. So when the idea for *Mary Ann* sprung up, I knew it was a book I had to write.

I'd like to thank the folks who have welcomed this project and boldly joined me for this tumble down the rabbit hole, offering their kind support and very good advice along the way.

Thanks to my cousin Diana Vencius for lending me her perspective and listening ear before *Mary Ann* had even made it to the paper. It meant a lot.

Thank you to my beta readers for providing invaluable feedback, catching the things my eyes could no longer see and helping to make me a better writer.

Many thanks to my cover designer Dave White and photographer Ben Yokitis for their time and talents. I presented them with this collection of mad objects and they transformed them. Hearty (heart-y?) huzzahs go their way.

I would also like to thank Jill Henkel for helping to name my walrus when my walrus-naming skills were not up-to-snuff. I firmly believe everyone should have a friend who's a talented walrus-namer. It enhances life considerably.

1

How many Unbirthdays was it for Queen Valentina so far this year? Three? Four? Mary Ann Carpenter wondered, as she wound along the path to her father's house. *At least three*, she tallied, the last one still quite vivid in her mind. Oh, the *fuss* Mr. Rabbit made about having his uniform just so, and the gift presented thus and his trumpet polished to a dazzling shine. As if Mary Ann would ever fail him in any of those tasks. As if she had some long history of negligence—of slatternly methods—and hadn't been running the household silently, smoothly, all along.

And now the fussing had begun anew. Mary Ann only prayed the Queen's latest gift would live up to expectations. The young housemaid had truly, if not also literally, stuck her neck out for this.

She wasn't even sure how it happened. Her employer had been working himself into the usual tizzy over royal gift-giving, and in a mad moment of actual vocalization Mary Ann heard herself say ... *words*: "My father could craft the piece for the Queen's special day."

She'd baffled herself with the very sound of it. This was a land where outstretched necks got the quick, jolly chop of the executioner's axe should Her Majesty not be properly delighted.

Now she wished she hadn't spoken at all.

Mary Ann's father was, of course, not only a talented contractor but also the finest woodworker around. He put real passion into the items he carved, and Mr. Rabbit had commissioned a piece that promised to astound. The sketches alone had been enough to send the furry gentleman's gloved hands a-fluttering, whiskers quivering in anticipation, sweet words predicting a future of royal favoritism, rich comfort and bright possibility.

It was with these thoughts that Mary Ann took the path from Neath back to Turvy, the land of her birth. When heading through Turvy, it was preferable not to think about the journey itself, or you'd never get where you were going. The topography was notoriously obstinate. It was better if you snuck up on your destination at a yawning saunter rather than have any direct sort of aim. In fact, it was best you wish to never arrive at all. It was the only sure way of getting there on time.

Mary Ann pushed back the low hanging bough of a tree—"I beg your pardon!" snapped the foliage, for the scenery did enjoy its umbrage—and she considered how her reluctance to meet with her father was a real asset to this sort of travel. It wasn't that she dreaded or feared or even didn't *like* Rowan Carpenter. It was hard to dislike someone you didn't know (though she understood some people managed it quite well). It was the simple not-knowing that made these family reunions so very, very awkward.

She found it funny that she could picture every curve, every line of her father's artistic style. But as for his views on the things that mattered (croquet and cabbages, tea trays and twinkling, or any of a hundred other subjects that drew people close), he stood a cipher. The only thing she knew for certain were his thoughts on child-rearing and they were this:

Children should be seen and not heard.
Also not seen.

It was a simple philosophy and more workable than one might expect. The thing was accomplished by making the child as useful as possible, as soon as possible, in someone else's paying household far, far away.

As Mary Ann ducked under a giant mushroom and searched for the connecting path through the woods, she admitted that, on the whole, Rowan Carpenter's approach had worked out sufficiently for both parties. Yes, there were adjustments to be made, sacrifices to endure. But if she hadn't found herself far away in that first useful position at the age of ten, Mary Ann Carpenter might never have become the person she was today.

She might never have discovered her powers of invisibility.

Ah, she remembered that first time it happened like it was a quarter past two, which it had been. She was serving as a lesser maid in Beatrice, the Duchess of Additch's household, a domicile of particular bustle and unconventional culinary habits. She could still picture the Duchess there, stuffed in the large armchair, squinting at the sampler that would ultimately bear her favorite morals. This woman was simply *determined* to have herself a hobby and had landed on needlework as a noble endeavor. Unfortunately, she was hopeless at needlepoint and even worse at threading the needle. After two weeks' effort, all she had to show for it was a sore thumb and a large and crooked red "T" in the far corner. It took so long to get there, she'd quite forgotten the phrase she'd planned to stitch in the first place.

"'T,'" she mused, drawing a finger over the thread, frowning. "What starts with 'T'?"

"Six o'clock starts with tea," shouted Cookie Mills, from the kitchen. "Should I prepare sandwiches, as well, Your Grace? I could do you some nice chili pepper ones, in a lovely peppercorn spread, with a tablespoon of beautiful pepper and—"

"Tablets! Tablets start with 'T,'" exclaimed the Duchess, a sudden light shining in her dark eyes. "I shall write down all my best, most clever aphorisms on pen and paper before I stitch them. And the moral of that is: don't count your letters before they're stacked. Or: a stitch in line takes time. Now where is that pen and paper?"

At the mere mention, Mary Ann flew across the room to a little desk and snatched up paper, pen and ink, setting them down on the table before her.

But the Duchess hadn't noticed. She was too busy looking under the seat cushions and peering into the flower vase. The Duchess even searched under the cat, much to the cat's splay-legged dismay. "Where *is* that pen and paper? Do we not have any? Are we completely out?" She shot a dark look toward the kitchen and raised her voice, projecting it Cookie-ward. "That soup last night was suspect. A bit inky, if you ask me. And far too pulpy and..." Then her eyes fell upon the table's contents, and the cat was tossed by the wayside. "Oh! Never mind! Here they are." As she said this, she looked hard at Mary Ann, standing there before the table.

No, that wasn't precisely true. What she did was look *through* Mary Ann, across the room and out the window and down the lane and across the field, like the girl was nothing more than a momentary vapor. "*I* found them! Right where I left them. And the moral of that is..."

Invisible. Mary Ann had felt it happen.

After that, it happened regularly. With every passing day, she noticed how she could be in the room, directly assisting with something, yet hear her employers divulge the most intimate secrets around her. She overheard all the neighborhood gossip. She saw all the ugly habits of grooming and not-grooming, boredom and binges. It would be powerful information, if Mary Ann ever cared to divulge any of it. But that would require her to share, and words felt so wasted when they were flung into the chill of the air. It was so much better to keep them to one's self, where they could gather together, still treasured, safe and warm.

"It's impressive how you do it," the cat, whose name was Chester, told her one day, after a particularly long session of invisibility. "I especially like how it comes over you all at once. I've never managed that myself. I'm always leaving bits of me behind, then gathering them up again. Can't resist. I always feel like something exciting will happen the moment I completely vanish. You must teach me."

But Mary Ann just smiled and stroked the cat on his soft, striped head. How could she explain that one could not teach what one did not understand?

And how long was it that she stayed in the Duchess' service? She considered this as she ventured down the path to her childhood home.

Four years, she decided it was. Four years, at an eighty percent invisibility rate, until she took the position with Mr. Warren Rabbit. Or, rather, until the position took her.

That was such a curious day; she'd been simply walking past his house from the market when the gentleman came scrambling out in a panic, pleading with her to help him find his reading spectacles. The whole thing smelled of desperation. Well, the task was done soon enough as she pointed them out there, on the top of his head. It was at that moment he decided what he really needed was a solid, clever housemaid on his staff. "Someone to fetch, find and point out spectacles, as necessary," he said. "I notice you happen to be in the garb of one such creature. Could it be? Are you … a housemaid, my dear?"

She indicated she was and he offered her the position on the spot.

As Mr. Rabbit's home was pretty and quaint and — most refreshing of all — it resided outside of a cloud of seasonings, Mary Ann agreed. When you were invisible, it was easy enough to leave a position. People only started asking questions when the chores didn't mysteriously get done.

Mary Ann was just wondering how long it had taken before the Duchess even realized she'd gone, when she snapped back to the present and noticed her father's domicile was but a few steps before her. *Lose yourself in thought, find yourself where you need to be.* And she took the path along the side of the cottage, to her father's workshop.

The scent of fresh sawdust hung in the air, a telltale sign of busy, creative fingers. "Father?" she called, "I've come about the mirror. You'd sent a rocking horsefly saying it's finished?" They were the best way to get messages quickly.

But a shout rang out. "No! Don't come in here, Mary Ann! Go away! It's not done, it's—"

She swung open the door and there stood two figures, her father and someone in a beautiful red-hooded cloak. The cloaked man was brandishing an elaborate axe. And before Mary Ann understood what was happening, he drew it back and sliced an arc through the air. The blow landed—landed directly into and through Rowan Carpenter's neck. The axe came away dripping red. Her father's head came away altogether, dropping to this villainous stranger's feet and rolling—hideously rolling to a stop on the floor by the counter. Mary Ann screamed and the figure turned. But Mary Ann was not invisible now and she didn't need to see the stranger's face to know it. All she could see was that cloak, the deep red, white and gold embroidered pattern like the back of a playing card, the unmistakable sign of the Neath Royal Court. Her skin went cold and before she could think, she was out the door and down the path from her father's workshop.

The footfall was a rush behind her, as she dashed madly off the path and through the woods.

The trees—old friends, these—called out to her in her wake. "Easy there, dear child! Have some respect for your elders!"

And: "Wherever is the fire, young human?"

And: "Mind the roots, please!"

"Behind me. This person chopped down my father!" she explained breathlessly, not daring to slow. "And now he's after me!"

"Well, that's a leaf of a different color!" said the Oak. Then: "You, sir! Where do you think you're going? This young lady says you've been causing trouble. Let us have a look at your face."

Mary Ann could not help herself. Still running, she turned to see. The trees had the stranger caught in a tangle of limbs and vines. An oak branch reached out and pulled the cloak away.

The Knave of Clubs? The valet to Neath's King and Queen of Hearts was the one who murdered Rowan Carpenter? The markings on his tunic were unmistakable. She saw the man was still wielding the axe and seemed to be struggling for momentum to chop himself free.

There was no time to gape. Mary Ann's feet seemed to recognize this first. They'd started off before she could even gather up her skirt, and they sent her thumping through the forest blindly fleeing Turvy.

It being Turvy, however, the more desperately she longed to go home, the further away she got. Fear had made her fast but forgetful. Soon she found herself deep in a part of the land that she didn't know well. What's more, she began to realize that returning to Neath was likely the worst of all choices. After all, that was the valet's home, too. A few inquiries about the daughter of Turvy's famed carpenter and this valet to the Hearts Royal Family would find her in a heartbeat. It was not only risky for her, but dangerous for Mr. Rabbit. Not to mention, the risk of returning to Mr. Rabbit without Queen Valentina's Unbirthday present.

Death would forgive her sooner.

Out of breath, hope and energy, she slowed, and then stopped, scanning the forest as her pink-striped morning uniform stuck to her sweating back and legs. The trees had given her the head start she'd needed to elude her pursuer. Now it seemed like all the terrors that had been streaming out behind her like hat ribbons had finally caught up. She sank onto a rock beside a sundial and wept.

2

"Don't you think that's a curious way to water the flowers?" asked a voice a few moments later. Mary Ann peered through her tears to see a tove standing there, one clawed hand holding a rain umbrella, the other tucked into the pocket of his pale green morning jacket. He regarded her with bright brown eyes in a face of somewhat patchy black-and-white fur.

For a moment, this appearance distracted her from her troubles. Weren't toves primarily known for their fine burrowing skills? How did he keep the jacket so clean? And was he actually speaking to *her*?

The short horns on his head made him look very alert and attentive, which he was, since she still hadn't answered his question. One small, rounded ear gave a twitch while he waited.

"Very curious," she admitted finally, drawing a clean handkerchief from her pocket and hastening to wipe her face. "Though I wasn't watering. I was crying."

"Well, could you cry at some other location? You see, despite all my best efforts at flood remediation, my roof needs work just there. And while the tree canopy does help block—"

She squinted at the creature. "You can see me?"

"Certainly. A tove's eyesight is excellent." And in a tone

suggesting he wanted to be helpful, he added, "Perhaps you're thinking of moles."

She wasn't thinking of moles; she was thinking of Mary Anns. It was very odd, everyone seeing her properly today, while any other day she could count on only the briefest interaction with Mr. Rabbit or the staff, and never the lot at once. She decided it must just be a low invisibility day. "Where am I?" She sniffed, dabbing her eyes.

"You're in the Tulgey Barrens, along the Wabe."

Ah. It had been so long since she spent much time in Turvy, she'd quite forgotten it. It was best never to dwell on places here, since the land was prone to shift and change when it grew bored with itself. It was better to put one's efforts toward other, more tangible tasks.

"And forgive me if I overstep, but why were you crying?" asked the tove. "Is it all the raths around here? They make a pitiful caterwaul, I know, but it's nothing to take to heart. They're not in any pain. Just a bit mome these days. Mating season, you know."

Mary Ann hadn't heard any raths today, mome or otherwise. But the tove's voice was so soft and sympathetic, and Mary Ann wasn't used to consolation or pity. Suddenly she was overcome by visions of her wretched circumstance, of swinging axes and spinning heads and the death of a man she abstractly loved but did not know.

She was awash with frustrated tears in no time.

"Oh, now that won't do," said the tove. "Oh, really now, miss! Crying does so much property damage around here. In fact, there was a tear-related flooding incident in Neath earlier today. That wasn't you, was it?" He searched her face for an answer. "No?...Well, you'll just have to come in."

Not knowing where In was, she wiped her eyes and let the tove lead her to a small circular door just a few feet away, embedded in the ground beneath their feet. The tove flung open the door, then shimmied down a ladder into a warmly flickering pit. A second later, a clawed arm popped up and motioned her down, as if it were the invitation itself and not the logistics that had stalled her. "Come! Come, come." It would be a tight squeeze, and the ladder was unlikely to hold her. But she wrapped her skirts around her legs and jumped into the hole.

The drop was short and the home, surprisingly accommodating, so long as she remained seated. (Which she did.) She imagined the ceilings were quite high from a tove perspective, and the space was pleasantly tiled and wallpapered. There was a water stain on the dining room ceiling. The whole place was furnished with beautiful little sofas, tables and chairs, sporting a carved design that was so familiar, Mary Ann froze at the sight of it. "Rowan Carpenter's work?"

"Custom!" said the tove proudly. "Why, I'm one of the biggest collectors of his smaller work in all of Turvy! Extraordinary, isn't it? Just look at those lines!" He stroked the wooden arm of a sofa. "How do you know of him?"

"He's my father," she murmured, and then amended, "Was."

The tove chuckled. "Changed his mind, did he? Backed out of the job?"

"I saw him murdered moments ago," said Mary Ann.

She should have, perhaps, eased into this topic a bit more.

The tove let out a quick "ulp!" of the throat, pushing down any additional insensitive words that had a chance to erupt. He took this moment to do a quick pour from a decanter into a tiny crystal glass, then a quick sip from the cup. He repeated the move with a second cup, but offered that to Mary Ann, which she waved away. The tove paused, hand pressed to his mouth. Then he was ready. "Murdered..." He shook his head. His voice was all air. "Such a genius...A true artist...Start with the event and proceed backwards from there."

Unaccustomed to being the focus of conversation, Mary Ann described the scene as succinctly as possible. She explained how she couldn't return to her employer without the mirror, she couldn't return to Neath without risking her safety, and she couldn't return to her father's for fear the Hearts' servant might still be in the area, searching for her.

The Tove agreed it was a muddle. "And this Knave of Clubs. Does he often commit executions on behalf of Neath's King and Queen?"

Mary Ann said she hadn't heard of it, but also had no idea of what the man was capable. She relayed how the fellow had become one of Queen Valentina's servants when the House of Hearts troops bested the House of Clubs in a particularly deadly round of War some years ago. The Clubs had been the last royal family standing between Valentina and her total rule of the Neath territory, and those alive in the aftermath did well switching their allegiance to her swiftly. The Knave, Jacob Morningstar, was among them when the Clubs' deck was cut, and he became a particular favorite of the court in due time.

"Could your father have done anything to displease the Royal Family?"

That, Mary Ann could not say. Whether formal execution or outright murder, the results looked much the same, she feared. Either way, any resolution would require her to bring charges against a highly-regarded servant of the Royal Family—and that was impossible for someone of her status. "I do not hold hope for justice," she said finally. "But I would settle for answers."

"And answers you shall have," said the tove. "Here, drink this." He poured from another decanter and held out the cup.

"Again, thank you, no. I'm really not—"

"You'll be safe here today…tonight…but my house will be safer if you are a bit, shall we say, more the appropriate size?"

She smiled. So it was DwindleAde, the popular drink that helped with those awkward size adjustments. She accepted the cup, sipped, and found herself in the spacious sitting room, properly able to, in fact, sit.

"I know someone who may be able to solve at least one of your problems," the tove continued. "We'll go there in the morning."

She nodded. And a sudden heavy sadness rolled over her again, accompanying this thought: "I suppose I shall also have to bury my father." Being smaller only meant the weight of her troubles had come along proportionately.

"We'll take care of that, as well," said the tove.

"But what if Jacob Morningstar's still there, waiting?" In another flash of memory, she pictured the cloaked figure in the workshop's half-light, holding that axe. Her heart beat so hard it was pounding itself a march.

"He can't wait forever," said the tove. "He's still a valet. He has regular duties at the castle, doesn't he? He'll have to be back by morning, surely."

While she appreciated his caring consolation, Mary Ann felt unconvinced.

"I'll help you with the burial tomorrow morning," said the tove. "I would be honored to do whatever I could for such a fine artist." He uncovered a dish and held it toward her. "Cheese?"

"I'm not very hungry, thank you," she said, while the tove helped himself to that and some wafers. "You've been very kind. And I realize I don't even know your name."

"Douglas," said the tove. "Douglas Divot. I was named that because I dug less than the others in my litter. Late bloomer, you know." And he sliced off a bit more cheese.

"Mary Ann Carpenter," she said, feeling somewhat sorry she had no interesting factoid to share regarding her name. But Douglas didn't seem to mind. He sat with her there for a long time, telling her tales of Tulgey Barrens, his life in the Wabe, and details on his favorite cheeses.

Then he showed her to a guest room, furnished with more of her father's work. It was a very pretty room, the wallpaper patterned in cheerful tove burrows. She realized she could hear a sound now through the ceiling. It seemed there were raths, after all. Calling...calling...To no reply.

She closed her eyes, thinking it would be a million years before sleep would find her, after the day she'd had. Yet, it wasn't long before she found her consciousness slipping away to the mournful outgrabe of the mome raths.

3

"Do you have the Burgeonboosh?" Douglas Divot asked.

Morning had come, and the inevitable, unenviable tasks with it. Now, as they approached Rowan Carpenter's property, so still and silent ahead, Mary Ann pulled a little cake from her apron pocket, and Douglas did the same from his jacket. She took one small bite of her portion, and he his, and in a flash, Mary Ann was back to normal size and Douglas, twice his usual.

Their first stop was the shed, arming themselves with the most ferocious garden implements the little outbuilding had to offer. They checked the craftsman's cottage first—no sign of Jacob Morningstar; that was some relief, at least—and then moved on to her father's workshop. Mary Ann's heart beat a Lobster Quadrille as she swung open the door to this latter building, bracing herself for the tragic scene before her. She'd pictured it in her mind a thousand times already and every time she'd hope it would not be as bad as she'd imagined.

Of course, it was every bit as gorrible as one would expect, and then just that much more.

For instance, her imagination had not accounted for the presence of the workshop's tinier residents. Overnight, flies and ants had taken over, transforming her father's toppled head into more of a vague head-shape, black and rippling with movement. Enough blood had pooled from the neck and body, partially drying around both, that it combined with the sawdust on the floor to create a startling russet and tan carpet. The neck, she noticed, revealed a perfectly smooth cut and she wondered at it now. How had this been possible? She'd seen the incident with her own eyes, of course — a single swing, impact, lop. Mary Ann had chopped enough wood in her lifetime to know that things simply didn't work that way, not even in Turvy. The men had both been standing, so it wasn't even as if gravity had been on Jacob Morningstar's side. Physics in the land was, yes, always somewhat subject to whim. But she felt fairly certain that this was not the work of any ordinary axe.

"Where would you like to bury him?" Douglas asked, his voice startling her out of these thoughts.

"Under a Tumtum tree, I think," Mary Ann heard herself say. That particular wood, with its swirls and burls and twists, had been one of her father's favorites.

Douglas nodded. "If you help me carry him, I'll burrow out the grave," he said.

So they heaved the body first, struggling through the doorway and ultimately resting the remains in the grass along the desired locale. Mary Ann took a moment, grounded herself and went back in for the head.

The flies and ants were none too pleased about the disruption, levying their complaints quite loudly as she did what must be done:

"Hey, buzz off!" one said.

"Where's breakfast going?" asked another.

"Aw, have a heart, lady! I've a family of thousands to feed," an ant pleaded.

Having cleaned the most wretched of household items in her eighteen years, Mary Ann had long ago lost her queasiness over muck and bodily fluids. But now, the texture of cold skin and the sandpaper stubble of her father's jaw were pressing the boundaries of her revulsion. Each stood as a terrible reminder:

"As of yesterday, I was not a thing."

As she shifted the head to open the door, Rowan Carpenter's stained and matted hair—or what there was left of it, for it was never ample—fluttered so humanly in the breeze. It was one image too many. She ran back to the yard, reuniting head with body like a hot potato, and grateful to have the item out of her hands. Some people longed to get a head in the world; others, not so much.

While Douglas made progress with the hole, Mary Ann put herself to work doing what she did best: cleaning. In Turvy, if you planned to do a job properly, you did it backwards. So she scrubbed up the blood, then fetched water from the well for scrubbing, then swept. In no time, the workshop was considerably improved, the only evidence of the deed being the reddish-brown floorboards where the blood had soaked in.

The stains will likely be permanent, she thought. Rowan Carpenter will forever be a part of this building.

She was turning from her work when she noticed the Queen's present propped against a wall. It was a mirror, carved with intricate, twining hearts and roses. He had made it full-length, so Queen Valentina would be able to see every inch of her fabled elegance at once.

The piece had been stained a ruby red so the grain of the wood shone through. Her father believed that one should always remember and honor the first artist of the piece, the tree itself. The Queen would adore it; there could be no alternative. But given its size and Mary Ann's current situation, how to get it to Mr. Rabbit without Mary Ann risking herself?

She would think of a way.

In the meantime, she decided to make a headstone, and thought nothing more fitting than using a Tumtum panel her father had planned for a small tabletop. She pondered what she wanted it to say. Then she found a jar of stain and a brush. And with them, in her tidiest backwards printing, she wrote:

ROWAN CARPENTER
Contractor. Woodworker. Visionary. Dad.

Never had so much good
Been done with a bit of wood
As when the man did and would
Transform it.

Now art alone must linger on
As artist leaf't us, fallen, gone
This cold decay upon the lawn,
We mourn it.

Mary Ann reread it. She wasn't much of a writer, she knew. She liked to read whenever she got the chance, but as for writing... housemaidery tended not to encourage one's more creative side. She decided the plaque would have to do — though it occurred to her, there was one thing it still needed.

She stepped outside to see if one tradition from her childhood was still intact, and she was not disappointed. Yes, there was the pile of oyster shells up against one side of the house. Rowan Carpenter would use them whole for mosaics and chimney breasts, and crushed for paving walks and drives. They were as much a part of the man in her mind as the wood ever was. And they were in seemingly-endless supply, for they were the product of a man with an abiding passion for seafood. The man who, during the dinners of her childhood, was outright competitive over the stuff, curbing her portions in order to enhance his own. Sometimes he made feeble, flushing excuses about it. And sometimes he simply slipped oysters from her plate, one by one, through sleight-of-hand.

She had such mixed feelings about it, finding it both amusing, yet also something like a small, old scar that was still-tender from past treatment.

She gathered up some shells in her apron and carried them back to the workshop. With glue, she was able to assemble a rather beautiful wreath.

She was just putting the finishing touches on it when Douglas entered, a clump of grass stuck to one horn, his claws caked in grime and some of his own shed fur.

"I'm ready whenever you are," he said.

She nodded. "I'm ready now." And gently, she set the wreath upon the plaque she'd made and they withdrew to the back garden.

Toves did know their precision digging; the grave was a perfect rectangle, just the size of a carpenter in-complete. Mary Ann tried to keep her mind on the positives of that—her good fortune in making a kind friend who could spare her this difficult step—as they moved her father's body, then the head, into the grave.

"A shame to see the end of an amazing artist," said Douglas, wiping his damp eyes on the forearm of his jacket. "It must be doubly hard for you, though."

Mary Ann murmured noncommittally and put her energies toward shoveling in the hole. There was a part of her that wondered if she didn't grieve the experience and the situation more than she did Rowan Carpenter himself. The artist was a loss to the world. The father was a heat shimmer along the distant road of childhood.

With the dirt in place, Mary Ann added the plaque, then set the wreath across the grave to finish drying, its mother of pearl glinting in the morning light.

"Are you ready?" Douglas asked, resting a grimy clawed hand on her shoulder, a sweet consoling gesture. "Would you like to say some words?"

To the wind, she released only the words that mattered. "I'll find out why this happened." And as the words took flight, an idea emerged:

Answers may lie here.

So they gave the place a rudimentary search. They started on the cottage and rummaged through the cabinets. They moved to the bedchamber and went through the drawers. Mary Ann peered under the bed and poked in the fireplace. But the sad fact of it was, they were no better informed about murderous motives than when they'd started.

"We'd best go," said Douglas finally, glancing at a pocket watch while Mary Ann stood in disappointed silence. "I'd like to clean up and take you to that friend of mine. I feel confident that he can help."

"This? This is your friend?" asked Mary Ann breathlessly as she stood before the manor house. It was a sprawling edifice of red brick, ringed by red waters, over which a red drawbridge extended.

"It's the home of the Lord Carmine," said Douglas. "He's a Baron, you know. I excavated a moat for him in preparation for the Battle of Square Four some years ago. He's promised me a favor."

"And how can he help me?" Mary Ann's mind was swimming. How closely did the Royal courts of Turvy and Neath intermingle, anyway? Did this Baron have pull with Queen Valentina of Neath? Did he know the Royal valet, Jacob Morningstar? What if King Rudolf or Queen Valentina were the ones who ordered Rowan Carpenter's death? Wouldn't that be a bit close for comfort? Wouldn't that be a bit…oh… *incredibly stupid* for her to even broach the subject? No matter how Mary Ann looked at it, she could not see how this Lord Carmine could assist without putting her in even greater jeopardy.

She said as much. But Douglas just smiled, a rather toothy, tovey smile. "All in good time, Mary Ann," he said, squeezing her hand. "All in good time."

There was a thick rope by the door and Douglas pulled it. A bell within rang. The front door opened a crack and Mary Ann could see the eye and the long nose of the First Footman, a sleek, noble-looking fellow of the equine persuasion. "Yes?"

"Douglas Divot to see the Lord Carmine," the tove said, with an impressive air of confidence.

"Oh, yes, sir! Do come in," said the First Footman. "Wait here, please." And he trotted off to notify the Baron, leaving them in the good hooves of a Second Footman, who happened to be a donkey. It seemed Douglas Divot did have connections.

Mary Ann noticed on the wall of the grand entrance hall was the taxidermy head of a tremendous beast, a creature with great bared fangs, jagged fins jutting from the side of its skull, horns projecting from the top and large, glassy red eyes at center. It was a shock to see it, mainly because she knew this beast. She'd seen the drawings. "Oh my goodness! Wasn't that—?"

"The Jabberwock?" said the donkey footman, with a smug, sideways glance. "And you should say 'is,'" he corrected.

Mary Ann frowned. The Jabberwock looked very Was to her. She suspected the Footman was simply being an ass.

"The young master's work," the Second Footman continued. "Lord and Lady Carmine's son, Sir Rufus, is a knight to the Red Queen, Rosamund. He slays the Jabberwock tomorrow, as prophesized. Day after, he'll commence training for it. And sometime after that, he'll quest for the Vorpal sword to do the deed. I'm sure you've heard the poem?"

Mary Ann nodded, for the epic was well-known in Turvy, and long before she was born.

"We're very proud," said the Second Footman.

Douglas Divot beamed. "As you should be," he said heartily.

"Proud? Who's proud?" came a voice, and an older man entered dressed in sumptuous red robes. His beard was ginger with a touch of grey, his mustaches russet and silver. His face was flushed in the hue of a tomato experiencing dyspepsia.

"The Lord Carmine," announced the returning horse footman and both footmen bowed.

Mary Ann made a quick curtsey as Douglas bowed, too.

"My Lord, I was telling our guests about your son's upcoming Jabberwock quest," the donkey footman piped up.

"Oh yes! We're very proud," said Lord Carmine, confirming it all round. "The lad's a hero. Or will be, when the deed's officially done. Callooh, callay and all that." He clasped his hands before him. "Now who have we here?" And his eyes lit on the tove. "Why, Devon! —"

"Er, Douglas," Douglas muttered.

"—A delight to see you as always!" continued Lord Carmine.

"And you, My Lord," Douglas said.

"What brings you here today?"

"Well, My Lord, I was rather hoping to ask a favor," said the tove.

"Ask away, dear fellow! The old moat is sound and sturdy as ever it was. Why, if it hadn't been for your clever thinking back in the battle days, we'd have been overrun by those Alabastards in the blink of an eye and we'd all be speaking Blanco-Turvian right now."

Mary Ann had met a number of people from the White Kingdom of Turvy and they'd spoken quite the same language as everyone else. She did not point this out.

"I was wondering," began Douglas, seeking to change the subject, "whether you might be able to offer a housemaid position to my friend here."

Mary Ann turned to Douglas in her surprise. *That* was his plan? Admittedly, it did solve her food and shelter problems, but it did very little in terms of murder-solving.

Lord Carmine appeared equally baffled, but for wholly different reasons. "Your friend?" The man blinked and looked all round. "Where are they, then? Have they run off? Security breach! Security breach! Man the what's-it and ready the thingummy!"

And the footmen trotted off in different directions trying to look busy doing something until the man calmed down a bit.

Lord Carmine leaned to Douglas, fear spanning his face. "Your friend isn't one of those sly spies from the White side, are they? Perhaps just posing as your friend seeking to infiltrate? I know how those slippery monsters think!"

"Why, no, sir," said the tove. "She's—"

"I am here, My Lord," Mary Ann said. And she waited the moment for Lord Carmine to finally settle his gaze upon her.

"Ah! There you are!" he said. "Where'd you come from? You do realize, vanishing while seeking a position somewhere does not reflect well on you, young lady? In fact," he considered it further, "vanishing doesn't reflect at all."

"Yes, Your Lordship."

"See, you vanish afterwards, once you're hired and become just another one of the help," he explained. "Not before. Right now I need to get a good look at you."

And this gave Mary Ann an idea. "I thought I'd vanish first, My Lord, to get it out of the way," she said.

There was a blink. A pause. Then the Baron's face brightened. "Ah!" He tapped his temple. "Thinking ahead, then. Planning! Very bright girl! No sense waiting until you're hired to do the needful things. You're a go-getter, you are! You'll be getting the Go and fetching the well water in no time."

"Yes, My Lord, thank you."

"And since you're already working the position, I suppose that means I have to hire you," Lord Carmine said.

"If it's a proper Turvian job, hiring would follow the work, My Lord," she agreed.

"Frabjous, then! Welcome to Carmine Manor. You will report to the housekeeper, Mrs. Cordingley. She'll assign you your chores...If she hasn't already...?" He raised an inquiring eyebrow at her, and she shook her head no.

"Ah, well. Not everyone is quite so enterprising as our young...What did you say your name was?"

She hadn't, but admitting that might throw cold water over her proactive reputation. "Mary Ann, My Lord."

"Marion," Lord Carmine said warmly. "Excellent! You'll find Mrs. Cordingley somewhere around here, Marilyn. The cook will know." He pointed. "That way."

Mary Ann followed his gesture down a long corridor. She paused, turned and looked at Douglas.

"Well, what are you waiting for, Darienne?" Lord Carmine asked. "Your cleaning quest awaits! Off with you!" And he made a shooing motion, like she was more goose than girl.

Douglas gave her a wink. So Mary Ann mouthed her thanks and scurried off down the hall.

The kitchen was much larger than the one at Mr. Rabbit's, and a lot quieter and less pepper-centric than the Duchess'. There were two people in the room at the moment. The tall, round one wore a cook's apron that appeared to contain a stain-smeared history of meals, past and present, making it possible to read it like a menu of all the dishes one had missed. The other person was a mite of a woman in a red housekeeper's uniform that was so stiff and starched, Mary Ann felt sure the lady's clothes would shatter in a strong wind.

Before the housekeeper was an enormous tray bearing an equally large plate and the cook was stacking food onto it in perilous proportions. She said, "Right, then! One big helping of adversity, hard-boiled…A side of irony (it's so important to get enough irony in your diet, I always say) … Some bittersweet, topped with shredded expectations … All seasoned with a sprinkle of dehydrated tears. To drink? A cup of hot, steeped wit. And for dessert? A slice of right-side-up cake."

The housekeeper nodded and hefted the tray to her shoulder.

"Mrs. Cordingley," Mary Ann began, "if you please, I'm—"

"Oh, and don't forget this!" said Cook, ignoring the newcomer. "This is *everything!*" and she dunked a pocket watch into the tea. For a moment, Mary Ann thought the weight of the pocket watch might be the whole project's undoing. The housekeeper wobbled and swayed like a willow in the wind, but somehow managed to regain her footing. She started away on rubbery knees. Mary Ann trailed after her.

"Pardon me," Mary Ann tried again, "are you Mrs. Cordingley? I'm supposed to report to you for housemaid work. My name is—"

"No time now, girl. I must take this up," Mrs. Cordingley told her, looking pained but still trying to keep a stiff upper lip about it. "So start with the fireplaces. Then fluster the moldings, massage the brass, milk the jugs, tickle the ivory and when you're quite done with that, report back and I'll give you some *real* work to do." She tripped a bit on the first of the steps leading up from the kitchen and weaved ominously.

"Oh, my!" Mary Ann rushed toward her, arms outstretched, trying to anticipate the direction of the inevitable tumble. "May I help you? Where are you taking it? I could carry half and together we could—"

"You just never mind," Cordingley said, ultimately stabilizing herself once more and turning away. Her voice echoed in the stairwell, "Off with you! Those moldings won't fluster themselves!"

It was after no guidance and considerable trial-and-error, Mary Ann found where the cleaning implements were stored and she began work on the fireplaces. She sought them out among the maze of rooms, polishing the facades and sweeping the tiles first, then shoveling out the embers, all properly backwards and Turvian. Next, she moved on to the baseboard moldings but had some trouble getting a good fluster up. Most of the woodwork that edged the rooms was fairly stoic, so you had to threaten it with sandpaper and wire brushes, before it got truly upset and sweated itself into a nice, oily polish.

In the case of the entry hall, however, even the sandpaper wasn't an incentive. So she found herself uttering the most heartless of threats: "Oh, so that's it! That's how you want to do things! I'll get a match then, shall I? A lit match? Is that what you want?"

Well, the moldings changed their behavior soon enough at that. And it was just in time, too, because the door burst open and a crowd thundered in. The group was led by a young man in light armor, assistants at his side with hounds and horns. All of them were clad in the reddest of red tunics, boots and leggings, chatting and singing, barking and tootling, as were their penchants. All them, that is, except for the young man in the armor. That one moved silently forward then stopped in the middle of the room, staring at the Jabberwock head on the wall as if in a trance. His face, a white canvas with a collection of red spatters across the nose and cheeks, grew three shades paler at the sight of the creature. In a moment, he was so pale, the White Queen would have merrily tucked him into her Royal Guard. He let out a miserable sigh as he clutched his rumpled ginger curls, an action which sucked all the life from his entourage like a flame in a vacuum.

"Sir Rufus," one of the squires asked, "what's wrong?"

"N-nothing," he said after a moment, in a voice as hollow as a haunting soul's. "All of you, wait in the drawing room. No—not you, Russell." He indicated one man. "You come help me with this armor." Sir Rufus moved suddenly toward the staircase, where Mary Ann had been flustering the spindles. Before she could even crawl out of the way, he was right there, stumbling over her. A moment later, he had drawn a sword—not one of the Vorpal variety, she noticed — and whirled around, scanning the area. "Who did that? Where are you?" He finally spied her. "Oh." The pale face turned pink. The small blue eyes surveyed her sharply. "Whatever are you doing there?"

"Crouching, Sir?" She indicated the woodwork.

"I see. Well, one has quite enough problems without also being on the alert for rampant crouching." He sheathed the sword. "Really, miss, if you must insist on it, at least crouch taller, would you? Where people can see you properly."

"Yes, Sir," said Mary Ann.

And at that, he looked somewhat mollified. He spun once more on a booted heel and clanked off, followed by the one called Russell.

By tea, Mary Ann was hardly able to believe it was the same day she'd buried her father, it all seemed so very far away.

There was a constant bustle of activity at Carmine Manor. For one, Mary Ann had never before worked at a place with so many servants. There were the footmen, Cook and Mrs. Cordingley the housekeeper, of course. But there was also a somewhat piscine-looking parlor maid called Mabel, a red-cheeked scullery maid called Emmaline, Lady Carmine's personal maid who was an aloof, elegant girl named Celeste, and several others she had yet to meet. All but Celeste had been brief and busy, but still welcoming. Celeste was busy, too, though mainly in having personal words with a lanky young carriage driver. From what Mary Ann overheard, those words were more neigh than yea.

With tea, Mary Ann learned what was expected of her at mealtimes, after meals, and what tasks should be done before the house had settled down for bed. By this point, bed was sounding very pleasant, indeed.

"This is our room," said Emmaline and she swung the door wide to the female servants' quarters. There were three large beds in the room. "So now it's you and me, and Mrs. Cordingley, and Cook and Mabel. Celeste sleeps downstairs off of Lady Carmine's room. Mrs. Cordingley gets her own bed—this one." She pointed. Even the bed looked starched. "But you can bunk with me, here." Emmaline hopped onto the bed by the window. "I'm happy to have a bedmate, actually. I don't like the dark much. Terrified of it. They poke fun of me sometimes, Mrs. Cordingley and Mabel do, but there's just something about these dark old houses that give me the heebies. Do you like it? The room, I mean, not the dark. Though, do you like the dark? Not fond of it, me. That's why I have the bed by the window. Little bit of light, you see. Comforting."

She paused for answer and possibly for breath. Mary Ann wasn't sure which question to address first, so she just smiled and thanked the girl.

"What is your name, by the way?" asked Emmaline, pulling back the covers and removing her work cap. "You see, no one's quite sure. Someone thought it was Marilyn, but then

Marion, Darienne, Terrilyn and Tamsin seem to have happened somewhere along the way. Of course, that's Lord Carmine for you. Very nice man, a very fair employer, but terrible with names. Why, in my time here, I've been Imogene, Emily, Amy, Allison and even once Ignatia, which I'm quite grateful was never an idea that popped into my parents' minds, that's for certain. The only ones he gets right are Mrs. Cordingley and his son, Sir Rufus. Only he never calls his son 'Sir,' as that would be silly," said Emmaline, imparting that extra bit of wisdom. "So, what's your name again?"

"Tamsin," said Mary Ann, selecting from the menu of names presented to her. She liked the sound of it, and until she knew more about Lord Carmine's royal connections, she suspected it was a lot safer than her own.

"Tamsin's a nice name," agreed Emmaline. "We're both lucky we're not Ignatia, eh?" she philosophized.

Mary Ann agreed it was fortunate. And perhaps somewhere, some poor Ignatia felt her ears burning. But Mary Ann was able to borrow an extra nightdress from Emmaline, who simply couldn't *believe* she'd come to work with no possessions at all, and it wasn't long before the other staff filtered in, readied themselves, and the lamp was put out. The draft from the window ruffled the curtains and blew across Mary Ann's face. Someone snored, she noticed, and given the number of occupants in the chamber, it was hard to pinpoint the guilty party. She was quite sure it wasn't Emmaline, who was still and silent for possibly the first time since Mary Ann had met her. But the remaining three across the room were still suspect.

She thought the bone-weariness of the day's events would carry her on the waves of sleep, a current of snores to rock her, and for a while this did prove true. But then the sleep gave way to fitful dreaming. She saw funeral wreaths of oyster shells wheeling their way across her view. Wreaths of shells, mother of pearl flashing at her in the light. It made her squint and wince—until the buzzing started. The flies buzzing in her ears, in her mind. A cloud of flies, blocking the light, darkening her view. She found herself dumped on a sandy beach, sopping.

She tried to stand but she couldn't bend. She was stiff as a board, floating, suddenly made of wood, carved wood floating on a choppy current out to sea. But the flies followed, landing on her, and oh, how she wanted to swat them away! The buzzing was so loud now, she woke up, arms flailing. In a moment, the buzz had melted into the sound of rain, pattering furiously against the slate roof above their little attic room. The precipitation mixed with the gentle sound of snores.

4

Morning arrived with the swift, careening intensity of a runaway carriage and Mary Ann rolled out of bed and into her new housemaid's uniform feeling bleary and sore. This uniform was certainly different than the ones she'd worn in Neath. For one thing, the whole ensemble was red—no particular surprise there. But the bodice was smooth and unadorned, there was no apron at all, and the skirt had the sleek, flared look of a horn, which kept its shape through a hoop sewn into the bottom hem. The cap was unlike any she'd seen. It was a sphere that perched on the bun of her plaited, upswept hair. She suspected the whole thing would take some time to get used to. The base hoop was awkward and unpredictable, and it forced her to account with greater accuracy her width between doors. She discovered this last feature the hard way, when trying to leave the bedchamber.

It was after she fortified herself with a quick slice of bread and butter, and a cup of water, that she proceeded to the morning chores.

Today, she'd been tasked to gather fresh flowers for the manor. Mrs. Cordingley said the ones from yesterday had escaped sometime last night and tucked themselves back into bed. Rousing them, let alone persuading them to uproot themselves into pots, was a challenge.

"Please," she urged a belligerent begonia, trying to keep the note of desperation from her voice. "You'll like it in the pot. There'll be fresh water and a change of scenery and…"

"Too early," moaned the blossoms, as if as one. "And the house is *so* drafty." They gave a collective shudder and pretended to close back into buds. Mary Ann knew they were faking because one kept peeking.

"You, then," she moved on to the daisies. "What would you say to a little adventure indoors? I have a nice sunny window all picked out for you!"

"Go deadhead yourself," one of the larger daisies snapped. "You coerced our relatives into your pots of despair, then never watered them. They endured an excruciating death by dehydration! You think we don't find out these things? It's all over the grapevine!" And the daisy made a leafy gesture to the arbor alongside the mansion. "We're onto your torturous ways, you fiend!"

"Now, honestly, I'm afraid you have it all wrong," said Mary Ann. "I would never—"

But the daisy was unmoved. "Deny all you want. We know it was you. We recognize you by your red petals."

She looked down at her housemaid uniform and smoothed the skirt on reflex. "But we all wear red pet—"

"How are you getting on?" This last voice came, not from the flowerbed, but from behind her. And Mary Ann turned to see Douglas Divot, claws clasped before him, looking intrigued.

"At the moment?" she said. "I fear the household staff has sown the seeds of discontent."

"Ah. Well. I'm certain you'll get to the root of it eventually," said Douglas. He assessed her weary smile. "You look tired, my friend. Didn't you sleep?"

"Dreams," she murmured. The feeling of sand in her shoes and surf swirling through her dress, that sense of being wooden and paralyzed, was still a very real and lingering sensation. And in this waking moment, it reminded her of something. "You know, my father's business partner has no idea what's happened. I shall have to talk to him—and sooner rather than later. Perhaps he might also shed some light on Father's relationship to the Royal Family of Neath."

"This partner, is he a craftsman, too, then?" As he tugged at his collar, she could tell the tove's mind was filled with uncomfortable questions. Rowan Carpenter's work was always billed as a solo act. If he had a partner in the creative end of things, how much work had he really done himself? Was it all left to an apprentice and was Carpenter a mere figurehead? How would this affect the value of Douglas' collection?

She realized she had to put that to rest swiftly before the tove hyperventilated there on the spot. "Mr. Banks is purely in sails," she told him. "He sails from place to place selling Father's finished pieces and arranging new commissions."

In a moment, Douglas' expression brightened. "Oh, yes!" He let out a relieved sigh. "Him! I've met him several times. Large, boisterous fellow, right? Prominent in the smile department?" He mimed tusks in duo.

"That's the one."

"Well, I'll join you, then. Frabjous fellow. Love to have another chat with him."

Love to secure a few last works for his collection, Mary Ann thought cynically. But she could hardly blame the fellow. And he'd been *so* generous with his assistance. "I have some chores to do just now, but perhaps I could steal away after the midday meal."

"I'll come back later, then," Douglas said. His gaze went to the defiant flowers. "And hopefully this little war of the roses you're having will prove to be mulch ado about nothing."

The nice thing about housemaid's work was that one could be physically occupied with a task, yet mentally caught up in solving one's father's murder. As such, Mary Ann's body went about her work efficiently, while the events of the past two days turned in her mind.

So lost was she in thoughts of royal connections, paranoid intrigues and potential confidants that she'd been working in the entry hall for almost twenty minutes before she realized the Jabberwock head had, at some point, vanished from the wall.

"Peculiar," she said and went back to sweeping. She did not envy Sir Rufus one whit.

"Well, it looks like Mr. Banks is not out on a sails call, at least," Mary Ann said to Douglas Divot later that day, indicating the bright and shiny sailboat with its crisp sails docked along the river. They proceeded down the path toward the gentleman in question's cottage. She hadn't yet raised her hand to knock, when the front door flew open and there stood her father's business partner. He was a large, well-dressed fellow, clad in many shades of exotic silks from waistcoat to cravat to stockings, almost as if a textile factory had exploded on a mountain.

He was also a walrus.

"Why, Mary Ann Carpenter! That's you, isn't it? How you've grown!" He leaned down to hug her, a flippery embrace. Then his attention shifted to Douglas. "I'm J. Sanford Banks ... Sandy, if you like," he said, extending the flipper to the tove and assessing him with interest. "Now, I *know* we've met before. Dougal, is it?"

"Douglas," Douglas said, looking pleased to be remembered. "Douglas Divot."

"Indeed! Douglas! Yes! I quite apologize for not recalling it straight away. One of our most treasured repeat customers. A man who knows fine art when he sees it. Wonderly to meet you again. What brings you both here?"

"Is there somewhere we could perhaps sit down, Mr. Banks?" Mary Ann asked. She recalled a little something about one of Mr. Banks' personal quirks and a calm, quiet setting would be a small step to mitigate its display.

"Of course," he said. And he led them through a beautiful home—all rich wooden beams, oyster shell-tiled fireplaces and more striking fabrics—to a porch overlooking the river. The river around the dock was teeming with aquatic life. And the little room itself simply overflowed with original Carpenter furniture. The sight made Douglas' face all smiles. Realizing he was under Mary Ann's observation, he struggled to transform his expression into something more solemn for the occasion, but his awe and excitement lingered on the air.

They sat, and were offered tea, and Mary Ann wasted no time explaining the reason for their visit.

Mr. Banks took the news rather better than she'd expected. The weeping was as loud as anticipated, a series of bellows reminiscent of a lighthouse in fog. But there was virtually no gnashing of teeth, and he'd improved considerably in the tearing of hair department. This last point may have been largely due to the fact that time and temper had left him nothing but bristles about the temples and cheeks.

She let the display of emotion play itself out, and in time, the fellow was dabbing his eyes so they were able to get back on course. "You knew my father as well as anyone. I'm curious: what was my father's reputation here in Turvy?"

"As a fine woodworker and a clever architect, of course. The pinnacle in quality craftsmen," said Mr. Banks.

"I mean, rather, what did people think of him personally?" said Mary Ann. "Was he liked? Were there any spats, any enemies? Can you think of any reason he might have been killed or ... or perhaps ..." she took a short breath, " ... executed?"

Well, this unleashed a second round of sobbing, albeit a lesser wave than the last. "Your father was a wonderful man... Wonderful man!" Mr. Banks blubbered through the tears. "Everyone loved him! Worshipped the feet he walked on and the hands he worked with and the thinker he did thoughts with. And—"

"So his relationship with the Turvian royals was—"

"None at all," he said. "He stayed quite clear of the Turvian royals, both Red and White—and anyone else for that matter. You see, I do most of the face-to-face business. Always have done. Your father is...*was*...more of a behind-the-scenes man."

She nodded. "And what about his connections to Neath?" She'd been easing into this question.

"Oh, Neath," he said, his tone falling flat. "Funny, I heard back in Neath they're having some problems of their own. Some transient has been stirring up trouble, flooding things, wrecking property, making a mess of the Queen's sporting events and such."

Douglas said, "How awful!"

"Your father wouldn't have been involved in any of that, would he?" Banks asked Mary Ann, the used handkerchief now mopping his brow.

"It doesn't sound like him." But Mary Ann's voice sounded uncertain, even to herself. What had she really known about Rowan Carpenter?

"What a tragedy ... A tragedy, I say," began Mr. Banks, clearly gearing up the ocular moisturization process again. "It's hard to conceive that there will be no more new pieces of his work. What a talent he was! Like that mirror he was working on for Queen Valentina. The one you helped commission. Sublime! Did you see it yet?"

For reasons she could not explain, she shook her head no.

"Well, that wasn't just special because of the glass," continued Mr. Banks. "No, indeed, it was a masterpiece of craftsmanship, every inch of it!"

Mary Ann thought back to the mirror sitting in her father's workshop, propped against the wall. While Rowan Carpenter certainly had outdone himself in terms of wood-carving, the glass had appeared quite standard. Beveled, yes, but nothing unique in that. "Was the glass very different?"

"Why, different? My dear, you couldn't get more different, if you painted it black and called it a kettle!" said Mr. Banks. He leaned in and lowered his voice, his breath smelling noticeably of fish. "This glass has special transporting properties. All you have to do is say the right word, and it's an escape hatch. Perfect if any nasty political uprisings should happen to pop up. I hear royals love that sort of thing," he said, and added, "Escape hatches, not uprisings. Not fond of uprisings, royals. Yes, they quickly get full-up of those."

"An escape hatch to where?" asked Mary Ann.

"Oh, now, there's no need to concern yourself with that, Miss Mary Ann. That's neither here nor there." Mr. Banks waved it away with a flipper and mopped his brow again. "It's also not Hither and Yon. Have you been to Yon? It's lovely this season. Should have been considered for the piece, but— alas, I'm not in control of these things."

Douglas asked, "Don't you know where it goes, then?"

"I *do*," Mr. Banks gave him a very narrow look. "And all I am privy to say is: it's a one-way trip and its secret will be divulged in due time to the recipient herself. Safer that way for all concerned. Now," Mr. Banks heaved himself from his chair, "I hope you won't think me rude, but I have a late afternoon appointment, and I must go while the tides are right and the wind's at my back. A sailsman's work is all ebb and flow, don't you know? Navigating uncharted sales quarters and whatnot."

They said they did have an inkling of the challenges he faced, and he escorted them to the door. "It's been lovely seeing you again, Miss Mary Ann," said Mr. Banks. "And you, Mr. Divot. Next time, I hope to meet under gladder circumstances." And they had only taken a step away before Mary Ann heard the door shut and lock.

5

"I want to take a better look at that mirror my father made," Mary Ann told Douglas, on the walk back to Carmine Manor. "I saw it there in his workshop. Can't say I noticed anything unusual about it, but then again, I got only a glance. Pity we don't know the secret word that Mr. Banks had mentioned."

"Perhaps it's written somewhere in your father's things," suggested Douglas. "Any ideas where that might be?"

Out of the corner of her eye, Mary Ann thought she spied something move in the grass along the road.

"Mary Ann?" pressed Douglas.

"Oh, sorry," she said, finding nothing, and resumed. "There weren't any work papers in the house when we searched, were there? So they must be somewhere in the workshop. A shame we never got that far." She glanced up at the sky. It was two o'clock-ish. She'd been gone longer than she'd wanted, and she hoped no one had missed her around the Manor or she'd have ruined her employment status before she'd even begun. "There's no time to search today, either, unfortunately. It will be tea soon." She picked up the pace. "Alas ... Perhaps tomorrow."

Douglas' shorter legs were working hard to keep up. "Do

you think that looking-glass had something to do with your father's death? Someone trying to prevent Queen Valentina from acquiring an escape route?"

"I'd say it was possible," she mused, "but then, why not smash the mirror or steal it? The murder would be unnecessary to achieve that end."

"It is a puzzlement," said the tove.

Soon, they were approaching the road to the Wabe. "Well, here's me," said Douglas, hooking a thumb Wabe-wise. "Best of luck, now. Remember, don't try to get there too quickly or you'll be very late, indeed."

"Thank you. Good day to you, Mr. Divot," and she waved as he ambled down the road into the forest green.

Left with her own thoughts, which had become manifold in recent days, she was pleased to find herself on Lord Carmine's property in no time. The Manor looked so placid from a distance, and as she passed the stables, she considered it quite possible she hadn't been missed at all. But if she had? She would come up with a convenient excuse. Any number of invaluable household tasks might take a person out of reach for a few hours, mightn't they? And she was just deciding whether she wanted to say she'd been perturbing milk into butter, or putting lighter jackets on the library books to suit the warmer weather, when a figure emerged from the stable house like a red-headed explosion.

"Ridiculous!" spat Sir Rufus. "They knew what this day is. Where are they?" To Mary Ann's surprise, he directed this question quite specifically to her.

She stopped. "Excuse me, Sir?"

"I'm supposed to quest for the Jabberwock today," Sir Rufus said. "The single, most important day in the history of my life—and jolly important for the realm of Turvy, as well. Poems have been written about it, you know."

She did know.

"And yet no one's here to help me with my armor, prep my horse, wave flags and say a little, 'You can do it, Rufus. Make us proud by not dying gorribly. Stick it to that Jabberwock!' and so forth. I'm fighting knee-quivering terror here on behalf of the kingdom and there's no one round to appreciate it. Hardly makes it seem worth all the hype."

She understood his dilemma. "Perhaps that paper says something?" She pointed. It was a leaflet tacked to the door of his horse's stable.

He grumbled, marched over, grabbed it and read. "Squire practice?" His outgrabe might have rivaled the mome raths'. "But that was this morning! They should be back by now. It's heading toward brillig. I swear, it's a concerted effort to wound me, in a very real fashion."

"Well, I'm sure you're aware, Sir, that travel in Turvy can be challenging. Particularly when you want to get somewhere very badly. The roads tend to—"

He moaned, head sinking into his hands. "Oh, curse it! — That must be it. Curse *it*, this stupid land of ours, and its rampant idiosyncrasies." He kicked a rock. "Now all the people who were supposed to help me with this epic journey are likely ten squares away, milling about a field, scratching their heads and wondering how the flappin' Jubjub they got there, when they were only going to the stables."

It was highly likely.

"Well," said Rufus, "there's nothing for it, then. There's only one thing we can do."

Go back to the Manor, Mary Ann thought sensibly.

But Sir Rufus sighed and motioned to her. "Come along, miss."

"What?!"

"Let's get this over with. You and I are going on this Jabberwalk."

As she worked with him to saddle his horse, she explained she'd never squired before. As she helped him into layers of battle gear, she told him she'd no experience at all with armor.

As she packed the last of the saddlebags, she expounded on her complete lack of specialized knowledge of Jabberwocks, both wild and domesticated, beyond the lines of one very old poem. And as she rolled up the travel hammocks and loaded them onto the horse, she could tell that Sir Rufus was not remotely listening to her.

Then a glorious idea popped into her head. "If I recall the poem correctly, it never did state a date, did it? It only mentions 'brillig.' Perhaps you could wait until your squiring group finds its way back and do the deed some other brillig," Mary Ann suggested.

He shot her a look. "I take it you're not familiar with the first version of the poem, in its original Olde Turvian?"

That she was not.

"In Olde Turvian, 'slithy' was a condition that toves are known to experience during the month of Jamberry. We call it 'molting' now. It got misinterpreted over the years to mean lithe and slimy."

Now she thought about it, Douglas *was* a bit patchy and shedding, wasn't he? It did seem odd, considering how fastidious he was overall. "Which still means," continued Mary Ann, trying to find some wiggle room in the thing, "that you could do your quest any day this month."

"Ah," the knight raised a finger, "but the poem has another clue to our event's timing. You see, 'mome' wasn't always 'mome.' The original word in the early version of the poem was 'morroam,' which referred to the first feasting day before the rath's late spring migration. And that happens on the sixteenth of the month, like clockwork. A sloppy scribe wrote it down as mome a century later and bungled the whole thing. So you see, it must be done today. Also," he said, "the Vorpal sword showed up in my scabbard." He held up the item in question, a weapon with a long shining blade, serrated teeth at the base, and a fearsomely molded hilt.

There was no getting round it. One cannot argue with magic swords and the feasting patterns of Olde Turvian raths.

So off to the Tulgey Barrens they went, Sir Rufus on his

trusted stallion, a chestnut horse by the name of Goodspeed, and Mary Ann on the only remaining horse in the stables, an elderly rose grey mare called Lolly.

It became clear how powerfully none of them, human and equine alike, wanted be on this journey by how fast they found themselves in the deepest, darkest part of the Tulgey Barrens.

"Now, this is important," began Sir Rufus in hushed tones, for hushed tones seemed just the thing in this part of the forest, "the Jabberwock is like no other creature in the land. Research suggests it stands at over twenty feet high. Its claws are so sharp, it can rip right through non-Vorpal steel. Its jaws—well, you saw the head. Powerful and razor-like. It has breath like an old rotted onion and leathery wings and a whiplike tail. Its singing voice is—"

"It sings?"

"Right before it goes in for the slaughter," he said. "Also in the bath. So keep alert; you'll need to discern which is which."

Suddenly, she understood the need for squire practice and wished she'd gotten a bit of it.

The trees grew together more densely as Mary Ann and the knight proceeded on their journey. Goodspeed expressed some opinions about the expedition ("These shoes hurt ..." "I'm thirsty..." "My saddle itches..."), while Lolly's ears twitched, listening for dangers ahead.

They reached a marshy part of the wood and Goodspeed came to a sharp stop. "Nope, sorry. This is me done," he said.

"What? Why?" Sir Rufus asked. "*Fine...We'll fix* the saddle."

"It's not the saddle," said Goodspeed, "it's ... my Uncle Reggie died like this."

"He died chasing the Jabberwock?" Perhaps Sir Rufus and the horse normally didn't chat that much.

"'Twas a squirrel, sir," said Goodspeed. "But, oh, what a fury of a squirrel, he was! Clawed, fanged, conniving and — and—"

Rufus raised a skeptical eyebrow. "Ripped him to shreds, did it?"

"Lured him into a swamp and he drowned. A swamp just

like that one." The horse pointed with a hoof.

Rufus sighed and dismounted, grabbing the horse's face and giving him a black look. "You're supposed to be my noble steed."

"Yes, Sir. And it's no bull when I say I'll be waiting for you right here, if—er, *when*—*when* you make it back."

Mary Ann dismounted, too—not so easy in that awkward housemaid dress — and called to Lolly. "Your uncle wasn't killed in a luring-by-squirrel incident, was he?" But Lolly had fallen asleep standing up. "Oh, never mind."

They grabbed their saddlebags and hammock rolls, and Sir Rufus his shield and sword. They would continue the journey on foot.

They sought their manxome foe for what seemed like a very long time, slogging through marshlands, searching the intermittent areas of solid ground for claw prints or the drag of a tail … Checking the underbrush for broken branches … Listening for unexpected singing, or the sounds of someone having a bath.

Mary Ann supposed they were making history — weren't they? —in the pursuit of the Jabberwock. Or making past, if one wished to be pedantic. But she couldn't help but think she had a lot more pressing matters to which she should be attending right now. Like dusting, fetching water — oh, and finding out why her father was killed.

She was thinking very hard about this last point—so hard, she was surprised to hear her own voice say, "What does one do about a murder in Turvy these days?"

"Oh." The knight seemed taken aback at the suddenness of the conversation. "Well, I suppose that depends on whether you're committing or prosecuting. If you're planning to commit one, I wouldn't recommend it from the beginning. Just resist the temptation and don't look back, is what I say." Sir Rufus squinted in thought. "Unless it's Jabberwock-related. In which case it wouldn't be so much a murder as a slaying. Slaying is pre-approved, you see, whilst murder makes it hard to get yourself invited round to holiday dinners."

"No," said Mary Ann, "no murderous plans on my part. I was just wondering what the protocol was for, say…witnessing a general murder here in Turvy? Hypothetically, of course."

"Generally speaking," he began, "that's determined by the Square in which it was committed. I understand Square Twelve has a person who solely investigates questionable deaths. But that's because part of Twelve is located on mead mine and people vanish into it regularly; I heard the same fellow's in charge of a rehabilitation program." Sir Rufus pushed aside a branch. "But in Square Six, all cases go to the Earl there, and in Square Eleven it's the Duke. And then if it's the border between squares, an inter-lord coalition's involved and the two groups have to duke it out."

"Or earl or baron," said Mary Ann.

"Precisely!" said Rufus. "Then, if it can't be agreed upon there, it gets bumped up to the Red or White Royals. It's all about jurisdictions."

"What about this Square?"

"Oh, well, Square Four," he said, "it gets brought to my father who dispatches his guards to investigate the situation. Then he rules on the evidence. Funny you mention it, actually," Rufus said, "because he hired two lead guards not long ago who've really taken to the position. Father's impressed."

"And what process does Lord Carmine use in these cases?" asked Mary Ann.

"First he decides if it's a forward or backwards murder. If the evidence suggests it's done forward—that is, the planning first, then the killing—there's nothing to be done but find the killer and bring him to justice; the murder can't be avoided. But if it's a backwards murder, then that would mean the killer might still be gathering resources and planning after the fact. So there's a chance of stopping the thing altogether."

"But the victim would still be dead," said Mary Ann.

"Never underestimate the power of poor follow-through," said Rufus. "It can undo a backwards situation like that." He snapped his fingers—or would have, if he hadn't been wearing metal gloves.

Mary Ann mulled all this over a moment. "So what becomes of the murderer if they're found guilty?" she asked.

"Typically, a public execution and all the murderer's possessions go to the family of the victim. Unless, of course, they have something my father likes."

Well, at least he's up front about it, thought Mary Ann. "And if the murderer is not Turvian?"

The knight considered this. "I believe the rulers of the killer's homeland would have to get involved."

"So if it were a citizen of ... say ... Neath that did the murdering," Mary Ann hoped it sounded like some random choice, "the case would go to Queen Valentina?"

"Very likely." He mused on this a moment further. "Yes... yes, I imagine it would. And perhaps it has, but I can't recall any such case." Sir Rufus eyed her. "What brought all this on?"

"I don't know, Sir," said Mary Ann, who thought quickly. "It's very likely follow-up to a backwards political justice conversation we'll have some future day. I look forward to it!" She offered him her most demure, most housemaidly smile and promptly went invisible.

"Yes, I suppose..." His tone sounded unconvinced, but he did leave it at that.

They went on in silence for some time more, before the sun worked its way toward the horizon and Sir Rufus spoke again. "Miss? Where've you—? Oh." He fixed on her. "There you are. We should make camp, while we still have daylight. This is a good place," he said, indicating a small grove of trees and a rocky clearing. "I was hoping we'd already be done with this Jabberwock thing by now, but it seems our guest of honor is uncooperative. You'll be all right with a night in the woods?"

"A knight or a night?" she asked. "I expect it depends on the character of both."

At this he flushed, muttered, "I suppose that's true. I can only guarantee the one," and fell back into silence. They set down their gear and for the next few minutes, Sir Rufus clanked around gathering wood and Mary Ann set about unfurling the travel hammocks.

She had managed to untangle them and was about to tie the first to an accessible tree when she heard a tumbling sound. Looking up, she saw Sir Rufus standing frozen in the waning sun, an armful of logs at his feet. His gaze was drawn to the path before them.

"*It...is...here...*" he breathed, fear in his eyes, his long face ghastly pale under his helmet.

Mary Ann turned slowly in the direction of his gaze to see two red lights hovering in the dusk. With them came a sound, a mournful burbling melody like a warbling bird drowning in a babbling brook.

Sir Rufus dove for his scabbard, seized it, and brandished the sword with a bright, metallic sound.

"Ah, young knight," said the Jabberwock, its voice cold and cavernous, "here you are. Just as the poem foretold."

"If you know the poem, then you know this conflict does not end well for you," Sir Rufus called out. "So I'll give you one chance. Turn around now and leave this Square forever or face the Vorpal blade."

"You know as well as I that in Turvy there are no absolutes. The poem could change at any time. Perhaps," mused the Jabberwock, "it already has." And the creature moved closer, picking up its tune once more.

"Sing all you like. I hope the song soothes you through your death throes," shouted Rufus.

"The music is for you, Sir Knight. It is your mourning song." And the Jabberwock rushed forward, a flurry of claws and wings.

There were several things the poem did not document, Mary Ann noted from her quiet place among the trees. It didn't say how the Jabberwock shot fiery breath over the knight and how he grabbed up his shield just in time, as heat poured over him, scorching the metal of the gauntlet that braced it.

The poem also did not detail the way Sir Rufus was swiftly left with no strategic alternatives but to back away from the beast, backing deeper into the wood until a single step sunk him down...down...knee-deep into the marshland, the weight of his armor working so cruelly against him.

It did not describe the way the Jabberwock was rapidly upon him, claws reaching, song shrieking in the late afternoon air, as Sir Rufus held aloft the Vorpal sword and countered the talons with every strike.

It also didn't mention how Mary Ann Carpenter, housemaid and backup squire, looked frantically around, grabbed up one of the hammocks and silently moved behind the hovering creature. She took a deep breath, wished herself fortune and tossed the rope contraption over one of the monster's flapping, leathery wings.

The reaction was instantaneous. The wing beat wildly, only tangling itself further in the web of rope, causing the creature to teeter and drop unceremoniously onto the ground of their campsite. In a moment, the monster had whipped around trying to grab at the ropes, but its arms were too short to reach.

It sent around its long neck and head to finish the job. And that, in its snarling frustration, was when it laid eyes on Mary Ann.

"Now, where did you come from?" it hissed.

Mary Ann snatched up the second hammock, picked up her skirt and raced around the beast. Housemaid's work makes a person quick, light on their feet and strong, yet even so, she only just dodged a blast of flame erupting from the creature's jaws. The Tumtum tree behind her was not so lucky and shrieked in pain.

But the Jabberwock was still tracking her. Rufus, she saw, had finally emerged from the marsh onto solid ground and was closing in fast. If she could keep the monster distracted a short while longer, they might be able to...

She paused and flung the second hammock, aiming for the creature's head, but the Jabberwock was slippery and swift. The makeshift net careened halfway to its target before the creature opened its jagged maw and set the rope ablaze, mid-air. Orange ashes tumbled to the ground.

"Silly girl!" cried the creature. "You can't fool me twice with the same trick."

"I wouldn't dream of it," said Mary Ann. "This one has a twist ending."

And SNICKER-SNACK! The Vorpal blade did its duty before the Jabberwock knew what hit it. Over and over again, Sir Rufus plunged the blade into the creature's hide with a slick, sickening, slicing sound.

The Jabberwock sank down onto the sandy earth. "This…isn't…the way…the poem went," rasped the creature.

"This is Turvy," said Sir Rufus. "There are no absolutes."

The creature was twitching and twisting now. "My name," it burbled, "never even made…the poem…"

It hadn't occurred to Mary Ann that the Jabberwock might have a name. "What is it, then?" she asked, suddenly feeling as sad as she was curious.

"Tell them …" The blood was running thick and yellow from its mouth now. "Tell them it was…Rumbledring."

Mary Ann promised she would, but the creature gave a last shuddering breath and she couldn't be sure it had heard her.

And now here was Sir Rufus with the Vorpal sword again. "Move aside. I have to cut off the head."

Mary Ann winced. "Oh, but Sir…"

"Yes?"

"It had a name." She used "It" only because she never learned whether it was Madam or Mister Rumbledring, and looking to see would be but one more indignity to the poor, slain creature.

"See here," said Sir Rufus, "do you think I like this? Was this how I wanted to spend my Jamberry evening? No. But the head was on the wall of the Manor as long as I can remember. Clearly, I beheaded it." He frowned. "Or will do. Besides, if we take care of this now, we can reach the road through the Tulgey Barrens before dark."

Mary Ann nodded but reluctance must have clung to her face.

"The lack of head will not affect its current health," he reminded her.

He had a point. He had several. So Mary Ann nodded again

and moved out of the way. She was packing up the parts of their camp that hadn't been charcoal-broiled, when she heard the final blow that separated head from neck. And the marshes ran red. Of course, that was their natural color.

"You have your gear?" Rufus called now.

"I do," she said. And as he carried the Jabberwock's head, she took his saddlebag as well as her own. She was glad to. She had reached her quota for handling decapitations in the past two days.

"Then we're off," he said. "The Jubjub birds may be to bed, but the Bandersnatch still roam. And I don't know about you, but I prefer never to meet one. Let's go gather Lolly and Goodspeed."

They had not gotten far from camp when they saw it, and if it hadn't been for the last streams of sun beaming across the woodland plains, Mary Ann didn't think they would have seen it at all. It was not a Bandersnatch. It looked like someone had taken a pile of rocks and stacked them into a careful pyramid. She pointed out the shape, in silhouette now, to Sir Rufus. "Look! Is that some sort of religious space over there? Or a sundial? It's rather pretty."

But Sir Rufus did not find it pretty. He groaned. "Oh, of all the cursed things…I simply cannot believe…" He gritted his teeth and motioned. "Come along, miss." And he headed straight toward the structure.

She followed. "I'm sorry: what are we doing?" She could see the pyramid more closely now. The objects seemed to be silver-grey, ovoid, with a slight pearlescent sheen.

They were not rocks.

"Jabberwock eggs," confirmed Sir Rufus.

"But how is that possible?" asked Mary Ann. "I thought there was only one Jabberwock." She couldn't imagine how that worked. She rather wished she'd peeked now.

"You only need one for this sort of thing. Jabberwocks are funny that way. Fortunately, they only lay eggs every three hundred years." The knight drew his sword.

It had been a day for interesting Jabberwock tidbits. And

now Mary Ann saw the awful truth. "So it was protecting its nest? The poem said nothing about it protecting its nest."

"Epic poems leave out much of the fine print," said Sir Rufus miserably.

"There must be twenty eggs there," she said.

"And twenty future Jabberwocks, if this thing goes forward."

Mary Ann knew where he was headed with this, and she understood it. But it still felt wrong. "It'll be the end of the species then," she said.

"Twenty hatched Jabberwocks and it'll be the end of Turvy."

Mary Ann braced herself. "Heroism isn't very cut and dry, is it?"

"Sometimes it's just cut," he said, and applied the Vorpal sword to the task at hand.

When they stepped inside Carmine Manor, the first thing Mary Ann noted was the empty space over the fireplace in the entry hall that would not be empty for long. The second thing she noticed was the crowd that oozed through the corridors, like a spilled bucket of treacle, into the room to greet them. All the squires had returned and the staff joined, too, everyone clapping and cheering. And emerging from the middle of this merry band of supporters came none other than Lord Carmine.

"And hast thou slain the Jabberwock?" Carmine asked in his most booming voice.

Sir Rufus squinted at him. "Olde Turvian, Father? Really?"

"Oh. Well…" The elder man shrugged, "I felt I should keep to the poem. It's my one bit of dialogue." He cleared his throat and resumed, "And hast thou—?"

"You can see I have the head right here." Sir Rufus held it aloft.

The crowd gasped.

"Er, yes, quite," Lord Carmine was still trying to stay on track, "then, come to my arms my beamish—"

But Sir Rufus waved him off. "Oh, hug yourself, Dad. I want to get out of this armor and have a bath. Got half a bog in my boots." He thrust Rumbledring's head at his father and turned. "Tell Mother I'm home and I'll come in to see her shortly. Squires? Some help, please?"

Having missed their questing opportunity, they were more than eager to assist with this. Mary Ann heard one of them explain they'd somehow ended up in Yon...

Apparently, it *was* very nice this time of year.

So as the squires and quest fans surrounded Sir Rufus with drink and praise and the chance for dry feet, Mary Ann drew back and went invisible again. It was bound to happen in situations like this, of triumph and glory. And such was the right order of things, she was sure. She slipped up the stairs to the servant's chamber, washed away her souvenirs of sweat and swamp, and changed straight away for bed. Tonight, hers was a weariness from within and nothing but sleep would satisfy it. She was nearly safely off in blissful slumber, when Emmaline entered the room, bounded onto the bed like a puppy, nudged her and whispered, "Is it true? Were you on that Jabberwock quest with Sir Rufus all this time? Celeste and Mabel say I've lost what good sense I had, but now I *know* I saw you both—"

But Mary Ann didn't want to talk about Jabberwock quests and she certainly didn't want to talk about Sir Rufus. She faked a reasonable snore until Emmaline resigned herself to conversations lost, and did whatever it was she did when she wasn't sleeping, scrubbing pots or talking.

6

Emmaline was still brimming with questions by morning, but Mary Ann found that a bright new day filled with chores had a handy way of swapping the epic for the practical in short order. Mary Ann was grateful for it, because she had more important concerns on her mind than knights and monsters, and who squired for whom. Like: when she could sneak away to her father's workshop and do a little poking around there. She planned her getaway right after the early afternoon tasks were done.

When she did approach her father's workshop, it was with care, wondering if she would ever again set foot on this property without a tinge of fear. She looked for fresh footsteps pressed into the path. She listened for any sounds of movement within, then she slowly pushed open the door, flinching at its shy creak. A quick scan of the room showed no one in wait. She looked down and rubbed at the red stain on the floor with the toe of her shoe.

Her attention moved from there to the mirror. It was special glass, Mr. Banks had said. An escape hatch to somewhere. "Say the right word and you were there." She peered into the mirror. It reflected the room behind her like any standard looking-glass. She pressed a hand to the glass and it left five little oval smudges just as it should. She ran a hand along the frame, but there was no trigger, no special lever, nothing out of the ordinary to suggest this was anything but your standard mirror. She peered around the back of it: standard wooden backing, no secret password inscribed.

She searched the frame for repeating patterns, carefully hidden words in the whirling, twirling, carved vines. She focused and unfocused her eyes, hoping something clever might pop out at her.

But nothing did.

Had Mr. Banks been fooling with her or had the glass been swapped by an intruder for something less exotic? She saw no signs of tampering around the inlay. It was all very curious.

And that curiosity brought her to her feet, which led her to her father's bench — a wooden piece that no one would ever have guessed he'd made. Stylistically, it was very spare, none of the embellishments he was known for, none of the fantastic pulls and fittings his clients received. But the drawers slid smoothly as Mary Ann examined their contents. And the chair next to it was very comfortable as she sat to examine the items she found.

She went through bills of sale, which appeared quite boring and unhelpful. She ruffled through commission requests. She spied thank you notes. And she found her father's accounting books.

On this last one, she yawned — not wholly due to the dullness of the subject matter, but because there never did seem to be enough sleep lately. She forced herself to focus.

Her father's accounts were meticulous, she discovered, everything tallied forward and backward and even sideways. He had every item he'd ever crafted logged in this book, from the cost of materials to detailed specifications of the piece, to special features, color and price. It was only toward the end of the book that there were half a dozen items that were circled in red ink. She recognized the hand as her father's. "Check with Banks" was the phrase next to them, also in red. It seemed the down-payment had been received for each. The final payment column was blank.

So Mr. Banks either hadn't yet collected the money from the sales or he never distributed it to her father. It didn't seem like much motive for murder, but the discrepancy was worth noting. She set this log aside.

She went through receipts for his general household expenditures, food, supplies…Nothing seemed particularly odd there. There were no potential magic words scrawled down anywhere that she could see, and nothing seemed to connect him with Jacob Morningstar or the Neath Royal Family at all, beyond the commission of that mirror for Mr. Rabbit.

And what to do about that mirror? She turned to face it. Originally, she'd thought she might get the piece to Mr. Rabbit in time for Queen Valentina's Unbirthday celebration in nine days hence, but now she wasn't sure how she'd manage. It was such an awkward position in which to be—witness to the Who, When and What but not the Why. Stuck between lands and invisible in both. Missing but not missing at the same time. In danger but possibly not in danger…Pursued and forgotten… Makeshift squiring and maid-shifts tiring…

Monsters who weren't entirely monsters. Monsters with names: Rumbledring.

Murderers who were very much killers. Killers with names: Jacob Morningstar.

Magicless magic mirrors and no instructions to be found.

Nothing amiss. Just those missing final payments…

Well—she stood and sighed, grabbing the accounts book— there was nothing for it. She would have to take a quick jaunt to Mr. Banks' home and ask him about the payment situation. With the money owed on hand, she could buy a new nightdress and replace the other essentials she'd had to leave behind. It would be a welcome resolution. It would be nice to have one thing that did not lie Between.

But when she reached Mr. Banks' lovely abode, there were no lit lamps by the windows of the little cottage and his boat was absent from the dock. Off on a sails call, perhaps? Trying to earn the most from that back catalogue of finished projects? Or undertaking the unpleasant task of notifying clients that their commissions were canceled due to tragic circumstance?

She supposed she would be in charge of her father's part of the business now, at least for a while, wouldn't she? She would get a cut of the remaining stock that sold. This would be her inheritance.

The front door to Mr. Banks' cottage, she saw now, was ever-so-slightly ajar. Perhaps the man was here after all and someone had just borrowed his boat. "Mr. Banks?" She knocked and poked her head inside. "It's Mary Ann Carpenter, again…Mr. Banks?"

Silence.

She moved through the house to the back porch, that tranquil spot with the view of the river. Up the river, down the river, there was no sign of the fellow's boat. Their teacups, however, were just as they had been the day before. Though now the teapot was cold and the tea leaves clumped, moist on their way to mold.

Mary Ann stepped from the porch into the house, a sick feeling forming in her stomach. She ventured into the bedchamber. The bed was made. She threw open the wardrobe doors. That was empty … No, wait, not entirely empty. One cravat had escaped, trailing across its floor, wrinkled and forlorn. It seemed Mr. Banks had made a grand exit.

Mary Ann Carpenter did the same.

She was almost back to the manor house, wrapped up in thoughts of boats and bookmaking, business partners and buggering off, when she heard a voice say, "Very rude of you, you know."

"Beg pardon?" She turned.

"Begging isn't necessary, but a brief apology would do." Sir Rufus was leaning on the Vorpal sword. There was no trace of expression that suggested he was joking. He assessed her coolly.

"I apologize, Sir," she said, with no sincerity whatsoever. "Please apply it to a topic, as necessary."

"Very well, miss. I thank you," he said, and she turned back to the path. "Wait: where are you going?"

"To the Manor, Sir. I've chores to do."

"Then who will help me with my Jabberwock training?"

This seemed to be the maddest question in what already was turning out to be a rather mad day. She wondered how she could answer it and still be at all polite. "Well, the squires, Sir, I'm sure would be most happy to—"

"Of course they'd be happy. But this isn't about pleasing them. We don't all go round trying to figure out how to please the squires, do we?"

She thought it was probably best not to respond.

He exhaled in frustration. "My squires weren't with me when I slayed the Jabberwock, were they? You were. You were invaluable at every step. So you're the one to help me with my training. It's simple sense."

Sense doesn't enter into it, she thought. "Regrettably, Sir," she began carefully, "I don't know anything about sword training."

"Well," he sniffed, "not knowing about something hardly prevents a person from doing it. Lots of people teach things about which they haven't the slightest inkling. You can learn it afterwards. There'll be plenty of time then." He held out a sword to her, a non-Vorpal one. "Come on…" He shook the weapon impatiently, waiting for her to take it.

She sighed. She decided she would go along with the plan for now. He would change his mind and give up on the folly once he discovered he was trying to get blood from a stone. "If you wish, Sir," she said and accepted the weapon. It did have a nice weight to it. Not too heavy, but well-balanced.

She wasn't sure how she knew that.

But the maddest thing of all was, an hour sparring with the sword and Sir Rufus proved that she did, indeed, know more than a little something about swordsmanship. Ideas and very good advice flowed from her like rain through a downspout and it was clear that this was some serious backwards training she'd gotten.

Surely, it must be a mistake. Whoever would care to train a

housemaid in sword fighting? The whole thing was absurd.

They were right in the middle of a Reverse Pass (it was startling how the term popped into her mind), when she noticed some movement out of the corner of her eye. The object in question was yellow, low to the ground and coming on fast. It was so peculiar that both teacher and student paused, breathless in their work, to further examine it.

This thing was sprinting through the yard and it had no business sprinting at all. The creature was the skin of an exotic fruit; Mary Ann believed it was called a banana. Yet, on its face —if you could call it a face, for it was only a few face-implying brown spots below the black top of the thing—were spectacles. And these were attached to a papier-maché nose and moustaches. Mary Ann had to admit, it wore the whole ensemble quite successfully for not having any ears to keep it in place. She burst out laughing. "Whatever is that?"

"Absolutely no clue," frowned Sir Rufus. Now he turned the blue-eyed scowl on Mary Ann. "Why are you laughing?"

Having to explain it drained away some of her own mirth, she found. "Well, it's quite funny, isn't it, Sir? How it runs on the flaps of its own fruit peel feet?"

But Sir Rufus' long face just grew longer as they watched the creature continue on down the path and vanish. It was making excellent time. "I wouldn't know." Sir Rufus sighed. "I lost my sense of humor several weeks ago, and I can't find it anywhere. Without it, everything has seemed rather bland, irritating and pointless. Wouldn't have even done that Jabberwock business, if all of Red Turvy weren't relying on me."

"Ah …" Suddenly, this explained so much about her interactions with the knight. "Where do you recall seeing your humor last?" Mary Ann asked.

"Oh, around my Unbirthday," he said. "It feels like ages ago. I remember laughing at a joke my mother made. I've not had so much as a snicker since then."

"Perhaps I can help you search for it," Mary Ann offered, wondering why she was adding another obligation to her to-do list. "What does it look like?"

He shrugged. "Never seen it. It's humor. Sneaks up on you, doesn't it? Strikes you when you're not looking. But I'd know it if I saw it. That's for certain."

"Then how can you be sure it's even gone?" she asked.

His expression was defiant. "Okay. Tell me a joke."

Mary Ann blinked. She hadn't bothered to learn many jokes. She'd never had anyone to tell them to. She thought about it a moment. She *had* heard this riddle once…"Why is a raven like a writing desk?"

"I don't know," said Rufus, "why *is* a raven like a writing desk?"

"Because Poe wrote on both," said Mary Ann.

Rufus raised an eyebrow. "And who's Poe exactly?"

"Haven't the foggiest," said Mary Ann.

Rufus squinted. "Not a very good joke then, is it?"

She was hoping it would make more sense to him. "I could come up with another one," she suggested, trying to help.

"No, don't bother." He was so crestfallen. "The point is, that it appears my humor is gone forever. Imagine, living here in Turvy with no sense of humor. What will become of me? I'll be an outcast. I'll be shut away in the Manor Tower just like—" And his face reddened, as if all of his freckles had finally bandied together to form a unified front.

"Like…?" The word hung on the air. Mary Ann waited, almost afraid to move and disrupt it.

"Never mind." He cleared his throat. "It's almost tea time. I'd best let you get back. Will you train with me again tomorrow?"

"Sir, I'd love to but—"

"I'll clear it for you."

And Mary Ann walked back to the Manor wondering at many things, not the least of which being how she'd somehow ended up teaching knight school.

The tea preparations were well underway when Mary Ann arrived. "Why, there you are!" said Cook. "Mrs. Cordingley was looking Nowhere for you. She'd looked Everywhere first and then gave up."

"Oh dear," the housemaid said. "I'm so sorry. Sir Rufus had asked me to help him trai—"

The woman thrust a platter into Mary Ann's hands. "Well, you can help me tray now. Take that into the dining room."

Mary Ann sighed. She imagined Emmaline was somewhere close-by to handle the thing, but it was going to be quicker and easier to simply do as requested. She performed the task and as Mary Ann returned, she noticed Mrs. Cordingley coming down from the back circular steps, carrying another silver platter of empty plates. These steps, it dawned on her, were the very ones that led to the Tower.

"Is someone up there?" she heard herself ask aloud. It was a terrible thing when one spent so much of one's life in one's own head; too often and too late, one discovered thoughts had inadvertently oozed into the open.

"What business is it of yours?" snapped Mrs. Cordingley. "Remember yourself, miss. You're the housemaid."

"There's house in the Tower," said Mary Ann hopefully.

"No house with which you're welcome to concern yourself. Now off with you! Go fetch washing from the line before the dew gets on it!" she shouted. Mary Ann scrambled away, though down the hall she could still hear the lady add, "And stay away from the Tower!"

The Tower was very dark now that evening had fallen, a weak candle the only companion Mary Ann had dared on this excursion. She'd been thinking about it all day, and the question was not so much, "To defy or not defy orders?" as it was,

"When is the perfect moment to do so?" Mrs. Cordingley and the rest of the women staff were in their quarters, having been dismissed for the night and settling in for some quiet time. Mrs. Cordingley and Mabel were darning the items that were still too proper for a full damning. And Cook and Emmaline were both pouring through recipe books, making notes, stomachs rumbling a duet with dreams of future dinners.

From this placid scene, Mary Ann had stepped out, invisible, wearing her borrowed nightdress and on bare feet. It was so easy to slip away when others' minds were occupied. Yet, now that the opportunity had presented itself to ascend the Tower stairs, the housemaid's legs felt heavy. The day of sword-fighting, crime scene investigation, walrus-tracking and even a fair share of housemaiding had clearly taken its toll.

Mrs. Cordingley was right, of course: whoever was up here, living in the Tower, it really was no business of hers. A proper housemaid would respect the wishes of her employers and stick to the basics of flustering, fetching and folding. But Mary Ann was also aware that with knowledge came critical opportunities for self-preservation. In fact, oftentimes it was the only power someone in her position was likely to have. So she'd found making the extra effort to pry into the depths of her various employment situations was an added assurance of her continued survival.

There was but one door at the top of the Tower stairs, she discovered, and as secret things tended to be, there was a padlock on it the size of the palm of her hand. Mary Ann assumed the key was on the large ring carried around by Mrs. Cordingley. She examined the shape of the lock. Quite large, with a hole roughly the size of a small coin; that would help narrow it down, at least. Perhaps there would be future opportunity to slip that key away and give the room a proper investigation. But for now, Mary Ann settled for pressing an ear against the wood.

It was at that moment, a man's voice called out. "You stay there, you hear me? You've nothing to offer me! Not now, not ever! Nothing at all, I say."

She leapt back, startled. Surely, he couldn't be speaking to her, could he? How would he even know she was there? Did light from her meager candle seep so powerfully into the room?

"Hello?" Mary Ann whispered through the door. "Hello, who is this?"

And then came the laughter, deep, gleeful, and entirely disturbed. It was a one-hundred-and-eighty degree change from the voice's desperate tone just moments before. It took the breath right from her, and she started down the stairs, covered in chill, the maniacal cackling still in her ears.

She would have run all the way down the stairs and straight to her bedchamber had she not heard the clap of feet on the floor somewhere below. The echo made it hard to determine from where the sound came, so she stopped short halfway down the steps. She blew out the flame and pressed up against the staircase wall. The clapping was closer now and she realized shortly it was the First Footman whose name, she'd learned, was Mr. Francis. Clip-clop, clip-clop into the kitchen he came, a kerosene lamp in tow. A second later, she heard the swinging door of the larder. "Oh, yes! I thought we'd a bit of this left!" And Mary Ann suspected she knew his aim: the carrot cake with sugared fruit on top. At dinner he had stood tableside, and she'd caught his expression of wistful longing.

There was silence for more than a few moments and she wondered if the cake lived up to his dreams and whether it was worth the inevitable staff interrogations that would take place should that slice be missed tomorrow.

She supposed it was. Because he came trotting out now, wiping his face with the back of his wrist, bobbing his head in the light like a fellow who knew something good when he'd got it. And in a jiff, he had trotted off again into the night.

Mary Ann ran back into their quarters and hopped into bed, just as Mrs. Cordingley tucked her needle into the pincushion and said, "Lights out then, ladies."

Emmaline emerged from the unending feast of her mind, snapping the cookbook shut and tucking it under her pillow like the locket of a loved one. She turned an eye to Mary Ann.

"Why, you're very red, aren't you? Were you always so flushed or are you not quite well?"

"Oh, just Red Turvian born and bred," Mary Ann said.

Cook piped up, "The bread's tomorrow's task."

"Yes," agreed Mrs. Cordingley, stiffly. "Stop showing off and trying to get ahead, Tamsin. It doesn't become you. Makes you look arrogant."

Mary Ann wasn't about to argue. "Yes, Mrs. Cordingley," she said.

The lamp went out thereafter.

"Bewareeeee," said a voice light and squeaky. And it was a groggy Mary Ann who rolled over to her bunkmate. Had Emmaline started talking in her sleep, too? Between the mystery snorer and this ungodly murmuring, Mary Ann feared she'd never get a good night's rest.

"Bewareeee," said the little voice again, but it wasn't coming from Emmaline's side of the bed. It was alongside her own. "Do not pursue the death of Rowan Carpenter or you, too, shall meet his fate! Meddle again and it will be at your own risk!"

She was sure this was not Emmaline now and she was fairly certain she was awake. She grabbed the candle from her side table and lit it with shaking hands. Something moved as she shone it around the room. She didn't see anyone, but one thing on the floor did catch her eye. There were glistening droplets leading from the opened door to the side of her bed, and now under it. She leapt to the floor and dove under the bedskirt, trying to see through the dim. She heard a rustle, swore she saw the far edge of the dustruffle move, and heard something scurry around the other side. Mary Ann pulled herself out from under the bed just as the door squeaked shut.

"What are you doing?" This was Mrs. Cordingley's voice now, heavy with sleep. "Put out that light. I swear, you girls will be the death of me. I knew I should have taken that job at the laundry."

Mary Ann quenched the candle for the second time that night. And when dawn arrived, and the house came alive again, even the mists of sleep did not prevent her from leaping out of bed immediately and looking at the floor where the shimmering trail of droplets had been.

Of course, there was nothing there, nothing at all.

7

Mary Ann was starting to wonder what was real and what was not, these days. Not that Turvy—or Neath for that matter—would ever be called sensible. Or stable. Or not completely off its trolley. But when one lived there, one had certain expectations for the place. One learned to work around the land and each other's eccentricities. One sallied forth, pondered very little, and adapted nicely. But lately, life seemed to be somewhat more...itself...than even usual. Either the place was becoming much more Muchy or quite possibly, Mary Ann had lost the plot.

There was also the uncomfortable thought that, if the events of the previous night had been real, then someone knew exactly who she was, where she was, and that she was trying to solve her father's murder. She greatly preferred the "it was all a vivid dream" theory, to being found out and duly warned. She supposed a warning displayed at least some goodwill on her visitor's part; it was a greater courtesy than her father had gotten. But it did add certain complications to an already thorny time.

These were the issues she considered as she worked on the upstairs family quarters. She had just finished Lord Carmine's and Sir Rufus' chambers. The first involved more time gathering up bits and bobs than anything else; the elder man was prone to scattering his possessions over flat surfaces like a whirlwind ripping through a variety store. On the other hand, the young knight had a methodical precision to his belongings that made Mary Ann's job quite easy. She wondered if it had always been so, or if the joyful gleam of life having been stricken from him, Sir Rufus found what solace he could by ensuring his boots all faced the same direction.

With those rooms tidied, buffed and gleaming, Mary Ann now paused at the door to Lady Carmine's room. She had not, in her time so far, seen Lady Carmine aside from the portrait in the sitting room downstairs. That was elegant but a bit over-red to suit Mary Ann's taste: the ginger hair, red dress, red chair, red floor and red tapestry behind her suggesting that to the artist, too much of a good thing meant he was only just getting warmed up. Word had been, Lady Carmine was under the weather of late and shouldn't be disturbed. Someone did, indeed, seem to be in the room, for through the morning dim, light filtered around the door seams with the uneven flicker of a kerosene lamp.

She had turned away from the door, a certain squeak of her shoe on the floorboard, as a light, shaky voice called, "It's all right. Please come in."

Mary Ann pushed open the door and a rush of cold air surrounded her. The floor was a sheet of ice. There was frost on the windows. There was a light coating of snow on the blankets and side tables. A grey cloud perched right above the head of Lady Carmine's bed. It seemed a parasol had been set up to shield her from the most direct precipitation, but wind had blown it askew so the lady's long hair was frosted into a pale orange and her red bedclothes a pink. The poor woman was shuddering from the top of her head to her blanketed toes.

The first thing Mary Ann did was drop her bucket and scrub brush, and slide across the icy floor to put the parasol back in its place.

"Oh, thank you so much!" murmured the lady, her face

flushed with cold. "I daresay, I woke up with a much higher wind-chill than yesterday."

Mary Ann nodded and bee-lined for the fireplace. The fire was low, so she put on a few more logs and tended them with the poker. Wherever was Celeste? Shouldn't she be helping here?

"We haven't met, but I assume you're the new housemaid my husband was telling me about," rasped the woman. "He said your name is Marion? Darienne? Tamelyn? Tamsin?"

"Yes, My Lady," Mary Ann said. Now that the fire was showing some energy, Mary Ann moved to the bedding, shaking off a layer of snow and replacing the topmost cover with a fresh quilt.

"Well, which is it, dear?" the woman asked.

"Whichever is your preference, My Lady." She moved to the windows. They were completely iced over from the inside. She looked around and spied the silent butler on the table. That might work. She grabbed up the dustpan portion and used it like an ice scraper, in hopes of getting at least some morning sun in—until the next frost, anyway.

"You poor child," the patient was saying, and Mary Ann was surprised to still be on Lady Carmine's mind. "You've forgotten your name, haven't you?"

"Forgotten it, My Lady?"

"Oh, it happens," the woman said sympathetically. "Ask my sister. She forgot her name once. Terribly difficult for her." *Scrape, scrape, scrape.* "For a period of time she felt quite strongly her name might be Herbert. But Father's favorite hound was called Herbert, so it caused all sorts of confusion between the three of them. She came out of it quite well, though, once the hunting season was over."

Mary Ann nodded. *Scrape, scrape, scrape...*

"Do you recall anything about your background? Your childhood?" asked Lady Carmine.

"There is nothing much to tell, My Lady." Mary Ann had learned long ago, when people asked questions like that, they were typically using it as a segue to tell you about themselves.

"Nonsense, dear, everyone has a tale to tell," said Lady Carmine. "And it's so dull for me up here. Do you have any parents? Any family? Tell me about them."

"Well," said Mary Ann, hoping to stall and go invisible, yet finding herself noticeably Not. In her panic, she began, "My father was a botanist and sea captain for the Royal Red Navy and my mother, a favorite seamstress to the Red Queen…"

Once the fantasy started to unfurl, it took on a life of its own. In no time, her father had fought pirates, explored mysterious new lands, and put the fox in foxglove. Her mother had designed and sewn the Red Turvian flag and made Queen Rosamund's robes for Red Turvy's five hundredth anniversary celebration. Besides this, never were there two more doting parents. When he was on leave, her father would teach Mary Ann sea shanties and how they'd sing by the fire while her mother sewed. When he was away, he would send messages across the water by flamingo twice a day, telling them of his devastation that they had been so cruelly parted. Then her father died in a typhoon off Hither, caused by the poorly-timed head cold of a giant. Her mother developed a rare metal poisoning from sewing needles and passed soon thereafter. And that was the reason Mary Ann was alone in this world.

It was as Mary Ann finished her tale and came once more to her own body and mind, that she saw the window scraped clear of frost. Great steaming lies, it would seem, may have aided in its removal.

But Lady Carmine seemed none the wiser. "You poor child. What a sad story it is," she murmured, brushing snow from her pillow. "So much tragedy so young."

"I was fortunate to have had the time with them I did," said Mary Ann, sweeping off the tables, brushing the snow into her scrub bucket. This last statement has been the only truthful thing she'd said in the past ten minutes. And it was strange, because the image of sitting around the fire, singing, together and warm lingered in her vision, causing a melancholy feeling to overcome her. "I'll tell Cook to send up some more hot tea."

CLANG!
SNICKER-SNACK!
WHHONNNNNG!
SNICK!

Who would have thought it? But while Mary Ann had discovered that her inner landscape held an uncharted ocean of lies, Sir Rufus was, at his core, a man of his word. He'd said he would request Mary Ann's time to help him train, and sure enough, she had only begun to fluster the moldings when Mrs. Cordingley came rushing in saying Mary Ann had been excused from her chores for a few hours—that the knight wished her to report to the stables immediately. "Why he should want your help, I can't imagine," Mrs. Cordingley editorialized, "but it is not ours to question. He promised to have you back for lunch preparations. So go! Be quick about it, girl."

Mary Ann was nothing if not quick. She arrived at the stables in a flash and barely a moment later found her plain squire's sword clashing with the Vorpal one with a bright, ringing sound. (BWINNNGG!)

"You've got a strange lot of upper body strength for a girl," said Sir Rufus, scowling as the impact rolled down both their arms. It was a sensation that woke up the body and the spirit. (CHIIINNNG!)

"A regular exercise regimen of housemaid's work, Sir," she responded, as the swords clashed again. (JANNNNGGG!)

"Housemaid's work," he sniffed. "Are you sure you haven't been juggling elephants?"

She lunged, the move sending him a bit off balance. "If you'd prefer, we could trade our sword work for a week of laundry baskets, water fetching and potato bushels. I think you'd find it enlightening. And enheavying." As soon as the words were out of her mouth, she wondered why she said them. Why were these walls coming down between her brain and mouth, all of a sudden? Why was she so bold and boundless? So daring and deviant? It was absolutely scandalous. Perhaps it was so many days of poor sleep.

But Sir Rufus just grumbled as he regained his footing and went on the offensive. (CLANNNG!) He wasn't amused, certainly, since he was incapable of that these days. But there was no sense of malice or even that she'd overstepped her position.

She decided it was best to change the subject altogether, not because of him but for fear of herself. So first she instructed him to try a Diagonal Feign. Then she brought up the one topic she was certain they had in common. "It must be quite the relief to have that Jabberwock business behind you."

His sword met hers with some force now. (WHUMPPPPP!) And he said in a wretched tone, "Relief from dark of night only comes to those who can actually feel the sunshine."

Mary Ann rolled her eyes. So it was going to be one of *those* days, was it? She began to understand why the real squires had not put up more of a fight to perform this job. And a thought occurred to her. "Do you not have many friends in the Court with whom you could spend some time? Turvian courtiers or… or … ones from Neath?" The blade was like a fishing line; it lured him in.

"Waste of time," he said with a grunt of disgust and a parry, "all of them. I now see how shallow the fripperies of my existence to-date have been." (CLANK!) "Once, yes, I cavorted among them, all frabjousness and hey-nonny nonsense, but now I feel like I'm seeing everyone from this high tower and the perspective shows it for what it is." (ZANNGG!)

And that's when Mary Ann heard herself say, "Like the person living in the Tower here at Carmine Manor?" It was out before it could be stopped.

It got Sir Rufus' attention, too, his sword arm sinking to his side. "What?" He couldn't have looked more stunned if she'd slapped him. "Why would you say that?"

It was too late to go back now. "You said it, Sir," said Mary Ann, putting as much chirpy lightness into her voice as she could muster. "Yesterday."

"I did?" His expression was covered in hot, shocked shame.

She tried a Reverse Thrust. "Yes, Sir. You were talking of your lost humor, Sir. You said, 'I'll be an outcast. I'll be shut away in the Manor Tower just like…'"

"Well, I hardly meant to." As if intent negated it. "In fact, I mustn't say a word more. It is a disgrace upon my family."

"Ah." She used a Right-to-Left Sweep.

He countered. "A stain upon our name."

"Oh." They followed it up with a Bind and Reversal.

"A pox upon our nether-regions," he said.

"Ooh." She wrinkled her nose and tried to look anywhere but at the spot on topic.

"… Metaphorically," he added with some emphasis and a parry. "Anyway, the whole thing is simply too terrible to consider."

"I apologize for bringing it up," she said.

"Rightfully, you should." He did a Long Lunge now and she instructed him to adjust the back leg a bit. "Anyway, what business is it of yours? You don't need to know anything about my uncle. My father's brother. And how he's in the Tower, secreted away from everyone, because he is…" He exhaled, his jaw trembling with the word, "… sane."

Mary Ann's sword arm dropped to her side. "Sane, really?" She thought about her encounter in the Tower the night before. What she'd heard from that room did not sound sane.

But he just lowered his sword and nodded like they were on the same page with things. "I *know*," he said, still nodding. "I've never met anyone who wasn't mad before—have you?"

"I'm not sure. I mean, I've always thought myself fairly sane," she admitted, "but lately, I'm starting to believe that's only a symptom of my madness."

"That's how it happens," he said sagely.

She leaned on a nearby fence. "So when was the last time you saw your uncle? Do you not visit him in the Tower?"

"Father said it was too risky," Sir Rufus said, wiping his brow with his shirtsleeve. "We don't know much about sanity but there's reasonable evidence it's easily transferred from one person to another. Father said too much contact could cause an epidemic. Sweep across the countryside. Our land would never withstand it."

She'd heard Mr. Rabbit speak on this topic once or twice, as well. "Certainly, once one person starts making sense, it becomes so hard to stay immune. Unless a good cognitive dissonance is put into place swiftly, of course. And then —" Mary Ann broke off, noticing something low to the ground barreling toward them. It was that same creature from the day before, the banana skin that wore the panto disguise. Mary Ann had never seen the likes of it and was determined not to let it get away again unquestioned. "You there!" she called. "Stop a moment!"

"I can't stop to chat," it said in a high, cheerful voice. "I've got miles to go."

"Where are you headed?" she asked it.

"End of the line!"

"Which line?"

"Punchline, of course," shouted the creature. "No, no, I can't stay. It's not here and timing is everything, don't you agree?"

Mary Ann had no time to agree or disagree before it sprinted off.

She turned to Sir Rufus. "You don't think that could be your sense of humor, do you?"

"No," he said, looking horrified at the prospect. "Mine takes its time and laughs at its own jokes. Wait, where are you going?"

"I never could resist a good punchline," Mary Ann called, propping her sword against the fence and trailing after the creature.

"But we're right in the middle of — Oh, son of a Bandersnatch." He slung the Vorpal sword into its scabbard. "Wait for me."

They trailed it all the way to Tulgey Barrens before they lost the creature, somewhere between a toadstool and a toad sideboard.

"Well, that was a waste of time," grumbled Rufus scanning the brush. "Next time, perhaps you'll heed me before you run off chasing—"

Mary Ann put up a hand. "Shh. Listen." She could hear voices off to the left. "That way."

"The Wabe's that way."

"Yes, and this is a one-Wabe street," she said, and ducked down the path.

The clearing was busier than Mary Ann had ever seen it. Representatives from Lord Carmine's guard were milling about, some clustered in knots, some jotting things down, and all of them pondering about the large number of green, scaly, snouted creatures sprawled lifeless and dewy in the wet grass. There must have been thirty of them.

Rufus stepped forward, stress in his voice. "Great gryphons, what's happened here?"

"Be with you in one moment, Sir," said a uniformed guardsman as round as he was tall. The badge at his collar read, "D.I. Tweedle." He'd been talking to someone and Mary Ann realized the individual in question, blocked by the guard's personal self, was none other than Douglas Divot.

"So you say you were in your current domesticile, then, at the time of the incident?" asked Tweedle.

"Why, yes, sir," said Divot. "I had just sat down to a bite of cheese. I'd gotten this charming dulled cheddar from a lovely shop in Square Five earlier in the week — Weeze's Cheeses, have you heard of it? — when I heard the most awful commotion above."

Tweedle wrote that down. "Would you describe it something along the lines of an 'outgrabe,' sir?"

"I would not," said Douglas. "The raths have been

outgrabing for days, it being their mating season. And this sound was nothing of the sort."

"Then in your own words, please describe the sound."

"This was like a moaln, or perhaps a shriell."

"Moaln or shriell," Tweedle murmured, jotting that down, too. "Right. And then what?"

"Well, like I said to the other fellow, I came upstairs to see what the hubbub was about and there were all these raths, bent over, twitching, making this gorrible racket. So I sent a rocking horsefly to you all about the situation, and here we are."

"And during that time, they...?"

"They expired, Mr. Tweedle," said Douglas.

"And is that bowl always there, sir?" Tweedle asked, indicating an empty, shallow dish the size of a knight's shield.

"As a matter of fact, I've never seen that bowl before," said Douglas.

"And do you recall, what was in this bowl when you arrived on the scene?" Tweedle asked.

"Nothing, Mr. Tweedle. Nothing was in this bowl."

Tweedle nodded. "And who did you see put the Nothing in the bowl, sir?"

"Nobody," said Divot. "I saw nobody. I keep telling you."

"Right." Tweedle turned to one of the guards. "Put out a warrant for Nobody. We'll want to bring him in for questioning about the Nothing and where he got it."

The guard said, "Right away, sir!" and exited down the path.

"See here—" said Sir Rufus, tired of being ignored for so long. "What is—"

"We'll be with you in good time, Sir," said Tweedle, not even looking at him. "Important Square business, this is. Now," he turned back to Douglas. "What was—"

Another man stepped in. "— Your relationship to these raths?" He looked much the same as the first man, just as round and as tall, the very same broad face, the part in his hair sweeping the opposite direction. Only his badge said, "D.M. Tweedle." And his eyes were narrowed on the tove before them.

Douglas looked from Tweedle to Tweedle and said, "Well…
I…I was their neighbor."

"And did you get on with these raths?" asked D.M.
Tweedle.

"Well, yes, many of them." Douglas twiddled his claws
nervously.

Tweedle leaned down and looked him in the eye. "But not
all of them, sir?"

"Well, you know … one gets on better with some people
than others, of course. There were a frightful lot of them living
here and—"

"Funny, then," said D.M. Tweedle, stroking the spot where
his chin would be, were there any actual separation between his
face and neck, "how there's several many less raths now."

"Yes," said D.I. Tweedle, "most hilafrious, I'd say, there
being more fewer now."

"Hysterrible, even," said D.M.

"Are you implying something?" asked Douglas, eyes fearful.

"Did you not lodge a complaint to one…" D.M. checked
his notepad, "Rory Romulus Rath of Nineteen and a Half East
Wabe on the second of Jamberry?"

Douglas inhaled sharply.

"Well…?"

"Well…" The tove tugged at his collar. "I might have gone
over and asked him quite politely to cease tossing his bathwater
out on the main lawn. I mean, that spot, it's my ceiling, you
know. And I've been having trouble with it and was getting
some damage to—"

"We have witnesses that say you 'had your pollen up' about
it, Mr. Divot."

"My what?" Douglas' ear twitched. "I might have been a bit
emphatic about the topic but certainly not in such words, no."

" — And that you gave him a right talking to and told him if
it happened again, you'd be picking off his petals before Lord
Carmine in a public dispute case."

Douglas whirled on a patch of nearby tulips. "You awful
gossips," he hissed.

The tulips shrugged and turned their backs on him.

"So you do deny these statements?" asked D.I. Tweedle.

"No, I don't deny it," said Douglas, "but that doesn't mean I planned to kill him and his whole family."

"See here now," said Sir Rufus, "are you suggesting this tove is a mass murderer?"

Finally, the Tweedle turned to him. "Ah, Sir Rufus! Greetings! Middle of the morning to you."

But the knight would not be deterred. "I repeat: are you suggesting this tove killed all these raths?"

"To answer your inquizzation, D.M. Tweedle and myself are not suggesting anything as of this momentous moment. We are merely gathering the evidentiary cluedoms of the incidental peculiarities," said D.I. Tweedle.

"And the peculiar incidentals," added D.M. Tweedle.

"Preciseably!"

If Sir Rufus would ordinarily have found the pair charming, he certainly wasn't in the mood to do so now. His jaw clenched. "This tove is a good friend of Father's. He was instrumental in the Battle of Square Four. He's a subterranean architect of unmatched genius and a Square treasure."

"Nothing to worry about right now, Sir," D.I. Tweedle assured him.

"Indeedly," affirmed D.M. Tweedle, "we've got a watch out for Nothing. We'll know more once Nobody's been rounded up and debriefed."

"And with that, we'll have to ask you to please step aside, Sir and Miss. This is a crime seen, you know. And as soon as we find out who seen it, the sooner we can go home for a nice evening of pugilism and polishing our rattle collection. Tell your father, Sir Rufus, we'll have his report ready for him tomorrow morning."

8

"Ridiculous," Sir Rufus was muttering. "That anyone could possibly think Mr. Divot would off half his neighborhood on account of noise and wastewater violations ... It's beyond absurd. It's...it's...supersurd, really."

"From what I know of him, I'm inclined to agree," Mary Ann said. She'd been mulling over the topic as they'd journeyed back to the Manor. They were currently doing a combination of running, hopping and walking backwards in order to reach their destination. "Which leaves us with the curious issue of what did happen to the raths."

"Mass suicide, perhaps," said Rufus darkly. "The mating scene may not be what it once was. Also, living in a soggy hill, eating swallows and shellfish every night — it can't be too inspirational. The hopelessness, the lack of variety, the squishy socks..."

Mary Ann thought perhaps he was projecting, but she did not say as much.

Indeed, they went the rest of the way in silence and Mary Ann was glad for the quiet reflection, for something within her felt unsettled in a way she could not explain. She entered the Manor as if she'd never left and continued her day's chores, just as ever she had. Yet the sword work had been so mentally stimulating and physically exhilarating that something felt changed within her.

On further consideration, she realized what it was. It had never occurred to her until this moment that being a housemaid was not a specific requirement for her as a vocation. She'd no idea until she came to Carmine Manor that she could carry any piece of her heart beyond the woodwork and the good work of washing and stoking and sweeping and spending her whole life in half-light, half visible. And the very idea that it could be otherwise was so terrifying, so laughable, so absolutely mad that she had to scrub it from her mind like the good housemaid she was, for fear the stain might set. And then where would she be?

So unnerving was the concept, that she felt infinitely grateful to hear the buzz among the servants; Lord and Lady Carmine had been invited to Queen Valentina's Unbirthday party in a week's time. And this news was a relief because it shone light on the proper order of things once more. Everyone was very excited about the preparations that needed to be made for their departure: wardrobe chosen, garments stowed, the carriage polished, horses prepped and delights for the taste-buds packed for the journey. Lady Carmine's personal maid, Celeste, could not speak enough about how lucky she was she could attend this fine event, even if it were in a somewhat diminished capacity. As if just being in the same fragrant air as Queen Valentina and her court would fortify her.

"Why, we've never been invited before, and this is supposed to be her largest Unbirthday celebration ever! My sister lives in Neath, and she said there will be ice sculptures twenty feet high! And tarts and cakes and fizzy drinks and treacle fresh from the well and everyone dressed in their finest of finery, candy floss gowns and lovely codfish hats and the latest quadrilles. Also tarts and cakes."

"So you mentioned," said Mabel, the parlor maid, flatly, who appreciated a good cake now and then but not a vicarious one.

"Well, you wouldn't enjoy yourself, anyway," said Celeste,

adjusting a hairpin. "You've never been one for large gatherings. Besides, someone has to stay and keep the home fires burning. You're all so good at that."

Mabel grumbled under the half-compliment and Emmaline argued the point in open envy, but Mary Ann found the rigid social order of it all soothing. She walked away from her colleagues humming an old Turvian jig, applied herself to the stubborn grout of the tile floor around a fireplace and said three cheers for home fires and hierarchies. She suspected a good bit of her gratefulness also stemmed from the distance that would be assured between Jacob Morningstar and herself. He would be far away and occupied in Neath, and she could contemplate her next steps from the relative safety of Carmine Manor. She had a strange suspicion her mysterious midnight visitor might be otherwise swept up in the festivities, as well.

Then she recalled the little problem of the mirror.

Oh, that cursed mirror...Mr. Rabbit still needed it, and its delivery had already been delayed several days. She'd been hoping to find out more about the object before dispensing with it. But one did not turn up to an Unbirthday party for the Queen of Neath without a token of one's esteem—particularly not when one was the Queen's herald. Perhaps the fellow had found an alternate gift by now. But Mary Ann knew the gentleman's tendency to panic first and solve never. She did not wish to simply wait and hope that Warren Rabbit would show previously undemonstrated initiative and extract himself from his own problems. If she did not take action, she would be sinking a decent rabbit in the stew in a very factual way.

There were several issues associated with transporting the mirror, however, which she pondered the rest of the day. The main problem was that the piece was large, fragile and heavy. She would be able to carry it for some distance, but it would take considerable time and energy to move it safely all the way from her father's workshop in Turvy to Mr. Rabbit's cottage in Neath. The original plan had been for her father to assist her in this task. A two-person mirror-moving maneuver at minimum. Borrowing a wheelbarrow or even a horse from Lord Carmine would draw attention to both its absence and hers, so that was not an optimum solution, either. It was only as she was climbing into bed, she came up with an answer to her challenge that met all requirements satisfactorily.

"It's what?" asked Sir Rufus the next day, scratching the back of his neck.

"A quest," said Mary Ann, beaming. "A training quest. I know you've read epic poems. So you know knights do these things all the time. They go off in quest of a magical object and deliver it where it belongs. This is one of those." She tucked her long, plaited hair up into a squire's hat (she'd pinched someone's garb from the wash), and she jammed it down on her head.

"So, like retrieving a magic chalice and giving it to a chosen king?" Those pinpoint blue eyes regarded her suspiciously.

"Yes. Exactly so," she said. "Only our chalice is technically wall decor and our king is a bit on the fluffy side."

"'A bit on the—'?"

"Don't let that put you off. Remember: a good knight does not pick and choose his epic errands." And Mary Ann led a saddled Goodspeed from the stall.

"Perhaps," said Rufus uncertainly, taking the reins, "but a good day is me back in time for dinner and not on some wild goose chase."

"No goose," she said, assisting him onto the back of Goodspeed, "rabbit."

"Rabbit?!"

"It'll be good for you, fresh air and a quest. Hones your skills and chases the blues." She climbed up on Lolly, a task that, she had to admit, was much easier to do in squire's trousers. "You sulk when left to your own devices. It's important to keep your mind off things."

"The insolence," he said, with an amazed shake of his head.

"I swear, I have never had a squire speak to me so."

"Too true. But then, I am not really a squire." Mary Ann smiled. Hadn't she wanted that comforting hierarchy just yesterday? Where did this outrageous behavior of hers keep coming from? She'd have to have a long talk with herself about it later. "Are we ready?"

He sighed. "Fine, I'll do it," and put up a gauntleted finger. "But I want it noted, there's something very bunny—er, funny —about this whole thing."

"You're quite right. Very bunny indeed. So let's hop to it. I'll make up—um, tell you—the details along the way."

Keeping the quest theme going took somewhat more imagination than Mary Ann had anticipated. The standard premise of these types of adventures naturally involved navigating shaky, rope-bare bridges, outwitting neighborhood monsters with riddle fixations, and climbing castle walls — anything to prevent one from reaching the magical item in question too soon.

So Mary Ann took Rufus the worst way round to her father's cottage — an old trail that came and disappeared on whim, sometimes being woods and sometimes being a tiled and paneled hallway. And she spent the bulk of that time commenting on non-existent footfall behind them, the suspicious cracking of branches or creaking of doors, and asking him if he spied this or that mysterious figure ducking behind the tremulous Tumtum trees (or hall trees) ahead.

By the time they got to Rowan Carpenter's workshop, Sir Rufus of Square Four was jumping at the buzz of bees and brandishing his sword at snapdragons. It didn't do much for the poor man's anxiety, but it did draw him out of his depression.

She was starting to feel a little ashamed about her tactics, as the charade he endured was neither kind nor fair. But telling the fellow he was doing a noble deed by helping rescue a rabbit from the perils of poor gift planning never would have gotten the thing done at all. Anyone could see that. It was the simple fact that the truth lacked oomph.

Of course, there at the workshop, Sir Rufus had oomph enough for everyone. Especially, if you asked the red squirrel that happened to be sitting at the doorstep, munching a seed. Mary Ann imagined the dear thing had never seen the likes of it, a knight leaping from his steed, sword drawn, red banner flying, telling the rodent its magical disguise would not fool him and to step aside, monster, and let him pass.

Yes, really, once you get these things rolling, they pretty much run themselves, thought Mary Ann as the squirrel squeaked off.

"It didn't give me a riddle," said Rufus, disappointment sinking his tone.

"The least it could do," observed Goodspeed over his shoulder. "Never trust a squirrel."

"Well, I'm sure it would have loved to," said Mary Ann, trying to think of a proper reason why. "It probably had … um… a second knight job to get to." And she opened the workshop door.

Once they picked up the mirror, the task was rather straightforward. They lashed it to the back of Goodspeed, then made the trip from Turvy to Neath as efficiently as the land would allow. And soon, they were trotting down the path to Mr. Rabbit's home.

Mary Ann knew the moment they started down the lane, it did not make the right impression with its audience.

"This is the end of our quest?" asked Sir Rufus, wrinkling his nose at the place. "Well, it's not much to look at, is it? No motes to cross. No towers to scale."

"Triumph comes in all sizes and types," Mary Ann told him.

But it was true that the cottage looked worse for wear since the last time Mary Ann saw it. Ladders were propped against the house, for one. In some spots, the roof slate was completely missing. In others, it looked like it had a very bad night's sleep. The shutter on the main second floor window hung clear off one hinge. There also seemed to be damage to several cucumber frames along the side lawn.

The knight and squire dismounted and went to work unstrapping the mirror. "Indeed," said Goodspeed, stretching his back a bit, "this is the oddest quest I've ever been on."

"You only ever went on that Jabberwalk," sneered Lolly next to him, "and that, only by half."

"As I said. This being the oddest of the lot," Goodspeed doubled down.

Mary Ann and Sir Rufus approached the front door, the mirror shared between them. Mary Ann read the familiar brass nameplate: "W. Rabbit." That was one thing that hadn't changed in the past few days.

They had only just knocked when a voice came from behind them. "Beggin' yer pardon, sirs, His Honor is not home at the moment. Is there anything that I could be helpin' you with in his absence?"

It was Pat, one of two overalled handymen standing there. Pat was a stout furry fellow with a twitchy nose that had always made Mary Ann think he was telling lies. In actuality, it was probably just the effect of being a guinea pig. Hugh was with him. He was a guinea pig, as well. Less twitchy, though.

Mary Ann pulled her hat down lower on her face. "Where is Mr. Rabbit?"

"Yes," said Sir Rufus, coming to life, color flushing along the cheekbones, "We are here to bring him this magical questing relic. So he can use it to transform himself from his sorry rabbit state back into a prince."

Mary Ann knew she had gotten somewhat too elaborate in her quest story.

But Pat shrugged it off. "Oh, well, I don't know anything about that, sir," he said, who was never one to pry, "but there's a jam tart scandal on trial at the castle. His Honor is a herald for the Queen, don't ya know."

"A trial…" Mary Ann breathed, "Is everyone there, then?" She was thinking purely of Jacob Morningstar.

"Oh, everyone who's anyone in the court is there," Pat said.

"Even Nobody must have made it there by now."

"We saw him walking that way hours ago," added Hugh. "I looked down the lane and I says to Pat, I says, 'Why, I see Nobody for miles.'"

Mary Ann relaxed a little. "Someone should tell the Tweedles. They've been looking for Nobody for two days now."

Pat frowned. "Beg pardon?"

"How's that?" asked Hugh.

"Never mind," said Mary Ann. "What happened to the house?" She pointed.

"Not a Jabberwock, was it?" asked Rufus, looking worried this quest was going to grow very serious, very quickly.

Pat shook his head. "Oh, no, sir! Sure, at first we was certain it was some kind of creature what done it. But after further discussion, we suspect it was Mr. Rabbit's housemaid, Mary Ann."

"What? No, it was n —" Mary Ann caught herself and cleared her throat. "What makes you think it was m—her?"

"See, Mr. Rabbit sent her into the house to fetch his gloves and fan," Pat went on. "And in two shakes of a lizard's tail, someone inside went monumental. Parts of her were pouring out the windows. Parts of her were blocking the doors and the chimbley."

"Too much Burgeonbevv at the wrong moment, as I understand it," said Hugh. "You know girls these days, growing up so fast." He gave a sad shake of his head.

"And the creature looked like this Mary Ann?" Mary Ann asked.

"Well," twitch, twitch, went Pat, "the thing had yeller hair. And she was…a girl."

Hugh nodded.

Mary Ann felt vaguely like she should be offended by this. But she supposed it was hard to know what someone looked like beyond being blonde and female when they were invisible eighty percent of the time. "So what happened to her once she became a giantess?"

"Oh, she booted poor Bill Leafliver clear into the middle of next week. Then, while we was helping him, she got tiny and scarpered out again. And right good she did, because we've assault charges being brought up on her. It would be handled neatly already, if the Queen weren't being consumed by this more pressing tart business, don't ya know."

"In the meanwhile, Pat's drawn up some posters to put round," said Hugh. He reached around the corner and came back with a page that read WANTED in ink and had the rough sketch of a blonde girl—likely one far younger than Mary Ann, based on the clothes and loose hair. But there in the place where a face should have been was an empty sphere.

"I've still got the fiddly bits to do," said Pat. "You can't rush quality work, ya see."

"Of course," said Mary Ann. "Is Mr. Rabbit's house open? We'd like to just drop off this item for him. He'll know what it's about."

9

"What a quest we had today, eh, my friends?" asked Mary Ann brightly. They'd just crossed the border into Turvy, where it paid to distract oneself with conversation. She smiled at Sir Rufus, who had once again become a dark cloud in the saddle. "Did you learn a few things that will be useful in your knightly endeavors?"

"Indeed, I did," said Sir Rufus. "More than I ever imagined."

This was a sweet surprise, given the sour look on his face.

"I learned much about my teacher," he continued.

This sounded ominous. She countered it with the lightest tone she could manage, "Oh, indeed?"

A single nod. "You're that rabbit's home-wrecker."

It took a moment for the meaning of this to sink in under Mary Ann's hat. Even Lolly got it sooner, because the horse gasped.

"Excuse me?" said Mary Ann.

Sir Rufus removed his helmet and turned to her. "I saw that handyman's drawing, and it was the spitting image of you."

"I'm afraid I don't know what you're talking about." She was stuck on denial and couldn't unstick it.

"Come now. Her name is Mary Ann? And yours is…" He frowned. "Oh, you *are* slippery, aren't you? … What is your name exactly? It's very like Mary Ann, isn't it? I know Father mentioned it, but then Father's use of names is always more of an approximate than an actual."

"I can't believe we're having this discussion." Mary Ann tried to pull Lolly ahead as a gesture of her offense, but Lolly had one speed and that was arthritic.

"Besides that," persisted Rufus, "*she's* a housemaid. *You're* a housemaid…"

"So? People can be housemaids, can't they?"

"She's got your hair," he said.

"In a different style."

"And your eyes."

"He hasn't gotten round to drawing them yet."

"Well…she will do, when he's done," he spat.

"I understand now. There's simply no reasoning with you," she said. "You're mad."

"You're wrong there as well, Miss *Mary Ann*." He brandished the name like his sword. "I am all reason. I'm the one who's dangerously approaching sane, remember? I am cross, but hardly mad enough. In fact, do you know what I think? I think this wasn't a quest at all. I think we were simply delivering that mirror to that rabbit."

Mary Ann's limbs went cold. "And how do you figure that?"

"The recipient of our quest wasn't just any rabbit. It was Warren Rabbit, herald to Queen Valentina of Neath. I've met this fellow before and he is not now and never has been anything other than a rabbit." He shook his head. "Prince changed by a curse, indeed…Ha!"

Yes, that did pose a slight problem.

Mary Ann decided to change tactics. "Fine," she said. "Yes. I'm Mary Ann, the former housemaid to Mr. Warren Rabbit. But I did not damage the fellow's house. Clearly, some impostor came in and made a mess of things in my absence."

"Mmn," said Sir Rufus. And an disagreeable "mmn" it was.

In fact, the rest of the return trip hung on that "mmn," and likely would have stayed there, dangling indefinitely, had Lord Carmine's guards not arrived at the Manor at the same moment that the two crusaders did and jumped queue.

"Lord Carmine, sir!" D.I. Tweedle burst into the Manor and shouted down the vestibule, voice echoing. It proved an effective scheme, for the Baron joined them in a heartbeat. "Given the evidenciary cluedoms that've come to light, M'Lord, we've got a suspect in custody for the recent deaths on the Wabe. We would like your presence to oversee a mirrigation and—"

"But this is Douglas Divot!" said Lord Carmine, indicating the tove of interest. Now that everyone had filtered into the entryway, Mary Ann could see the poor fellow. There were shackles at his wrists and his claws had mittens over them. They drooped sadly.

"Yes, M'Lord," said D.I. Tweedle, reading off his notebook. "Divot, comma, Douglas. Species: tove. Occupation: digger."

"We know all that," said Lord Carmine. "I've known Douglas since he was but a tiny tove."

"But these new evidenciary cluedoms…" interjected D.M. Tweedle.

"Well? What are they?"

The guard looked pleased to finally get to the crux of the matter. "The raths, M'Lord," said D.I. Tweedle. "T'were poisoned."

"Poisoned?"

"Yes, M'Lord. Judging from the residue in the suspicious bowl, as well as the inner tummal area of the victims, it appears as if the raths was poisoned by shellfish with, er, poison in 'em. To be more pacific: oysters, M'Lord."

Lord Carmine stroked his chin. "So you're saying the oysters were bad."

"Very bad indeed, only not spoilt," said D.I. "This was not food poisoning. We know this because the poison rezzibules detected in the bowl and the bodies themselves all had the odor of bilberry jam."

D.M. explained, "Bilberry jam being the odor of zarlene oil, the household chemical substance commonly used to polish fine furniture. When, of course, it's not the odor of bilberry jam itself," he added, in case anyone was confused on that point.

D.I. Tweedle nodded. "So, given the situation, we would like your presence and use of your premises, M'Lord, as we mirrigate this suspect further."

"Fine," said Lord Carmine, with a concerned look to Douglas. "It's best we get this resolved as soon as possible. To the Mirrigation Room!"

"To the Mirrigation Room!" announced D.I. Tweedle, and everyone in the entry hall went pushing and shoving down a corridor so that even Mary Ann and Sir Rufus were caught up in the roiling crowd.

The majority of them ended up in a small room behind the Mirrigation Room, looking in at it through a pane of glass—a two-way looking-glass, it would seem. Mary Ann knew this because first one Tweedle and then the other peered into glass critically and licked an index finger to smooth his eyebrow, before turning around to the business at hand.

The most interesting feature of this room, she noticed now, was that every wall was paneled floor-to-ceiling with mirror. Mary Ann thought it very shiny and bright considering she hadn't known this place was here to clean it.

Lord Carmine took a seat at the table, a Tweedle to either side of him, while the downcast Douglas Divot sat perpendicular, facing three sides of mirrored wall.

"Right," began D.I. Tweedle, who seemed to be the one in charge of things. "This here is the Mirrigation Room. What you see before you are three special looking-glasses. Now, we're going to ask you some questions. And when you respond, the mirror will show us the truth of it. The mirror on your left will signal when the truth reflects poorly on you. The one on the right, when it reflects well."

"And the middle?" asked Douglas in a voice so small one would think he'd been swigging DwindleAde all the way there.

"The most important mirror of all, Mr. Divot," said Tweedle. "The one in which you must face yourself."

Back to her, Mary Ann could see his face reflected in the mirror; Douglas Divot swallowed hard.

"So let us begin. Mr. Divot," proceeded D.I. Tweedle, "did you know the following creatures located at addresses One to Forty-Nine-and-a-Half, East Wabe, Tulgey Wood, Turvy?" He flipped a page on his notebook. "... George and Eleanor Rath, Ignatius Rath, Terry-Belle Rath, Stephen J. Rath, II, Indigo Rath, Emily Esther Jane Rath—"

"Er, skip ahead a bit, would you?" Lord Carmine said here. "I'm supposed to attend an Unbirthday party in six days. I'd like to be done with this by then."

"Yes, M'Lord," said D.I. Tweedle. He turned back to the tove. "Douglas Divot, did you or did you not have issues with some of your neighbors?"

The tove was still molting around the cheeks and Mary Ann swore she saw him blush along the empty patches. "As I'd said before, one has nothing against most people, of course, but some people do require more patience and—"

The mirror to the left of him began to change. It showed Douglas Divot, yes, but a dark shadow of the tove chastising the neighbors over what appeared to be the bathwater incident, his corkscrew tail twitching, his horns glistening threateningly in the light.

"Oh dear," breathed the suspect.

"Ahh," said the crowd of observers.

"And, Mr. Divot, is it true that you not only have an extensive collection of handmade wooden furniture in your domicile, but that you keep a certain quantity of furniture polish at all times? Furniture polish made of zarlene oil, the very same chemical found in the oysters that killed your neighbors?"

"Er, well, yes, I do," Douglas' mittened hands were clenched tightly before him. "But it's such a common oil. I mean anyone has it who keeps—"

The mirror on the left was changing again. The reflection had shifted to images of Douglas Divot polishing his furniture with an almost obsessive level of detail. And everyone could see clear as day, the pot of zarlene oil in one clawed hand.

"Ohhh," said the crowd of observers. Mary Ann's heart raced; partially from the fact that there were magic mirrors, right here, working away before her, and partially the fact that things were not looking good for dear Douglas Divot.

The audience was on the edge of their seats. (It was a narrow bench.)

"Douglas Divot," and Tweedle's words seemed portentous now, "have you ever committed murder?"

"Yes," said Douglas shakily and everyone in the room gasped. "I murdered a whole block of a frabjous extra dull cheddar by myself at brillig yesterday. And I regret nothing. Nothing I tell you!"

And the middle mirror began to change, showing Douglas Divot greedily gnawing on a block of cheese the size of a dictionary. It was shameless. He didn't even get a plate.

In the back room, all the Square guards were talking at once.

"How can he face himself?"

"I feel bloated just looking at 'im."

"I prefer a nice Turvydale, me."

"Would you all please be quiet?" Lord Carmine demanded, facing the hidden room. "We can hear you clearly through that wall, you know. It's the same way you can hear us."

There was some surprise about this from the room's inhabitants but mostly mumbling of "Someone should've said, then," and: "Can't expect us to know everything," and: "That's them acoustics, innit?" But finally everyone fell to silence.

"Last question, Douglas Divot," D.I. Tweedle said, thumbs hooked into his suspenders. "Can you give us one reason you could not have committed this heinous crime against your rath neighbors?"

"Other than my shellfish allergy?" asked the tove.

You could have heard a pin drop. Then you could have heard any angels currently dancing on the head of that pin say, "Dear heavens, I hope we have emergency medical coverage for this."

It even took a moment for D.I. Tweedle to recover himself.

"I-Is that true, Mr. Divot?"

"Oh yes." The tove nodded. "I cannot eat, touch, smell or receive personal correspondence from shellfish without coming all over in hives. I'm sure if you check my property, you will find no hives there whatsoever. My residence and the surrounding area is completely beehouse-free. I believe the last time I found myself broken out as a beekeeper was after I was invited to a Lobster Quadrille five years ago. I shell never do it again."

And there was no question of the truth of the matter. Because the rightmost mirror began to glow a cheerful gold and recapped the Lobster Quadrille outbreak of five years past. In no time, the tove in the mirror was up to his nose in wooden boxes and netted hats.

"Well, then," began D.I. Tweedle scratching his head, "there's nothing for it. We have to set him free on circumnavigational evidence."

Lord Carmine looked puzzled. "I believe I'm not familiar with that."

D.M. Tweedle stepped in. "Circumnavigational evidence. Where we've gone round and round and round the matter, and it's no further solved than when we started."

"Ah! Then, case dismissed!" said Lord Carmine, and he looked quite pleased for it, too.

The Tweedles took a moment to unshackle Douglas Divot and the freed tove met the crowd of well-wishers in the hallway.

"Oh, thank goodness!" said Mary Ann, crouching to hug her friend. "We were so worried."

"Glad for your exoneration, Mr. Divot," said Sir Rufus, shaking the fellow's hand heartily. "My father's always spoken well of you."

Mary Ann turned to the knight. "The various mirrors in that room…Where did your father get them?"

So much had gone on, Sir Rufus seemed to have forgotten his earlier crossness with her. "No idea. Never sat in on a mirrigation before. In fact, I'm not really certain the room was here yesterday. Happens all the time, though; lose a room, gain a room. You know how it is."

She did. An extra room had shown up once at her father's cottage when she was small. She thought she'd finally gotten her very own bedroom—she was so excited! It was all she'd ever wanted . . . Until the next morning, of course, when she woke up in the flowerbed, a snail trailing across her face.

Such was Turvy.

She snapped out of this reverie in time to realize Douglas was saying something. "The only glazier I can think of would be in the market district of Square Five. Plaine's the name, I think. Gertie . . . Greta . . . something like that."

"And what is this sudden fascination of yours with mirrors?" Rufus asked. He seemed to be recalling he was supposed to be annoyed and planned to get back to it as soon as possible. "Not taking some other poor, trusting knight on a hare-brained folly?"

"Rabbit," said Mary Ann. "And no, Sir. If you'll excuse me, I've chores to do." With that she curtseyed—rather hard to do in squire's trousers, but she managed — and scuttled out.

10

Mary Ann bustled about the Manor the rest of the day, taking care of not only the chores she had missed earlier, but tomorrow's, as well. It was a nice feature of Turvy, really, that if you were very clever, you could clean the grates for today, and then clean them again for tomorrow in sequence, and it would keep nicely until another day hence. So the hours went by swiftly, filled with double-duty on all the major tasks she could think of, creating a sort of Mary Ann-ness about the place that should hold them for a while. She even peeked into Lady Carmine's room to see how she was getting on after the blizzard. The lady slept. The snow showers were down to sporadic flurries but the cloud over the bed was as large as ever, its color now a foreboding charcoal grey. Mary Ann shook her head sadly. There would be more to come.

The next morning, Mary Ann was out of bed and down the path from the Manor at first light, on her way to see a woman about a looking-glass. If all went well, she would be back in time for training with Sir Rufus and the household would be none the wiser.

An unexpected excitement was mounting in her chest. She hadn't been to Square Five since she was a child, and she looked forward to recapturing this time in the hustle and bustle of one of Turvy's major villages. It was just a shame it was for information instead of pleasure. She needed a few things, but all she could afford was free information.

Square Five, she was soon reminded, did present its topographical challenges. The streams that spread across the sector made the journey rich and varied, but were winding and on the soggy side. In some places, bridges had been erected, but in others, one had to hop across mossy stones or wade through the waters. These were not the easiest undertakings in a housemaid's dress and Mary Ann wished, several times during the course of the hike, that she'd had the presence of mind to clad herself in squire gear before she'd left.

Alas, some things could not be done backwards.

But she arrived at her destination in due time. The place had changed a bit since she was a girl, but then it did so constantly. At the moment, there was a cobbler—button boots in plum, apple and cherry were on special that day. She passed a place for spun wool and sundries, where shawls were the specialty and the sheep proprietress sat out front knitting them, putting much of herself into her work by way of will and wool.

The pawnshop looked lively this morning; it was doing a brisk trade among both Red and White Turvian pawns looking for a new shield, affordable armor or a book on how-to exploit the weaknesses of the opposing side and not get taken prisoner. The shop was split down the middle, Red and White, with two separate doors. But a quick glance through each battle guide sitting on the outside tables proved that it was the very same book for both groups, with a different cover and minor text edits for each.

If anyone noticed, certainly, no one seemed to be bothered by it. Then again, there had been peace for almost a decade between the two sides in Turvy, yet here was a store specifically catering to those who hated to let go of a good grudge once they'd got a hold of it. She supposed it made for a pleasant hobby.

It was only when Mary Ann came to a place with a sign that

read "Hats, Custom Hats and Royal Messenger Service" that her shoulders tensed and she lost her breath. (She found it again; she'd just dropped it nearby.)

Quickly, she surveyed the style of hats, the choice of fabric, the color combinations, the generous use of embellishments and decorative codfish ... All very distinctive and instantly familiar. But, surely, it could not be...

Oh, it *was*. Mary Ann could see the man himself bustling round the shop, arranging the hats with, of all things, a teacup still in his hand.

A very dirty teacup, Mary Ann noticed guiltily...

For she was the indirect cause of that.

While working for Mr. Rabbit this past year, the fellow had promised Mary Ann's assistance for two hours, three times a week to one of his acquaintances, Mr. Simon Milliner, hat maker of Neath. Mary Ann agreed to the work, not because she had much choice in the matter (despite his cuddly appearance, Mr. Rabbit was not one easily denied), but because some extra funds would be nice to sock away for the future. She'd even made the sock.

The problem with this particular position was not specifically Mr. Milliner, though the man *was* prone to the occasional rude personal comment. (She recalled him observing once quite seriously over a cup of hot chamomile how her face resembled a chipmunk in need of a hair restorative.) No, the real issue was that the man had somehow gotten on Time's bad side and was essentially cursed to perpetual tea for eternity.

Now perpetual teatime may sound like a lovely thing to those who are fans of the stuff. But it presents a certain series of problems in the housemaid/kitchen departments. Mainly, there was simply no way of ever ensuring enough tea, foodstuffs and clean dishes to support the effort. Mary Ann would just get done with preparations and set-up and, suddenly, all was dirtied and devoured again.

What's worse, because it was always six o'clock, Mary Ann's allotted two hours per day never came to pass. Hour after hour of work: still six o'clock. Eventually, she'd simply walked out of the engagement. Her talents for going invisible had never come in handier. Even Mr. Rabbit hadn't pressed the matter once she'd explained the situation. She'd apparently been gone four days in teatime, and now his socks needed mending and the linens changed.

On the up side, he never lent her services to anyone again.

Now, seeing Mr. Milliner here in Turvy with a second shop and a messenger's service to boot, Mary Ann felt nothing but ill-prepared and uneasy. She bowed her head and ducked past the front window, unsure about her invisibility status and hoping he hadn't caught a glimpse. Mr. Rabbit never had said what the hat-maker's reaction to her vacancy had been. She'd wondered if they ever got anyone to replace her. Based on that tannin-stained cup, she suspected not.

Mary Ann tried to put it out of her mind as she wound through the marketplace section of Square Five. Signs to various purveyors pointed this way and that, through tiny doors, sideways corridors and upside-down staircases while she scanned them for any mention of the glazier she sought. All the while, she could not shake a feeling that eyes were on her, trying to read her like she read those signs.

Then she saw it: "Plaine Ornamentation: Stained Glass, Looking Glass, Baubles, Beads and Buoys. Made-to-order!"

Mary Ann had ducked through the door in half a tick.

A little bell tinkled and Mary Ann was almost blinded by reflective silver and overwhelmed by color. There were stained glass windows and mirrors propped on tables, in wooden stands, hanging from the ceiling, tiled to the floors. There were bowls of round glass spheres and buckets of round glass fishing floats. There were mirror animals and glass insects and some glow worms wriggling around with real fire blazing within their glass bellies.

One of these dropped from some height onto Mary Ann's arm and she could feel the heat radiate from it. On closer look, she saw the creature had real stained glass eyes and...

"May I help you?"

It was a woman with very large spectacles whose lenses were

stained glass. She could not make out the woman's eyes behind them. The lady's dress was decorated with bits of mirror embroidered into it. Tiny mirrored buttons trailed down her bodice. Her shoes appeared to be stained glass.

"I hope so. I'm looking for a Miss Plaine. Forgive me, I don't know the first name. Gertrude or Greta, they thought it was."

"They, whoever they are, thought wrong," said the woman. "There has never been, nor will be, a Gertrude or Greta Plaine here."

It was a tone of dismissal, and Mary Ann dismissed. "Oh, I daresay. I'm very sorry to have troubled you." And Mary Ann stepped to the door, to double-check the name of the shop.

"Stop right there, young lady!" Given the sheer volume and sharpness of the voice, Mary Ann did as she was told. The woman went over, put an arm around her shoulders and led her back in. "I did not say you were in the wrong place, did I? But the name," she said. "The name is Gilda." She smiled. "Gilda Plaine."

"Ah." Mary Ann nodded.

"And what can I help you with, my dear?"

"I'm looking for a mirror."

"We don't have any," Gilda Plaine said.

Mary Ann looked from the wall, to the ceiling, to the floor, to the other wall and heard herself let out a little frustrated exhale. This was either going to be a long encounter or a very short one.

"We don't have any that are not already spoken for," purred Miss Plaine, following Mary Ann's gaze. "The work is custom. We don't keep stock. What you see here are samples, samples, and more samples." She picked up a small hand mirror with a stained glass dragonfly the same colors as her glasses and twirled it around. "Also samples."

"I see," said Mary Ann. "Well, I came because I thought you might be the one to make a very specific type of mirror."

"Ideal, then, you being in a place that makes many specific types of mirrors," she said. "What would you like, dear? Flat?

Convex? Concave? Full-length? Hand? Wall? We have tabletop mirrors, tables made of mirrors, and mirrors framed in old table legs. We've got mirrors that magnify, reduce, stretch, bend, or only show you the back of your head. We've got mirrors that make you look younger, that tell you when someone is lying, and show you when you're in love. We've got mirrors that know who's the most beautiful in the land and ones that, no matter how dreadful you look, will lie and say you're a dolly. We've got mirrors that won't fog, mirrors made of fog, and mirrors with foghorns in them (lighthouse keepers love them). So." She seemed quite out of breath. "What would you like to see?"

At this point, Mary Ann's head was spinning. "My! Such choice!" she said. "But I was rather hoping for... a mirror that led to other places?"

"Nope, don't have that."

The words fell flat.

"That's curious," Mary Ann continued, trying to put it politely, "because J. Sanford Banks mentioned you'd done one for a project of Rowan Carpenter's recently."

"Ah," said Miss Plaine, "well, that was a very special commission. Limited edition. One edition, very limited."

"And, um, who did you deal with for that commission? Mr. Carpenter, was it?"

"No, Mr. Banks. I always deal with Mr. Banks. I've never met Mr. Carpenter, though I appreciate his work. Simply magnificent! Genius! If this particular item I made goes well, Mr. Banks and I plan to secure a more lengthy partnership. My mirrors, Mr. Carpenter's frames. Frabjous possibilities. We're simply beamish about it."

Mary Ann nodded. "So if someone wanted a mirror like the one you did for Mr. Banks, what options would they have?"

"It was a transporting mirror. So the options are: go through the mirror or don't. Not a very good transporting mirror if you choose the latter, though."

"I mean about the location," said Mary Ann. "Where does the looking-glass lead?"

"Right now, all transporting looking-glasses lead to Thither. That's non-negotiable. It's the only place that has a receiving mirror installed, permanently. In the future, I like to think there will be mirror ports all across the realms. But right now, there's the one. Thither."

"And how is the passage in the mirror accessed? It isn't activated all the time, is it?"

"Certainly it's not," snapped the woman. "Why, you can't go just leaving it wide open all the time, can you? Toddlers and pets would be getting into it, the moment you looked away. You'd be losing toddlers and pets in droves. Piles of toddlers, lap dogs, cats and hedgehogs all piled up at the base of it. Very untidy and they'd have to start a Lost and Found. The authorities in Thither would be a-tither. It wouldn't do at all. You have to say the right word."

"Yes, but how do you know what it is? Does the client choose the word? Do you? Is it predetermined in some way?"

"No," the woman looked at her like she had apples for ears. "You just say the right word and go through."

"But where does the word come from? If I wanted to access the mirror to use it, how would I know what to say?"

"You? Clearly, *you* wouldn't," and she laughed to herself bitterly about this. "And you know what's more? I don't want you going through my mirrors. I think we're done here."

"Please, ma'am, I meant no disrespect, I just—"

"Out."

As she was escorting Mary Ann out, the housemaid tripped on something. She looked below and saw she had crushed one of the pretty little glow worms. It was all broken glass and a burnt spot on the floor.

"Oh dear! Madam, I am so terribly sorry! I'll pay for—"

Gilda Plaine looked at the broken insect and shook her head. "Pane in the glass," she muttered. "You. Gone. Now."

"I'm going. I'm going."

Mary Ann went.

She emerged onto the market street and bumped directly into someone, feeling even more of a fool. "Oh my, I do beg your pardon, it's—" She recognized the red tunic and looked up. "Oh! What are you doing here?"

It was Sir Rufus.

"I might ask the same of you," he said. His arms were folded, his face blinding in the daylight, his lips a thin, not-amused line. "Shouldn't you be housemaiding? Isn't there all sorts of ..." he waved a hand, "... housemaidishness you should be getting up to? Because I'm quite certain no one sent you on an emergency mirror errand."

"Oh. Ah..." She brightened. "Well-done, Sir Rufus!"

His frown deepened. "Well-done who?"

"Well-done you, Sir!" she said, infusing her voice with warmth.

"And what have I done exactly?"

"You passed."

"Passed? Passed?" He seemed to be scanning the various market tables to see if he'd passed something vital there.

"You passed an important part of your training. Just as I hoped. You've learned tracking today and done a splendiferous job of it, too. Perfect for a Jabberwock situation, don't you think? Huzzah for that fellow!" she said, pointing to him.

Before he could recover from this wave of enthusiasm, she cleared her throat and started down the street toward home.

He ran to catch up rather faster than she was wishing. "See here, *Mary Ann*." He always flung her name like a knife. "You're trying to distract me. Just now, you were at that glazier Douglas Divot mentioned yesterday."

"Was I?"

"It's all smoke and mirrors with you," he said.

"Don't be silly. It is not—" She coughed and waved away the cloud from the market incense vendor. "Oh. Yes, I see."

"You'll tell me what's going on." His expression was not dissimilar to the look he had when slaying the Jabberwock.

"In time, perhaps," she said gently, feeling very tired. "Right now, it's really nothing over which to trouble yourself. Besides, I have much to ponder."

11

The water pooling at the base of the Manor's grand staircase was not a good sign and the higher Mary Ann looked, the more enthusiastic the waterfall became.

"Oh dear, oh dear, oh dear," said Mrs. Cordingley, running in with an armload of fresh towels, trying to staunch the stream. "Oh dear and dear again!"

"Whatever is happening?" asked Rufus.

"Your mother, Mr. Rufus," said the housekeeper. "It's gotten worse. She's feverish and begun a thaw! I fear before it's over, we'll all drown!"

In a flash, Sir Rufus was dodging around her, up the stairs, and Mary Ann followed.

"I wouldn't do that, Sir, if I were you!" Mrs. Cordingley called. "You'll let out the—"

There were towels packed at the base of the lady's door. But Sir Rufus ignored them, yanking open the entrance, dragging the towels aside. A foot of water and ice came rushing out. It soaked their legs and poured down the steps.

"Oh dear, oh dear," continued Mrs. Cordingley, for lack of better analysis.

There was no denying it. Mary Ann had been right about

that foreboding cloud she'd spied earlier. Inside Lady Carmine's chambers, torrents of rain issued from it, the air was steamy as a laundry and every surface was either fogged, dripping, buckling or drenched.

"Mother," said Sir Rufus, leaping over a half-melted snowbank and rushing to her bed. "Are you all right?"

It was hard to hear him over the roar of the rain hitting the bed parasol. Thunder rumbled and lightning struck the marble-top dresser, leaving a scorch mark down the center. Mary Ann was glad Sir Rufus wasn't wearing his armor. He'd rust, if he weren't shocked senseless first.

"Oh, I'm fine, my dear boy," Lady Carmine said feebly. She reached out to stroke his cheek as rain soaked his hair and ran down his face. "You look tired," she said, brushing a limp ginger curl from his forehead. "Are you getting enough rest?"

"Mother, don't worry about me. What do you need?" Sir Rufus asked, taking her hand. "Fan, dry dressing gown … canoe?"

"Oh no, dear. Very sweet of you. Just maybe a little rest…"

Mary Ann moved to the pitcher on the not-so-dry dry sink and poured a glass of water. She handed it to Lady Carmine. "Drink this now," she said. "It should help."

Rufus scowled at her. "Water? Whatever is wrong with you? Wouldn't you say she's had enough?"

"She has a fever. She needs fluids. On the *inside*." Mary Ann added before he could object. "And a cold compress. And plenty of rest."

After the lady drank it down, Mary Ann poured Lady Carmine a second glass. "I know you might not want it, but do try drinking another one shortly. I'll just set it here." She left the glass on a nearby tray and attended to the compress.

But Rufus' expression was all incredulity. "Shall I just get her a straw for the floors?"

"Do I detect some humor there, Sir Rufus?" Mary Ann was dabbing at the woman's face with a cold wet cloth. At least the remaining snow had some good use.

"I'm perfectly serious."

"If you want to seriously help then," she said, "go find Douglas Divot. Bring him here."

Rufus raised an eyebrow. "Divot? What'll he do?"

"He's a digger and a builder. He's the one who built the mote around the Manor. He understands water flow. He might have some idea for stemming the damages indoors."

Sir Rufus stood there blinking.

"Well? It's not getting any drier, is it?" Mary Ann said.

He muttered something about if it weren't a crisis and it weren't his mum, he wouldn't stand for anyone talking to him like that. But all said, he did stand and he did leave the room in search of Divot.

"Will you drink just a little more water?" Mary Ann asked, helping the Lady, as the rain beat down. Her own clothes and hair were soaked to their limit and she mopped water from her eyes.

"I understand you've been helping my son with his Vorpal sword training," said Lady Carmine as Mary Ann set the glass down.

Mary Ann gave a start. The news had certainly gotten around quickly. "Er, yes, My Lady. At his request."

"I appreciate your support of him," Lady Carmine continued. "We all do. Remarkable girl you are, knowing what to do with everything from ill weather, to cleaning, to Jabberwock fighting. How did you learn the sword work?"

Mary Ann wrung out a blanket at the base of the bed. "I wish I knew, My Lady."

Pity came over her face. "Ah, you've forgotten it, haven't you? Along with your name." She shook her head. "So sad."

"No, My Lady, I believe it's backwards training I've gotten. I'll likely learn its origins in the future." She dodged a lightning bolt as she moved to open the window a crack.

"And do you enjoy it? The swords, horses and everything?"

It was a question Mary Ann had not expected. She'd never had an employer who asked her opinion on anything. And she surprised herself with her own answer. "I do, My Lady. Very much."

A nod. "Then: Cornelius Clashammer," said the woman.

"Beg pardon, Lady Carmine?" It was hard to hear over the rain.

"Oh, yes, people do beg him. Why, they come for miles to beg! But if it's right, simply asking Mr. Cornelius Clashammer to train you should do the trick well enough." Lady Carmine spied the confusion on Mary Ann's face. She gave a light, tired chuckle. "Clashammer is the trainer you should seek when the right time comes for your own sword study. All the way out in Hillandale or possibly Yon, I can't quite recall the locale at the moment. Nonetheless, it's well worth the trip, I hear. He trains all the best knights, the keenest adventurers. Frankly, we'd expected he'd be the one to show up and train Rufus. But I'm glad it was you. I'm sure you're much nicer." And she patted Mary Ann's hand.

Mary Ann suppressed a laugh at the absurdity of the idea, as she wrung out a table runner. "Can a housemaid *be* an adventurer?"

Lady Carmine smiled a sweet, weary smile. "Can a caterpillar fly, my dear?"

Mary Ann left Lady Carmine sleeping and slogged to the servants' bedchamber for a dry set of clothes. By the time she was done, Douglas Divot had arrived and was standing with the knight, Lord Carmine, and half the staff at the bottom of the staircase. They were discussing run-off and fluid dynamics and how they might rig a makeshift gutter feature to, at least, funnel the water somewhere sensible until the fever broke.

It was progress.

Mary Ann went about her chores reflecting on her morning's activities. So the mirror that was in Mr. Rabbit's hands—er, paws—contained a portal set to go to Thither. The question remained: how to trigger it. Also interesting were the preliminary plans for a whole network of transporting mirrors to be done, with frames crafted by her very own father. If it went forth, it would change much about the way one moved from place to place in Turvy, and Turvy did enjoy its traditions. But was that reason enough to dispose of the woodworker? It wouldn't sideline a project such as that, since they could always get another craftsman for the frames. The mirror was the key element there and Gilda Plaine was alive and well.

It was a puzzlement.

By evening, Mary Ann felt like she was standing in a bog of ideas and motive. Why would anyone kill her father? Especially when everyone knew of him and yet no one seemed to know him at all. In a way, she found this comforting. She wasn't an ignored daughter, trivial to his life. She was part of a great lively community of people he made efforts to avoid completely. She slipped her father's accounts book from under the mattress on her side of the bed and reexamined the details there. The money owed to her father by Mr. Banks was not insignificant. Why hadn't it been paid? Had it been collected? And if it had, where did the money go? That was something worth finding out. She had the client names there. She would just have to go to the source.

If Mr. Banks were skimming off the top, that might explain his abrupt departure. But was it reason enough to hire an assassin? There was no indication that John Sanford Banks knew Jacob Morningstar at all. And she knew that Morningstar was responsible because she saw it with her own eyes.

Yes, the only person who seemed to actually interact with her father had fled.

Unless…

Who do you talk to when you want to know more about a person who rarely leaves home?

You talk to his neighbors. And Mary Ann had a few candidates for that.

12

Hope sprung early the next morning. For one, Lady Carmine seemed to have taken a turn for the better overnight. The rainfall was down to a mist now, the temperature in her room had evened out with the rest of the manor and that pesky storm cloud had gone from charcoal to pearl grey. What's more, the patient was in good spirits. "So kind of you to check on me, dear," she said. "I feel like this front will clear any time now. And when it does, I will not forget your kindness."

"Just doing my job, My Lady," Mary Ann said.

"Ah, but you see, you aren't. Tending to me is not your job at all."

It's Celeste's, thought Mary Ann. That was the unspoken truth there. But Celeste was unhelpful in a crisis situation. She'd spent most of yesterday wringing her hands and having a bitter row with her beau, the carriage driver. She simply wasn't inclined toward wringing towels or readying rowboats.

"I'm glad you're on the mend, My Lady," Mary Ann said. She mopped the floor, wiped down the tables and stoked the fire, then went about the rest of her chores.

Her training session with Sir Rufus was hopeful too, but in an entirely different way. It was not jovial exactly, since he was incapable of that, but upbeat, perhaps. "Mother's doing better, you know," he said, swinging the Vorpal sword at what she knew was half-power. For some reason, he was holding back.

"I do," she said. As the swords made contact, she gave it all she had. CLANG!

"She credits you for her returning health," he continued. He put more energy into the blow, she noticed. SWWOOP — WHACK!

"She's the one who's healing." Mary Ann dodged and gave it an upper thrust.

"She likes you." WONNG!

"And I her." CRACK!

"It would be a shame to disappoint her, then." WHUMMM!

"I don't plan to." CHINNNG!

"And did you plan to disappoint Warren Rabbit?" A parry.

She moved to higher ground for a better angle.

Sir Rufus followed. "That's some strange business worth discussing, I think. That and why you keep vanishing during the day."

"Okay, that's it." Mary Ann dropped her sword arm. "You're doing it all wrong."

He blinked and lowered his weapon, too. "The sword work?"

"Not the sword work. Forget the sword work," she said. "You are the master of the house. I am a housemaid. I do my job properly, so you need never notice me. That's a tradition that's worked nicely for everyone for years and years and years. But you people—why, I've never met such a family and their habit of noticing housemaids!"

"Look, it's not that you're there and I see you, but shouldn't. It's that you're *not there* and I see you *not being there.*"

"My work is there, completed. That is all that matters. My presence is irrelevant. You shouldn't notice me to notice when I'm not there," she said and then considered it more. "Has anyone else noticed my absence?"

"Not as I'm aware," he said. "But I can make that happen, if you don't come clean."

"Coming clean is what I do." But she felt a twinge of worry over the comment that rippled across her expression.

He latched onto that swiftly enough. "Did you hear the news? There was a girl with golden hair who grew twenty times her size right in the middle of Queen Valentina's tart trial the other day."

She set her jaw. "Oh, was there?"

"Scared the jury to bits, I heard," he said. "What's more, they seem to think it was the same girl with the same *modus operandi* at Warren Rabbit's house. They said she called herself Alice, but alas, they're not sure if Alice isn't an alias."

"Indeed," Mary Ann said sourly.

"But you're right," he said, "she's not you."

"Excuse me?" She hadn't seen this part coming.

"She looks nothing like you. She's got different hair. And different eyes. And unlike you, she is just a child."

"And how would you know?"

"Because I saw the finished poster," he said. "And I see you." His gaze now was very direct and full of weight. And was that…a hint of a smile?

She had to admit, she did rather like his face in this light. It wasn't a handsome one—it was too long, with too many angles, the mouth too wide and the eyes too small—but it was a good one, an interesting one. And he was flushed, so the freckles weren't quite so intense.

She felt herself flush, too.

"Also," he said, "because I was with you when that tart trial was happening. Can't be in two places at once, you know."

"You're right," she said, feeling like there wasn't quite enough air in this outdoors at the moment. "And I need to go."

"What?"

"Lunch," she said.

"I can give you an excuse for lunch," he called.

But Mary Ann was already down the path.

Lunch was the same as always—helping in the dining room, watching that tray go up to the Tower and an old one return empty. So it wasn't until after clean-up and a few pre-tea chores that Mary Ann got a chance to scarper off. This time, she made good and certain Sir Rufus was not following her; after this morning, there was no predicting where that would lead.

She'd been thinking a lot about her childhood during the past day and it had occurred to her that the people who knew the most about her father and his goings on were the ones planted closest to home. So Mary Ann headed to Rowan Carpenter's cottage and called out to some of the locals.

"Pardon me? Hello? Do you have time for a few questions?" Mary Ann asked.

She looked up at the towering trees lining the house. One tree stretched its branches. "Time?" The voice was creaky and echoing. "Young lady, we have rings and rings of it. What would you like to discuss? Weather? Deciduous and conifer politics? Music perhaps?"

"I'd call it history," said Mary Ann.

"Well, we have seen peace and battle, we've seen sunrises and sunsets, we've seen kings rise and crowns fall. What would you like to know?"

"More recent history, I think. About this area, the owner of this property. I used to live here. I don't expect you to remember me specifically."

"Let's get a good look at you, girl," and the tree bent low, held up a pair of pince-nez in one branch before its gnarled face and squinted.

"I'm Mary Ann Carpenter. I lived here when I was, er, a seedling."

The squint continued a moment further, then the eyes, which looked like knotholes to the casual observer, went wide. "Ohhh, Mary Ann," said the voice. "Indeed! You climbed my branches."

"You played games with my dropped seedlings," said a second tree.

"You made beautiful fans with my fallen leaves," said a third.

"Yes," she smiled, "that was me."

"How many rings do you have now?" a Maple asked.

The visual was very unpleasant when applied to people, she thought, and she got a new insight into how trees must feel about it. But she had an answer. "Eighteen rings," she said.

"Not such a long time," said the Maple.

"A pittance," said a Tumtum.

"Hardly a dent in the universe," said the Oak.

Mary Ann nodded. "And it's because you all have been here and have observed so much, I was wondering if you had seen anything unusual lately?"

"We saw you and that tove put your father to mulch, if that's what you mean," said the Oak.

"Well, yes," she said, hoping not to dwell on that point, "but I was rather wondering whether you've seen anyone else show up here?"

"There was a Royal from Neath that came by. The one we assume cut down your father in the first place. But you were here for that."

Yes, she was here. They had seen some of it. She hoped that wouldn't cause her problems in the future. "And before that?"

"That walrus friend of his."

"Yes," said the Tumtum tree, "that walrus fellow came by perhaps once a week for over a decade."

Mary Ann said, "And did you ever overhear any of their discussions? Were they…friendly?"

"One time not long ago it got a bit heated," said the Maple. "I could hear the argument through the open windows. Your father said something 'would not do' and had to be rectified. I specifically remember that: 'rectified.' And then that walrus fellow said it was not to worry and things got quieter. Things must have been resolved because we smelled human food not long after that."

"I heard some laughter," said the Tumtum.

"And the walrus fellow came out looking jolly, picking at a tusk with a bit of wood, a spring in his step and his belly round," said the Oak.

"And you never saw my father with anyone but Mr. Banks?—Er, the walrus fellow," she clarified.

"Not in a number of rings, no. The walrus would come sometimes with some helpers to move a new piece of furniture. But there was always that walrus."

The Oak said, "Your father came and went himself, usually returning with a bag of supplies. Food or wood. But he was alone. He seemed to like it that way. He would whistle to himself. Oh, how he could whistle!"

Mary Ann had forgotten about that. The one fond memory she had of her father. The warbling whistle that could make the birds take notes on technique.

"He was all right, you know," said the Tumtum tree. "For a human. He never cut us. He always used only fallen trees to make his work. He gave them new life. Nobility. He helped them live on."

"Well..." creaked the Maple, "he could have left them to return to the earth, could he not? He could have refrained from mangling our friends' dead bodies for art... That might have made him better..."

The Tumtum tree leaned down and whispered, "Ignore Clarence. Nobody likes him."

Hm, Mary Ann thought. *The things one learns.* All this time, she'd no idea the Maple's name was Clarence.

Mary Ann thanked them for their time and headed down the path to her next stop.

"Hello?" Mary Ann called into the nest from the coop's stoop. "Hello?"

"Hello?" called a voice in return. "Hello?"

"Mrs. Nightwing? I don't know if you'll remember me. It's Mary Ann Carpenter, your neighbor Rowan Carpenter's daughter. I knew you and your husband when I was young."

"Oh, come in, child, come in! So nice of you to cawwwwl."

It had not been easy getting up into the giant Pine, even with the Pine's kind assistance, and Mary Ann entered the raven's abode now a bit strained, full of DwindleAde and out of breath. "Mrs. Nightwing, a pleasure to see you again." In fact, Mary Ann wasn't seeing much of anything yet as her eyes adjusted to the light in the place. "I was wondering if you had a moment?"

She was almost able to discern detail now. The bird was at a writing desk — an ornate one quite obviously designed by Rowan Carpenter. The bird's jet feathers looked glossy in the light of a candle. The candle was, in fact, the nub of a taper candlestick. At Mary Ann's new reduced size, it looked like a pillar. The bird wore a collection of assorted gems, glass and fragments of shell on strings around her neck. This glinted in the light, too.

"I always have a moment for an old friend," said Mrs. Nightwing. "Besides, I wasn't getting on much with this scene, anyway."

Mary Ann looked to the desk. "Are you writing another book? The last one of which I knew was <u>Lady, Croak No More</u>."

"Oh, dear child, that was twelve books ago," the bird said with a merry flap of her wing. "I've done very well in the suspense genre of late. There's been a huge market for my raven detective novels. The readers just flock to them, you know." She indicated a stack of books at one end of the room, presumably the library. They were almost the size of the raven herself and it must have been no end of trouble getting them into the nest. The covers were beautiful, ornate things, covered in twining flowers. <u>The Shattered Egg</u>, by Lenore Nightwing. <u>The Human</u>, by Lenore Nightwing. <u>The Talon Terror</u> by Lenore Nightwing. And so on.

Mary Ann looked back to the desk and pointed to a machine

there taking up the bulk of surface space. "Now, that contraption is fascinating! You simply must tell me what that is."

"Oh, that? Yes, I'm quite pleased with that. It's an entirely new way of printing words, my child. It's a bit like a portable press. You may recall, I used to dip my beak in ink to write. But it left such a dreadful aftertaste, it made everything from carrion to carpenter ants taste like ink. So now I have this little gadget."

Mary Ann leaned closer, captivated. "And how does it work?"

"Hunt and peck, dear child," said Mrs. Nightwing, "Hunt and peck. You just press the letter of the alphabet you want, like so ..." The bird demonstrated, pressing a key, which connected to a little arm on the machine, that in turn struck a ribbon with ink, then the paper. It was miraculous. It made a marvelously satisfying clatter. In a moment, Mary Ann could read the perfectly typeset word:

Nevermind.

"Actually," said the bird, rereading, "I believe that should be two words...Ah, well. That's why we have editors."

"It's remarkable," said Mary Ann. "I didn't know such a thing had been invented."

"It hasn't," said the bird with a wink, "but it will. Turvian invention, you know. Manufacturing first, then the invention. I've had this 'writetyper,' as I call it, for several years. And—" The raven gasped. "Oh, my goodness, where are my manners? Please, child, have a seat!" She indicated a chair made from twigs, twine and a sea sponge. As Mary Ann sat, Mrs. Nightwing held out a bowl. "May I offer you a beetle? Some grubs? They're fresh!" Indeed, they were, for they were still squirming around in the dish.

"Er, no, thank you. I've already had some grub this morning." But it was toast.

Mrs. Nightwing nodded, set the bowl aside, and perched

down in front of her desk. "So, about what topic did you come to speak with me?"

Mary Ann had been so interested in the writetyper she'd almost forgotten. "I was just wondering, since you lived so close to my father…Did he ever mention any…enemies?"

"Enemies?" The raven cocked her head thoughtfully. "Why, not so as he ever expressed. He is very much his own man, your father. He doesn't need an unkindness to make him feel comfortable."

Mary Ann raised an eyebrow. "What unkindness?"

"No, not an unkindness," Mrs. Nightwing went on, thinking. "A…murder?"

"I'm sorry?" By now Mary Ann's heart was thumping and her mind was awhirl. Had Mrs. Nightwing been witness to what had happened? Was word getting around? Did she have information?

"Perhaps that's solely for crows," the raven continued, almost as if to herself. "What do you humans call a group of your people who share space together?"

"A family? A crowd?" stammered Mary Ann. Now it was starting to making sense.

"Yes, just that. A crowd," said the raven. "My goodness, you've come over so pale, my dear! Are you quite all right?"

"Yes," Mary Ann pressed a hand to her face, "I'm fine. Fine now."

"I'll get you some water," said Mrs. Nightwing.

Mary Ann looked around the lady's home while she bustled off for the pitcher and a glass. In addition to mud, twigs, feathers, paper, fabric scraps and tufts of furniture fluff that comprised the nest's walls and ceiling, there was an odd assortment of objects included there, as well. Here Mary Ann spied a child's marble, there a die, there a thimble, all much larger than she was used to them being, given her current size. There were also some bits of broken bottles and a remarkable number of shoes. Tiny shoes—doll shoes, perhaps—since they were almost twice the size of the marble and all basically the same—shiny and white. It created an interesting texture to the place. "You have quite a knack for design. So many unusual objects you have worked together."

"Oh, these old things?" But Mary Ann could see the lady was pleased that she'd noticed. "I just pick up whatever's around. What people toss aside or forget. Waste not want not, we ravens always say. There you go, child." She handed Mary Ann a glass of water. "Would you like a maggot in it? I find it adds some flavor."

"Er, no, thank you. Plain will do." She took a long enough drink of the water that it made it worth the lady's trouble.

"So if you don't mind my asking: why do you think your father would have any enemies?"

Mary Ann had not been prepared for questions in return. She looked hard at the raven, whose face was open and sincere. Her eyes fell on the stack of mystery books that the lady had penned. (Or, more recently, writetyped.)

And Mary Ann found herself explaining the entire situation. "I'm at a loss, Mrs. Nightwing," she concluded somewhat out of breath. "I've no real power. I can't accuse a courtier of Neath of anything without putting myself in jeopardy. If I had any evidence beyond my own eyes — some motive, some tangible item I could bring forward as proof — then maybe. *Maybe* I could bring it to Lord Carmine. But the only one related to my father who seems to have any questionable intent is my father's business partner. And that man's suddenly packed up and left. Not to mention, based on what I've learned, he doesn't seem to have had much interaction with Neath. If anything, based on the account books, my father had more motive to murder him." Mary Ann shifted in her chair. "You write mysteries. You have a fine mind. What would your characters do?"

"Well," said Mrs. Nightwing, tapping the tips of her wings together in thought. "In my books, when my detective reaches an impasse such as yours, he usually sits down to examine his Ises and Isn'ts."

"Excuse me?"

"That is to say, he examines the things that Is that Aren't.

And conversely, those that Aren't, that Is. Or Are, rather." She settled into her chair. "Is that clearer?"

"Like a pudding," said Mary Ann.

Mrs. Nightwing gave a croaky laugh. "The trouble with our brains, no matter how fine they are, is that we often don't know what we don't know. I'm talking of the sort of thing we take for granted that Is, that in our minds simply Must Be, but not only Isn't but Never Has Been. We've accepted that thing unquestioned for so long, that it's Become. But it still Isn't. Not really. Those are the points my detective looks for. The Betweens. In Turvy, as well as Neath, my dear, we are filled to the brim with Betweens. We exist on Betweens. Nothing is what it is for long."

"I don't know what happened with Nothing, but Nobody is wanted for questioning in the rath case," Mary Ann said, trying to be helpful.

"Well, Nobody will get far on Nothing. Mark my words."

"How do I find my Ises and Isn'ts?" Mary Ann asked. Her head was starting to throb a little and she wasn't sure if it were from the conversation or her reduced size.

"I suggest you start at the beginning, child. Take the thing of which you're most certain, most firm, most unshaken. Then dismantle your truths from there. You'll end up with a terrible pile of bits and bobs, and likely some extra pieces. Still, knowing's worth the time for reassembly."

Mary Ann left Mrs. Nightwing with a small bag of grubs "to snack on for the journey home" and a spinning brain. It was the latter, she thought, and a need not to offend her kind hostess that led to her accepting the former. Especially since she wasn't quite ready to return to Carmine Manor yet. She had one quick stop she wanted to make first.

She sorted out her size issues with a bit of Burgeonboosh and turned at the lane that read, "Goodnuff."

Noting the fine weather, Mary Ann knew better than to knock at the cottage. Instead she went directly to the meadow in back of it. She could see Professor Cyril Goodnuff crouching in the brush, like a creature of prey himself, though a lumpy, awkward one in kneeboots and breeches. Mary Ann came up quietly but wasn't sure of the best approach to catch the gentleman's attention. Speak aloud and she'd startle the fellow to death, along with whatever he was watching. Tap him on the shoulder, and she might get caught in that butterfly net the man had at the ready. She settled for clearing her throat.

The man turned, grinned a grin broader than even that of Chester the cat and motioned her close, to come down into the grass where he crouched. He whispered, "Be very quiet, or the whole mission's done for."

"What are you doing?" Mary Ann whispered. She looked among the grass and flowers before them, but spied nothing.

"I'm trying to lure a Passing Fancy," he said and gave her a confidential wink, like she'd practically written the definitive paper on the subject, so he was letting her in on a good thing.

"I'm afraid I'm not familiar with what that is," she admitted, hating to disappoint him.

"Why, it's only one of the rarest and most unpredictable creatures in Turvy. No one has as of yet photographed one in the wild."

Then a thought occurred to her. "Does it wear funny spectacles and a false nose and mustaches and have a body like a banana skin?" It seemed very likely to be that thing she and Rufus had seen running around outside Carmine Manor.

But Professor Goodnuff quickly shook his head in the negative. "Oh, not at all. No, a Fancy's got legs like party streamers and a body like a cream cake, a head like a cherry and eyes like boiled sweets. So it is said, anyway."

To Mary Ann, it sounded more like the man needed his tea. "How do you lure it?"

"It operates entirely on its sense of whimsy. Goes however the spirit moves it. Follows the way of the wind…The twinkle in the eye…The rumble in the lower bowel."

"So, basically, you're just waiting in case it shows up," she said.

"Yes." He grinned. "Only way to catch a Fancy."

"How long have you been out here?" she asked, for what parts of his face weren't covered in wiry grey whiskers seemed to be quite sunburned.

"Four hundred and thirty seven days," he said. "But I feel certain today's going to be a lucky one."

"While we wait," said Mary Ann, who had been looking for a good way to introduce the reason for her visit (it *was* getting toward tea after all), "I don't know if you recall me, but—"

"You. Yes, you! You're the Yellow-Headed Mary Ann. Eats predominately seafood, berries and porridge and is recognizable by its distinctive yellow hair, full cheeks and overbite."

"Er, well, yes, I suppose ..." It was somewhat more flattering than Mr. Milliner's comments about her appearance, at least. "I am rather off seafood now, after eating it so often as a child but—" She tried to redirect the discussion. "I've come because I wondered if you'd spoken with my father recently."

"Your father?" He thought a moment. "Oh, the Great Taciturn Carpenter! Known by its rough, stained hands, sinewy forearms and stiff mandible."

It didn't sound that far off.

"Ah, by recently: how recent do you mean? You see for the last four hundred and thirty seven days, I've been enmeshed in this project of mine and haven't had much company."

Mary Ann decided to try another angle on this. "Do you recall ever hearing talk of any enemies of, er, the Great Taciturn Carpenter?"

"Well, there was, of course, your mother."

"My mother?"

"Yes, the Wild Roaming Clarissa," he said. "Same yellow crown feathers as yourself, erratic behavior patterns, mostly nocturnal. Oh yes, she was trouble. Predatory species."

"I can't say," Mary Ann replied. "I don't really remember anything about her."

"Sure, she left your father when you were just a tyke. But

she joined the White Turvian Resistance when the Battle of Square Four happened. Ran off to her White Turvian roots and became a pawn for the King and Queen of that side."

"My mother was White Turvian?"

"Yes, indeed," said the professor. "We knew when she married your father that the match was doomed from the start. But, every now and then you'll have that with varied species. I think it has to do with proximity, myself, and — You look surprised, dear girl. Didn't you know?"

"My father never spoke much about my mother," she said.

"Well, your father shipped you out to Neath, didn't he, before the battle made it to this Square? He tried to keep you out of it. So it's hardly a wonder."

"He told me I had to go because children were to be seen and not heard. Because I made too much noise and asked too many questions."

"Well, you did! That's a child for you. That's their job. But two things can be true at the same time and your mother was a traitor to the Red Turvian cause." He scratched his chin. "What's prompted all these questions about your father?"

"I'm not sure any more." Mary Ann rose to go. "Thank you, Professor. You've been very enlightening."

"A Running Joke," the man called to her.

"Pardon?"

"Your friend the spectacled, false-nosed banana skin. That's a Running Joke. To catch them, you need to find their source."

"The punchline?"

"Certainly not!" he said. "To really understand 'em, you need to get 'em where they start. You see, those chaps pop up wherever you find some particularly concentrated humor. Just spawns 'em right out. But don't you worry…You see 'em once, you're bound to see 'em again, until they completely wear out their welcome."

"Oh, thank you ever so much, Professor!" she said, a bounce coming into her step. "This is joyble news! Good afternoon to you! And best of luck with your Passing Fancy."

"I think today might just be the day," he said.

13

"It's a Running Joke," Mary Ann whispered as she passed Sir Rufus in the hall before tea.

He frowned. "What is?"

"That creature we've seen twice on the Manor grounds. I spoke to an expert in the field about it."

"Which field?"

"The one behind his house," she said.

He gave her a look. "I meant field of study."

"Oh. Well, he's a Turvian zoologist. He says it's a Running Joke."

"And this matters to me, why?" He folded his arms.

"He said they're spawned from concentrated humor. I have this feeling that if we find out where the Running Joke begins its journey each day, we'll find your wit and whimsy again."

He shook his head with an expression of actual pity on his face. "Mary Ann, that's mad."

"Precisely why it's worth a go," she said. "Do you or do you not want to get your humor back?"

"Of course I do," he said. "Yet, the longer it's gone, the harder it is to remember what it was even like when I had it. If I think very hard, I can almost remember the carefree times when humor both brightened the good days and soothed the bad ones. But it's fading fast."

"Then we'll make this a priority." She wondered about taking on too much, but the offer did have Sir Rufus looking a bit more hopeful.

"You!" Mrs. Cordingley seemed to have emerged from the ether. She snapped her fingers at Mary Ann. "There you are. Come here. Cook has an errand for you."

Watercress. The dinner salad demanded it, said Cook, and when your side dishes spoke, a proper chef listened. Of course, a proper chef didn't go fetch the ingredients herself. She sent someone less important to get them and Emmaline was already up to her eyeballs in gravy boats, tureens and silver polish.

That was all right. Mary Ann was never against getting some extra fresh air. She knew the patch of watercress of which the cook spoke, an enthusiastic little thicket of it along the banks of the Topsy River. Mary Ann had missed this river, having lived in Neath so long. She had vague memories of playing along it. It wasn't always here, of course. Sometimes it was a series of streams, sometimes a tiled bath and sometimes a gravel lot. But when it showed up, it gave so much.

She was pleased to see it was here at the moment. The trouble was, so many people were here, as well. Lord Carmine's guards trod the reedy shores, backs to her, right at the spot in which she was hoping to wade. "All right, men," said a fellow on a horse. "On three. One...two...three!"

It was obvious the job was completely unplanned, or the task would have been done backwards and neatly executed. But now she saw the men clasping ropes, straining to drag something from the river...

Something that was not very forthcoming. Initially, Mary Ann felt sour about the state of the watercress. They were crushing it, churning the waters and dredging up mud. What kind of trouble would she be in when she got back to Cook, watercresst-fallen and failed? Why, she would be…

Dead.

The body slid onto the bank, at that last great heave. At first, Mary Ann didn't recognize it, so tangled in vegetation as it was. But then she spied the color of the fabric. A bright pink. A cerulean blue. And patterned trousers, the silk now stained and sopping.

"J. Sanford Banks," gasped one of the men.

Oh no. She moved closer, barely daring to breathe, and could now see the fellow's boat, or rather, what was left of it—shards of wood spiking from between rocks.

"Drownded," assessed a Tweedle, examining the body. From this distance Mary Ann couldn't tell which Tweedle it was. Crouching, he was almost a ball. "Full of water his lungs are. Suffixiation."

"Suffixiation?! Not hardly," said his brother.

"Quite muchly. It put an end to him, didn't it?" said the first Tweedle, and the second Tweedle begrudgingly nodded. "There's the suffix. The suffix always goes on at the end."

"See here," began Tweedle Two, who Mary Ann could now see was D.M. Tweedle, and he was itching for a fight. He pointed to the body. "A bump on the head. A contuberation. That's the cause."

"That's the prefix," D.I. Tweedle corrected. "It fixed him good first. But the ultimate cause was the water in his lungs, which suffixed him. You cannot argue with that."

"I will in my report."

"Not if my report gets to Lord Carmine first."

For a moment, Mary Ann thought it would come to blows—there was certainly some posturing in that direction. But the tension eased and the other guards didn't seem to notice, anyway.

"How did he end up drownde—er, drowning?" Mary Ann asked quietly.

It took them a moment to fix their gaze on her. "Boat hung up on the rocks, didn't it?" D.M. hooked a thumb to the scene.

Mary Ann stepped closer. "But look: there's plenty of room for him to have sailed past them. And Mr. Banks was a fine sailor. How could this have happened?"

"Perhaps he got distractipated," suggested D.I. Tweedle. "Distractipated driving is responsible for one in five accidents."

"None such," said D.M. "This is the first boating accident we've seen."

"And how many accidents have we investigated?" asked D.I.

"In our billustrious career of three whole weeks?" He seemed to do some mental arithmetic. "Four."

"There you go. This is five."

Mary Ann moved to the river. "Is there any chance someone could have hit him on the head? Could he have been, er, clubbed first?"

"Well, he's the only one in the boat. So no one to do the clubbing." D.I. Tweedle eyed her narrowly. "Surely you don't think he clubbed himself, do you?" He turned, laughing to the other guards. "Look at her, she thinks he clubbed himself."

"Not no-how," laughed D.M. Tweedle. "He'd never get up the leverage!"

But Mary Ann was determined to make them see sense. "Couldn't someone have gotten aboard, struck him and then leapt off?"

Sadly, they didn't seem much interested in that idea. "Nah," said D.I. Tweedle. "Then there'd like as be footprints along the banks somewheres and we saw nothing of the kind in our investibles."

He hadn't finished his sentence before Mary Ann was already searching a short distance away upriver. And it wasn't long after that before she saw two solid boot prints in the sand. They were men's, full-sized and not at all a flipper. "Here!" she called. "Take a look at this."

The Tweedles and their men ran over. "Where? What?"

And in no time, they had stepped upon the very place Mary Ann had pointed out.

"Oh, them? Those are guard-issued boot prints, nothing to get yerself in a twist over."

"Well, they are now," snapped Mary Ann. "You've trod all over it!"

"What we need to do," mused D.I. Tweedle, "is notificate any of whom might be fambily to poor old Sandy Banks, eh? Send someone round to let them know and give our condolorances."

D.M. Tweedle was jotting this down.

"I'm not sure about any wee ones," D.I. continued, "but I know he had a friend in that woodworker fellow, that Carpenter who lives over at the edge of Tulgey Barrens. They was business partners, and this'll mean something to him."

"Frabjous, then send a group round right speedily."

When Mary Ann heard this, cold was the chill that ran down her spine. They were "sending someone round." And when they arrived, they would find the place completely empty and a fresh grave in back. What if they spoke to the trees? The trees had, at the least, seen Jacob Morningstar come and go, but not the crime itself. Just her and Douglas Divot carrying two parts of Rowan Carpenter to "mulch." The trees did seem to believe she was not responsible for the tragedy, but would the guards? Also, this put Douglas smack-dab in the middle of one mysterious death and another mass killing in just a few days. How would this be for him?

And what if they wanted to question Mary Ann? Everyone knew she was sent to Neath years ago. What if they followed the trail and tracked her down? What would she say? It was a little late to say, "Oh, by the way, I saw my father murdered and was afraid to mention it so I buried him quietly and cleaned up the evidence." Even if they did believe her and exonerate Douglas of any wrong-doing, she had very little confidence the Tweedles would be able to protect her from a determined assassin. The Tweedles couldn't protect themselves out of a paper bag.

She was in a cold sweat by the time she was done pondering the situation.

She pried herself from the crime scene and had started back to the Manor when she remembered the reason she'd been sent to the river in the first place, so she moved downriver to look for additional patches of watercress. It was action, at least. Something to burn off some of the fear, until she could think straight.

"You look like the weight of the world is on your shoulders," said a voice, and it was Douglas Divot.

"Funny," she said, "I was just thinking about you."

"Me? I don't weigh all that much," he said.

"But J. Sanford Banks does. Or rather did."

Douglas looked surprised. "He's reduced since we last saw him? Good for him. As long as he's healthy."

"He's dead," she said and she described the scene upriver.

"Perhaps it was a suicide," said Douglas, kneading his clawed hands in a worried way. "Could he have felt some guilt about your father? Could he have been involved in it somehow?"

"The Tweedles seem to think it was an accident," said Mary Ann. "But he had a head injury that I'm not fully convinced happened when his boat went down. And I found a boot print in the sand upriver from where the boat crashed and capsized. I'm starting to really believe he was fleeing something. Or someone."

"Well, it's not me," said Douglas.

"I didn't think it was," she said.

"I only met the fellow that time with you."

"I know."

"And when commissioning furniture," he said.

"Right."

"And I had to commission it, you know, because your father didn't do tove-sized pieces. DwindleAde won't work on it to make it smaller. You can't just rub it into the wood grain and hope for the best; it's got to be built small from the start."

Mary Ann looked at him hard. "That's very specific. It almost sounds like you tried."

The tove's ear twitched. "Er, I'm sorry," he said. "This whole rath thing has got me a bit paranoid. The Wabe is entirely too quiet now that everyone's gone. Even the other toves have left. They consider the place a bad neighborhood now and feel it's a hazard to even live there. I'm not sure I feel safe myself."

She pressed a hand to his shoulder. "Take it easy. Mind what you eat and drink. Don't fall for a bowl of seafood you find lying about in the woods."

"Oh, I'd never do that," he said. "There's the shellfish allergy. Also, toves eat cheese, you know."

She did know. "Cheese then." And rising, she took the watercress she'd gathered up in her basket and headed back to the Manor.

14

Judging by the laughter coming from the dining room, the dinner was a success — at least, as much as Mary Ann could hear it from the kitchen. The Earl of Scarlet was visiting from Square Three, a very bald, very boisterous fellow who the servants said always made for a lively time. It seemed the table discussion had largely turned to the travel for Queen Valentina's Unbirthday, which was impending, and to Lady Carmine's health, which was improving. Improving so much, it seemed almost certain she would be able to attend the event in four days time with no black cloud of illness hanging over her.

"I'm somewhat concerned about that walrus situation, though," admitted Lord Carmine, and Mary Ann drew close to the door of the dining room. Peering through a crack in the pocket doors, she could see the interest cross Sir Rufus' face as his father said, "Hate to leave with all of that going on, of course."

"All what?" Sir Rufus asked, in mid-bite of salad. "I thought it was an accident."

"Interesting thing about that. I received a rocking horsefly not ten minutes ago. Seems those Tweedle boys went to notify that Carpenter fellow — you know the one, the recluse? He works with Banks, sort of a manufacturing and sails partnership they have for the furniture business. Anyway, it seems that one's dead, too."

Sir Rufus' fork clattered to his plate. "What?"

"Hopping hedgehogs, Carmine!" exclaimed Lord Scarlet with a laugh. "Your people are dropping like…like…something that drops a lot, aren't they?"

"Apparently," continued Lord Carmine, not bothering to address his friend's simile issues, "there's a grave in the back of Carpenter's house, made with some care."

"Well, these things happen. Easy come, easy go. Circle of life and all that," Lord Scarlet said philosophically and helped himself to some more wine.

"How long?" Sir Rufus asked, sitting up very straight. "How long do they think the grave's been there?"

"Fresh grave," said Lord Carmine. "The ground still doesn't have any grass on it. I understand there's also what looks like a large stain on the floor of his workshop."

"And I'm guessing you're about to tell us it's not the kind meant to paint chairs," said Sir Rufus, narrow-eyed.

Lord Carmine reached for the butter. "Seems Tweedle and Tweedle both think it's a blood stain."

"You think the two deaths are related, then?" Sir Rufus asked.

Lord Carmine popped in a bite of buttered bread. "Not certain at this point. One theory is that there was some form of disagreement and Banks struck Carpenter in a fit of rage. You ever meet that Banks fellow? Very emotional. Cried at the drop of a hat. Hat didn't even have to be his. Something about headgear got the fellow weepy and out of control." He had swallowed the bread and took another bite. "Other topics did, as well, of course. Like I said, very emotional."

Sir Rufus said, "So they think Banks got angry or offended, and that was that?"

"Or hat was hat. Hard to say," said Carmine. "We do know Banks had owed quite a bit of money on that fancy sails boat of his. It was just about to be repossessed, when he suddenly paid it off in one go. So it could be a dodgy financial thing. Maybe Banks, having killed his friend and meal ticket and all, was overcome with regret, took to his ill-gotten boat and drove himself distractedly onto the rocks."

"Sure, things like this happen a hundred times a year," said Lord Scarlet affably.

Sir Rufus raised an eyebrow. "A hundred?"

"Or this once," said Lord Scarlet and reached for the salt.

"You said one theory," Rufus looked like he needed some wine now himself and poured a glass. "What's the other?"

"Ah, yes," said Lord Carmine. "Well, on account of Carpenter's death, they looked into who needs notification of the thing. The man had a daughter. Turns out, she was shipped off to Neath years ago for being troublesome. Carpenter set her up in a housemaid's position and now she's gone missing there, as well. Blew up Herald Rabbit's house first, though, and caused mayhem in a few other areas around Neath. There's a warrant out for her."

"So Carpenter's daughter is a mad housemaid, eh?" said Sir Rufus. His eyes darted to the door between the dining room and the kitchen. Mary Ann ducked away from the crack, but she wasn't sure it was fast enough. "Will you excuse me a moment?" Sir Rufus asked and he leapt up from his chair.

That second, Mary Ann was trying to put as much distance between herself and the dining room as possible. She rushed into the drawing room and grabbed a doily from a chair arm, using it to wipe the moldings. In a moment, Sir Rufus entered.

"All right, *Mary Ann…*" Just once, she wished he'd say her name nicely. "Mary Ann *Carpenter*, isn't it? It is time for you to talk."

So she talked. And talked of many themes. Of knaves and dads and walruses, Unbirthday gifts and dreams. Of why she fled to Tulgey Wood and whether friends had schemes.

He listened to it, listened to it quietly with intense interest. And when she was done, she took a deep breath, wiped her eyes with the dusty doily, sneezed once and waited. "Well?"

"I daresay, I didn't expect it to be in rhyming verse," he said, scratching his chin, "but it certainly all has come clear now."

She held out her wrists. "So I suppose you'll be apprehending me. Shackling me, taking me to the Mirrigation Room for further questioning, or tossing me in the dungeon until the Tweedles come."

"Dungeon? We haven't any dungeon," he said. "Father keeps his model train collection in the basement. And put your arms down, would you? Nobody's being apprehended."

"Really? Nobody's being apprehended?"

"Actually, Nobody was apprehended earlier today, but on a vagrancy charge. Not at all related to your problems."

She sank into a chair.

"Why didn't you just talk to me, or to my father, about this in the first place?" His expression was all sincerity.

"Because," she said, "I didn't know how much contact your family had with the Royal Family in Neath. I needed a chance to see what inter-realm relations were in the courtier circles. But I kept hearing how you were invited to Queen Valentina's Unbirthday event. And you knew Mr. Rabbit. I had no idea where your loyalties would lie in a case like mine."

He thought about this and nodded. "And you think Jacob Morningstar killed your father."

"I know it. I saw him do it with my own eyes," she said. "How much do you know about the man?"

"Not much," he said, "for now. But I shall see what I can learn. Tell me what day this happened specifically, and I'll see what information I can track down amongst my contacts."

Mary Ann hesitated and he added, "Don't worry. I won't mention anything related to you or what you saw." He rose.

So she gave him the details, adding, "And you really will do this for me?" After feeling so alone with her troubles, it was strange to think she might now have him on her side.

"Well," he said, "with no sense of humor, I feel compelled to shift from my past frivolous ways to one of service to the less fortunate." And with that, he vanished through the door.

If Mary Ann hadn't known better, she would have thought he was kidding.

"Ow, ow, no! Please! Stop! I never asked for this!"

The next morning, Mrs. Cordingley said it was time to beat the rugs, so she and Mary Ann rolled up and dragged out a few of the smaller ones into the yard and hung them on the line to give them a good thrashing. Mary Ann had expected the great amount of dust, but not the complaints and the trouble the things were giving them.

"What have I done?" asked a particularly vocal geometric-patterned one. "Just tell me what I did to deserve this maltreatment?"

WHACK! WHACK! "Shut your noise, you," said Mrs. Cordingley. "You give me lip about this every spring, you do, and I'll not have it again. Keep it up and I'll unravel you where you hang!"

And that set the carpet crying all the more.

It wasn't a wonder that Mary Ann never heard Sir Rufus approach. Instead, a hand gripped her shoulder but for half a moment she thought it was some fringe trying to strangle her in its defense.

"Oh! It's you!" she said, relieved.

"Mrs. Cordingley, I'd like a word with Mar — er, your housemaid a moment. I promise I'll give her right back."

Mrs. Cordingley beamed up at him. "Oh, you take all the time you want, Mr. Rufus, Sir. I'll still be out here with the rugs that need a good what-for when you're done." And with that, the beatings continued until morale improved.

"So I've asked around a bit," began Sir Rufus once they were out of earshot, "worked it casually into conversation amongst my father and the guards. It seems that Jacob Morningstar had quite the reputation during the Great War of Neath. Apparently, he was fierce on the battlefield, yet many in the Clubs family considered him a traitor because of the speed with which he switched to serve the Hearts' side. The general consensus is that if he were acting in the way you described, he'd be acting on Queen Valentina's order."

"Oh dear," sighed Mary Ann. "It is as I feared."

"But I have some questions. You said yesterday your father was beheaded with an axe. And that it was done in one chop."

"That's correct."

"One swoop, at a sideways angle and no hacking?"

"Er, yes."

"And it resulted in no jagged cuts or veins, just a smooth wound area that—" At what must have been her very pained expression, he said, "Look, I wouldn't ask, but this is important."

"Yes," she said. "It was a perfectly smooth, even cut and it took the head off in one lop."

"So it was a magic axe," he said.

"Well, one would expect so," she said, dusting off her hands. "I've never seen a normal axe cut like that."

"And who have you asked about it?"

"Asked?" She blinked in lieu of a better answer.

"You didn't trace the axe?"

"Er, not precisely *yet*..." She decided she was not going to be a liar these days, so she went on. "I mean, it's the Knave of Clubs' axe. Why trace it when we know who has it?"

"We know who has it now, yes. But this is not a weapon he was known for."

"What was he known for?"

Rufus looked at her hard. "What do you think he was known for? The Knave of *Clubs*..."

"Oh." She'd never thought about it. But then she hadn't any dealings with that pack of courtiers when she lived in Neath. It wasn't as if Mr. Rabbit needed a traveling companion when he went to the castle, or that the Queen ever popped by the cottage for tea.

"No, see, the axe is a new feature for him," said Rufus. "So I'm thinking, what we need to do is to have a chat with the people at the source of it. See what they know about it and him. Persuade them, if need be."

"All right, but magical axes... They're five brasses a dozen around here, aren't they?" Truthfully, she had no idea.

"Of course not," said Rufus. "If they were, everyone would have them and no wars could ever be waged properly. We'd just keep calling it a draw and have picnics instead."

She eyed him. "Are you sure that wasn't a flicker of a sense of humor?"

"No, it was sarcasm," he said. "Anyone can do sarcasm. It doesn't count. It's not funny, it's just contradictory and mocking."

"If you say so…"

"No, I know of only one place in which a person could get a good magical weapon such as an axe like the one you describe. So get tomorrow's chores done today. Because bright and early tomorrow morning, Mary Ann, you and I are going on a quest." He gave her a look. "A real quest this time. Not playing courier to a rabbit."

"Really, are you sure that's not hum   "

He glared and stalked off.

"Yes, okay," she called after him. "Sarcasm, Sir. Humor's loophole. As you prefer."

She headed back to Mrs. Cordingley and the rugs. From the noise of it, the lady was having a real battle with a knotted berber.

Mary Ann spent the day doing double-duty on chores and by afternoon, she had a good solid body of backwards cleaning that could run through in her absence. The last thing she had to do was a bit of sweeping and dusting in the kitchen area.

This was usually light work. Emmaline was quite competent about keeping their space clean, though Cook herself was not. The scullery maid wasn't as rigorous about it as Mr. Rabbit's chef, of course. But she was far more enthusiastic than the Duchess' Cookie Mills, who took cleaning with a pinch of salt (and a pound of pepper). Mary Ann never minded this work.

It was such a large, echoing house, that the kitchen with its low ceilings and timber beams felt especially snug and comforting. She liked the smell of lovingly-made meals and the scent of ingredients for dinners still to-be.

Mary Ann crept around the baseboards, giving them the attention they deserved, and finally reached the end of the woodwork at the Tower stairs. She noticed the first two steps there were dusty. She had, of course, been told in no uncertain terms that the Tower wasn't her concern. But dust did tend to trail so. And if you had dusty stairs, it was only a matter of time before someone whisked through, sending the stuff flying, only to have it settle on the dishes. It wouldn't hurt to just mop.

So Mary Ann mopped those first few stairs, then the next, then round and round, and before she knew it, she was up at the top of the spiral staircase.

She eyed the door. She never had gotten round to sneaking the keys from Mrs. Cordingley and having a look-see inside, had she? She pressed an ear to the chamber. Indeed, she could hear movement within. "Hello? Knock-knock," Mary Ann called, trying to sound friendly, even though she didn't have that key. "Is anyone in there?"

"Oh no," said a male voice in dread. "Not again! I won't do it. I won't do it and you cannot make me."

"Do what, sir?"

"I won't say it. I won't say it because it's not funny. Not in the least. So you can just forget about it. And if you bring that thing in here again, I will...well, let's just say you'll be sorry."

"If you please, sir—who's there?" she asked.

"Ah, see, yes, I knew it!—that's how it starts. Well, I won't be fooled. Change your voice if you like, but I'm not falling for it, funny voices or not—"

"Funny voices?" Certainly Mary Ann's voice hadn't gotten a lot of use until recently, but it hardly seemed fair to call it funny.

"*Very* funny voices," sneered the one from inside the room. "And not funny ha-ha, either, in case you get lofty ideas about yourself."

"Lofty ideas about myself? I'm the housemaid."

"Oh, I see. So now it's coming out. 'Knock knock.' 'Who's there?' 'The housemaid.' 'The housemaid who?' And then I suppose you say something like, 'The housemaid a creaky noise in the night...BOO!' or something to that effect. That's your game."

This was not her game. Nonetheless, Mary Ann decided to take a different tack. "Do you need anything? May I get you anything, sir?"

"What, like call me a coach? 'Okay, you're a coach!' Or perhaps you could bring me the favorite fruit of twins: pears! Or—"

"All right, I'll take that as a no, sir." And Mary Ann hastily mopped her way back down the stairs.

15

Mary Ann decided to mention the encounter to Sir Rufus the next day during their travels. "Are you sure it's your sane uncle in the Tower?" she began.

They were journeying over the hills of Square Eight toward the Lake District.

"Sure, it's my uncle," Rufus said, egging Goodspeed up the gravel grade. "My father told me so."

"Well, how can you be certain it's your uncle? You'd said you hadn't seen him. How do you know who's in that room?"

Rufus' eyes narrowed. "Come along, Goodspeed, let's put a little energy into it. We haven't got all day."

"Doing my best, Sir," said Goodspeed.

Mary Ann had to push poor Lolly to keep pace, and it still wasn't enough. "Really, now," Mary Ann called to the back of Rufus' head. "How do you know for certain?"

"My father said as much and that's good enough for me," he said. "Are you implying that my father, lord of the Manor and your benefactor, is a liar? Ha, coming from you, that's rich. You've lied to me more than anyone I've ever met."

"I explained about that."

"Yes, explained, I know," he grumbled. "Anyway, whatever

is your fixation with this? Why can't you just let it be?"

"Last evening I was mopping the Tower steps and the person in the Tower room…your uncle…spoke to me. He was completely nonsensical and also …" she chose her words carefully, "he told a joke."

"Joke?"

"Yes. A knock-knock joke."

"And why not?" asked Rufus. "I mean, he's supposed to be sane, not humorless. I'd imagine one can be funny and sane." Though he sounded like he didn't know for sure. "So let's hear it."

She relayed the housemaid bit.

Rufus shrugged. "Not funny to me," he said. "But then I'm no longer the target audience for this sort of thing. For that you need a merry, whimsical person."

Goodspeed piped up, "It didn't tickle my funny bones, either, Sir. But I prefer a good 'horse walks into a pub' joke."

"I like limericks, me," said Lolly. "'There once was a mare from Dumbstruck…'"

"I'm just wondering if it's your uncle at all," Mary Ann interrupted, trying to head off the ending on that limerick. "I mean…could it be your sense of humor in that room?"

"What? No, of course not. Just because it told a few jokes and spoke absolute babble …?" Rufus considered it, his face growing more concerned the longer he did. "I suppose it *could* be mine after I've enjoyed a jolly jousting day and few mushroom beers … I mean, that one Unbirthday party got completely out of hand…" He scratched his head. "We'll, er, look into it when we get back."

Mary Ann nodded, satisfied. The sun shone warm and pleasant on her back, and there had been something of a lightness in her body, around the lung region, now that she had shared the truth of her problems with Sir Rufus. She was buoyed by the progress.

She began, "So you said we're looking for a purveyor of magical things. An expert in these matters."

"Yes," said Rufus. "An enchantress."

"And she lives here?" asked Mary Ann. She peered through a telescope they'd borrowed from the Manor. "I'm afraid there's no cottage or castle for miles, as far as I can see."

"Quite right," he said. "Technically, she's a minor water deity."

"Oh!" said Mary Ann. "So she lives in one of the lakes." She closed the telescope with a snap. "Of course! I've read about that sort of thing in epic poems."

"Erm…" His eyes shifted.

"Not in an epic poem?" asked Mary Ann.

"Yes and no," he said hesitantly. "She's in the second piece written by the historic *Jabberwocky* poet, Sir Loral Clew."

"I didn't realize there *was* a second poem," she said. "Or a Sir Loral Clew." Until she'd met Lord Carmine and Sir Rufus, she'd always thought *Jabberwocky* was one of those tales no one person wrote and everyone keeps adding to. The kind of thing people long ago told around a campfire, back before the invention of bookstores and knitting needles. "How does it go?"

"Alas, there's no time," he said, looking suddenly tense. "This is it." And he jumped down from Goodspeed.

Mary Ann hopped off the back of Lolly and took in the view. Before them was a beautiful smooth lake, sprawling silver-gold in the sunshine. "Fantabulous…" Mary Ann breathed. "Enchanting…"

Rufus tapped her on the shoulder. "No. Here behind you," he said. "The other way."

She turned around, frowning at the road, the hillside. "Where?"

He pointed down. "There."

"The mud puddle in the ditch?"

"Shhh," he said. "Don't get snobbish about it or we'll never get anywhere on your axe issue."

"These minor water deities sound sensitive. I suppose I would be, too, if I lived in a mu—"

"Shhh. Now drink this." He handed her a corked bottle.

"No, thank you, Sir. I'm not really thir—"

"Do you want to find out about your axe or not? It's DwindleAde. Take one sip."

She sighed, wondering how she was supposed to have known that; it wasn't as if the bottle were labeled "Drink Me." But she sipped, and as she handed it back to him, she already found herself getting smaller...smaller...and the grass around the puddle getting bigger...bigger...

"My, that dandy-lion is enormous!" she said as it roared and snapped at her. "There, there, kitty," she said soothingly. "We won't be in your way long."

And now Sir Rufus had joined her.

"What next?" Mary Ann asked, once he got to proper size.

"This," he said. "And I can't believe I'm doing it." He cleared his throat and in a loud voice, he recited:

> "O, Puddlefae of mud and clay,
> I beg you hear my call
> I come to thee for blade to see
> The Jabberwock doth fall."

"Catchy," said Mary Ann approvingly. "What now?"

"According to the poem, we wait in 'teemish phantication,'" he said.

"I'm not sure I know how to do that," said Mary Ann.

"Shhh."

That part must not have been all that critical to the process, anyway, because the mud across the surface of the miniature lake was already bubbling and rippling. And up, up, up rose a figure clad in silt and grass. Her hair was a mass of slick fallen leaves, her eyes like shining black river pebbles. And she opened her mouth and a voice like an entire brood of tiny tadpoles echoed: "Are you the Red Knight? What are you doing here so early? It's not Joyble Day."

"Er, I recognize that, My Lady!" Rufus said, managing a stiff bow. "Terribly sorry for the inconvenience."

"I should say so! Come back later," she said and started down again.

"Wait!" he shouted, then remembered himself. "If you please, Madam. We are looking for a magical weapon."

"What did I say? Joyble Day. You'll have to wait. I swear," she directed this bit to the dandy-lion, "knights these days are so impatient! Not like in the good old days, where they knew they couldn't rush a proper prophecy poem."

"We're not looking for the Vorpal sword," Mary Ann added quickly, before the lady's ears submerged again. "We're looking for a magic axe. We wondered whether you might have given one to someone."

This got her attention. "Magic axe…"

"Yes," Mary Ann felt hope rise within her. "One that can cut anything in one chop, clean and neat. It's silver with a bronze handle and some fiddly thingies etched into the blade."

"Do you know of such a weapon?" asked Rufus.

"Puny mortals," she began, looking them straight in the eye, "in my possession, I have had magic swords, daggers, rings, shoes, a tea set and even, one time, an autonomous cape. But never in my eight thousand years have I been keeper of an axe."

Rufus sighed and nodded. "Thank you, My Lady. I'm sorry to have troubled you." He bowed, Mary Ann curtseyed, and they started away.

"I do have this magic rake," the lady called, reaching into the mud and drawing out a full-sized garden implement, holding it aloft. Difficult to do because it was a hundred times her size. She was apparently very strong.

"Er, no, thank you," said Mary Ann. At the look of disappointment on the enchantress' face, Mary Ann added, "It is a very nice rake. But…"

"Not the ticket, then, eh? Ah, just as well," she said, dipping it back into the mud. "Probably best it never caught on. Imagine being forever known as the 'Lady of the …'" She couldn't bear to finish it. "… Never mind. But if you absolutely have your hearts set on a magic axe," the enchantress continued, "what you want to do is to go down the road, make a left, over the bridge and you can't miss it."

"Miss what?" asked Mary Ann.

"The Ace of Spades Magical Hardware Shoppe. They have *everything*." She pointed to Rufus. "Come back when your poem tells you to, young man. Not a moment before."

They swung open the door and a little fanfare played from somewhere. It was a nice touch. "Ace of Spades Magical Hardware. I'm Ace, the proprietor — how may I help you?" asked a gentleman in a red patterned apron.

At first, it gave Mary Ann a start, because the fabric precisely matched the cloak Jacob Morningstar had been wearing at the time of her father's death. But then she realized that this man was much older, a barrel-chested fellow with a quick smile.

"Do you carry any magic axes?" Mary Ann asked, glancing around. It was floor to ceiling items for sale in there, so she thought it quicker to ask.

"Why, young lady, magic tools are my specialty and my selection is all you could axe for. In terms of practical implements, I've got hatchets, felling axes, mauls and broadaxes. I've got single-headed, double-headed, bardiches, and claw axes. I have accessories for them and a no axcuse axchange policy. All I'll need is a proof of quest in the form of an epic poem or legend and two forms of portrait ID. Now in what might I interest you?"

Mary Ann said, "Well, I'm looking to trace a specific axe. I'm not sure what kind it was," and she went on to describe it.

"Oh, that one!" said Ace. "Yes, well, that was quite a while ago—and I'm sorry to say, that was a one-of-a-kind."

"So you know it?"

"Absolutely. It was Queen Valentina's. Or, rather, for the prop section of her production company, back before she ruled Neath."

"That's right," said Rufus, sounding like his memory had

been tickled a bit. "Originally, she was a famous stage actress or some such, wasn't she?"

"Oh yes," said Ace. "One of the greatest. She was mesmerizing; you couldn't take your eyes off her. They were doing the play *Pack of Lies* at the time. We should have realized she was taking her leading lady role as Queen a bit too seriously when she insisted, in the name of theatrical realism, to use actual magical weapons for the beheading scenes. It was the beginning of the end for many of us then. It's when she first licked the bloody taste of power off those rosebud red lips of hers. After that, there was no stopping her. I was surprised how many followed suit."

"Is that why you're in Turvy?" Mary Ann asked.

"Indeed," he said. "Self-exile. It was a choice between shuffling along behind her, being cut from the deck or leaving the pack altogether. I couldn't abide the takeover, so here I am. I have no regrets."

Mary Ann said, "We think someone's used that axe to dispatch an enemy of the Crown. We're just not sure what her grudge would have been."

"It's Valentina, so…what day is it?" He gave a bitter laugh. "Her grudge could be anything from not red enough roses to unlicensed soup."

Rufus said, "And you're sure the axe was in her possession?"

"As far as I know, it's been displayed in her castle armory ever since her takeover of Neath. If you check her portraits in the Royal Gallery, I'm sure you'd find it hanging in the background of at least one painting."

"What can you tell us about the Knave of Clubs during that time?" Now that Mary Ann had a decent source of information, she wasn't going to miss out on a single question.

"Knave of Clubs … Who, Jacob Morningstar?" At their nods, he said, "He's a two-faced son of a stacked deck, that one."

"How so?" asked Mary Ann, surprised how quickly Ace went from friendly to bitter.

"For one, he has no sense of pack loyalty whatsoever. Once he saw Valentina, that was it. He signed up as the valet just to be close to her, if you ask me."

"What does the King have to say about that?" Rufus asked.

"Oh, him. He hardly enters into it. He's scared to death of her. I think he lets her keep those Royal Theater shows running that she stars in, and indulges her in the croquet tournaments and Unbirthday parties and whatnot, just to keep her busy and out from under his wig."

"Wasn't Jacob Morningstar a trained military man at one point?" Mary Ann asked. "That's what we'd heard."

"Oh yes. He was a whiz with that club on the battlefield. The 'Bludgeon of Blackwater,' they called him. And that's what I mean about the valet position. It wasn't naturally his skill set. Yet, now he spends his days making sure the King's wardrobe is pressed just so and that the Queen's bilberry jam sandwiches are cut into heart shapes." He considered this. "Unless, of course, your suspicions are right and he's gone into the execution game again."

"That's rather what we're trying to find out," said Mary Ann. "Thank you, Ace." She shook his hand. "You've been very helpful."

"I'm happy to provide any support that adds a little misery to that heart-faced harpy." He walked them to the door. "And if you find yourself in need of a magic screwdriver, hammer or scythe, I'll hope you'll come back to ol' Ace for a visit."

"Thank you, we shall," said Mary Ann.

16

"And you're absolutely certain your father had no connection to Queen Valentina's court?" Sir Rufus asked Mary Ann as they made the return journey to Carmine Manor.

"As I said, I can't be certain. But I looked through my father's books, which were detailed, and his correspondence, which was limited and I never spied anything that raised a flag. The only thing connecting my father to the Queen was that looking-glass. But it wasn't like the mirror was a request from the Queen or her court. It was my gift idea. Mr. Rabbit signed off on it, but I arranged the thing."

"Curious," said Rufus.

"Then there's the question of Mr. Banks. He was only involved with the mirror glass portion of the gift. But first he was acting queerly and now he, too, has died."

"Strange," said Rufus.

"The one thing they have in common is the gift to Queen Valentina. But that could have been stolen or broken at any time, depending on the murderer's motive. Yet the mirror remained safe and intact."

"Peculiar," said Rufus.

"Also, my father was beheaded with an axe…"

"With a magic axe," corrected Goodspeed, who liked to be involved in most discussions.

Mary Ann nodded. "… With a magic axe from the Neath Royal Armory. Mr. Banks, on the other flipper, ran aground in his boat, possibly because he was hit on the head first, knocking him out and causing the crash."

"Odd," mused Rufus.

"Two deaths. Two entirely different techniques."

"Three, really," said Rufus.

She turned to him. "How do you figure that?"

"More than three, really," he continued. "If you count the raths. Thirty-two deaths, three entirely different techniques."

She blinked. "Do we count the raths?"

"I don't know," said Rufus. "Do we?"

It hadn't occurred to her before. She'd been so focused on the tragedy in general, and the death of the raths not being done by Douglas Divot, she'd not spent any time considering who it was or why. "What did the Tweedles decide on that?"

"I hadn't heard."

"Well, that's worth knowing," said Mary Ann.

"Indeed," said Rufus. "Do the raths, by any chance, have any connection to the mirror?"

"I can't think of any," she said, shifting in her saddle. "The only connection of which I know is Douglas Divot."

Rufus squinted in the sun. "How so?"

"Well, that expansive furniture collection of his—the one he likes to polish—was made by my father. Commissioned one piece at a time."

"But, of course, he didn't know Mr. Banks…"

"Yes, he did. Well, acquaintances, anyway. Mr. Banks was his sailsman. Mr. Divot commissioned projects through him."

"So Divot was neighbors with the raths, collected your father's furniture and commissioned the pieces with Mr. Banks?"

Mary Ann winced and groaned.

"How much do you know about Douglas Divot?" Sir Rufus asked.

"He was very kind to me the day my father died. He has excellent taste in home furnishings. Also: he likes cheese. You?"

"Been around for ages in the neighborhood. Was on the Red Turvian side in the Battle of Square Four. Fine moat digger."

"Any alliances to Neath?" Mary Ann asked. And she hated to ask.

"I don't know," said Rufus. "But I'll find out. Quietly. Can't rely on you to do it because you've become a real chatterbox."

It was late by the time they arrived at Carmine Manor, the sun dipping behind the horizon for some shuteye. Mary Ann was ready for some sleep herself, though the moment she stepped into her bedchamber, she was pounced upon by Celeste, who was lying in wait like a prettily-dressed Bandersnatch. "There you are! Where have you been? We received notice that the King and Queen of Red Turvy, and their entire entourage, will be arriving tomorrow and staying the night. There was so much extra cleaning that went on today and you weren't here for any of it."

Mary Ann set her borrowed satchel down on the bed. "Why are King Garnet and Queen Rosamund coming here?"

Mabel the parlor maid said, "So they and Lord and Lady Carmine can all travel together to the Unbirthday party. You know how Turvian travel is; the more people in your travel group, the more distracted you are and the faster you get there. They're trying to amass all the Red Turvian nobles so they can make short work of the journey."

Celeste said, "But that's not the point, Tamsin," for everyone had finally settled on that name. She slapped a hand down on a table. "The point is: there was this tremendous load of preparations to be made, and I had to step in and handle all of your chores, while you were off doing who-knows-what."

Mary Ann had some doubts about the scope of her actual efforts, but did not say so.

"She was helping Sir Rufus," said Mabel, giving Mary Ann a sly look. "Didn't you know, Celeste? She's his new pet."

"He's been so deeply unhappy these past weeks, I think it's rather sweet he seems to like Tamsin," said Emmaline, propped up in the bed with her cookbook.

"Oh, it's all sweets to you," sniffed Celeste. "It's completely inappropriate, and you know it."

Mary Ann knew it was best not to even address this. She went about trading her travel clothes for night clothes and washing in the basin. She could see in the mirror, however, that Celeste lingered.

"Anyway, I'm simply dying to see what Queen Valentina wears to her party," Celeste was saying. "My sister in Neath said she once saw her perform in the theater there. *Hearts Afire* was the show, I believe. She said the Queen was astounding, completely slayed them."

"Literally?" asked Mary Ann, recalling what Ace had said.

"Oh, you're not going to bring me down with your negativity," Celeste went on. "I'll be sure to tell you all about the event when I get back."

"Mm," said Mary Ann. She had no doubt.

Speaking of which, there were some questions that Unbirthday fete might help answer, Mary Ann thought. Not that she could trust Celeste with any of them. Sir Rufus, on the other hand …

She moved to the little table in the corner and began to make out a list:

1. **Jacob Morningstar.** Does he attend the event? What is his demeanor? Has he been absent from the court lately? If so, when, and what was the excuse? Has anyone noticed anything unusual in his behavior? Is he armed? With whom is he socializing?
2. **The axe.** Where is it? Does Morningstar carry it? Is it hanging in the Royal Armory?

3. **The mirror.** Looking at the attendees when the mirror is unveiled, what is the reaction? Does anyone seem surprised or unhappy? Does Rowan Carpenter get mentioned and what is the reaction to that?
4. **Rowan Carpenter.** Drop name in conversation. Does anyone seem to know he's deceased? What is the general opinion of him? Enemies?
5. **J. Sanford Banks.** The same. How known is he in Neath? Has word of the boating "accident" reached Neath? What is the reaction? What is the opinion of Banks?
6. **Clarissa Carpenter.** Is she there from the White Turvian side? Does she mention Rowan Carpenter? What are her feelings toward him? Does she have any connection to Morningstar?

Mary Ann reread her work. There was probably more that she was forgetting, but she felt it hit the main points nicely. She would approach Rufus about it tomorrow, to see if he'd care to be her eyes and ears at the event. She smiled to herself, for he had really taken to the detective work, and she had a powerful feeling the request would not be denied.

She picked up the little paper, blew on the ink and folded it, tucking the page under her pillow. A glance at Celeste caught sharp eyes lingering on that list. "What was that? A love letter?"

Mary Ann felt her face go hot. "A letter home," she said. She had never written a letter home in her life, but perhaps this Tamsin had people somewhere who cared for her. Mary Ann let herself think about that, as she climbed into bed, and she thought about it more as her head hit the pillow. She'd told Lady Carmine that her parents had both passed away, but perhaps Tamsin had siblings ... Yes, two grown sisters! With families! And a grandfather. A wonderful fellow with great snowy white mustaches. Who told stories and used to slip her sweets when no one was looking.

Unfortunately, these warm images didn't carry into her slumber. They melted into woodland chases by unseen pursuers, mad dashes over a drawbridge that dropped her into the middle of Queen Valentina's castle, winding her through unknown halls and tunnels. Soon she was plummeting off a precipice into the river, which was a hundred miles deep and sank her straight to the bottom among the catfish and oysters and clams, who would not help her…who kept grabbing at her shoes as she tried to reach the surface…white shoes that were uncomfortable because they were far too small. And she realized as she was drowning that they weren't even hers. How had she gotten them? She did not want to drown in someone else's shoes. She woke up gasping for air.

17

The next day, the arrival of King Garnet and Queen Rosamund of Red Turvy was like a dam breaking, torrential people pouring into Carmine Manor with a sound and fury that made Lady Carmine's recent flood seem like a leaky water pump. Mary Ann had never seen so many children, so many courtiers, so many servants, so much luggage, so many carriages, all of it in varying shades of red and all of it moving, talking or wanting something.

For the first three hours, Mary Ann ran everywhere she went. Ran to fetch, ran to remove, ran to assist, ran to slip away without disrupting anyone. She met the demands of Mrs. Cordingley, the royal guests, the royal guests' courtiers and the royal guests' courtier's maids. She'd lost track of who was whom as she heard the names: Ruby, Magenta, Cherry, Redmont, Redfern, Lord Cerise and so forth. Mary Ann had no idea how the Manor was going to accommodate them all, but Mrs. Cordingley said she thought she noticed a new wing had shown up on the left side of the house overnight, so they would make do with that until it vanished again. Hopefully, it would hold out until everyone was on the road in the morrow.

It was as Mary Ann hustled into the kitchen to fetch tea for a waiting lady-in-waiting that she came to a short stop that almost launched her head-over-tea-kettle...

The Running Joke was there at the base of the Tower stairs.

"You!" she said, pointing rather rudely on reflex. "Where did you come from?"

"A long tradition of slapstick in theater," it responded. "But no time for a history lesson. I simply must dash."

It headed toward the back door, while Mary Ann herself wasted no time running the opposite direction. She recalled seeing Sir Rufus in the parlor, so to the parlor was where she ran. And sure enough, there he was, sitting tensely on a sofa, looking glum. It appeared another Red Turvian knight — an older, beefy fellow — had him cornered in conversation. "So you really let that Jabberwock have it, what?" And the man clapped him hard on the back. "Who's training you? Cornelius Clashammer? Why, I was going to train with him myself. Went all the way to his place in Thither for the interview process, only to have his servant stop me at the door and say he was full-up. You ever been to Thither? No? Well, it's not like popping round to the corner store. Least he could do was invite me in for refreshments and use of the facilities. Anyway, the chap is clearly overrated. So I got myself a *real* trainer, name of Notlob and—"

Rufus saw Mary Ann at the door, motioning frantically. Looking relieved, he bounded up from his seat. "Pardon me, will you?" he said, extracting himself from the knight.

Mary Ann and Rufus stepped into an empty corridor. "What is it?" he asked.

"I saw the Running Joke," she whispered. "In the kitchen, by the Tower stairs."

They had been so busy since returning from the axe quest, they hadn't time to address the "supposed-uncle-in-the-Tower" business. Determination crossed Rufus' face now. "Right. This has gone on long enough." He stepped back into the room. "Father? A word?"

"Of course, my boy," said Lord Carmine. "What's on your mind?"

Mary Ann expected him to draw his father aside. Instead, his eyes went cold and hard, and in front of all the company, he asked, "Is my sense of humor locked in the Tower?"

This certainly got Lord Carmine springing from his chair. "Nonsense, my lad, perhaps the stress of training has strained you." He laughed in a forced way before their guests and shook his head. "Young people these days…I'll only be a moment." In the hall, his face clouded over and he hissed, "What is wrong with you, boy? That's your Uncle Edmund in the Tower. We've spoken of this already, haven't we?"

"Yes, but—"

"Please, son," Lord Carmine got a grip on the knight's arm, "you understand we mustn't let everyone know he's sane. It would be a terrible stain on our family."

There was something about Lord Carmine's pleading tone, or perhaps the paternal vise-grip, that made Rufus all the more resolute. He squared his shoulders, narrowed his eyes and said, "Listen, Father: since my humor's been gone, we keep encountering a Running Joke on the property. An expert was consulted on the matter and we learned that Running Jokes are spawned by concentrated humor. What's more, that very Running Joke was just seen in the kitchen by the Tower stairs. There's nothing funny about that kitchen, so something is going on."

Lord Carmine scratched his cheek. "Nothing funny in a kitchen? Well, I don't know, dear boy…I quite think sieves are funny, don't you? With all their holes, leaking and straining things? And—and spatulas! Isn't spatula a funny word? Rather like a vampire who runs a tavern kitchen." Lord Carmine certainly was trying hard.

"Fine," said Rufus flatly and started away.

"My boy, where are you going?"

"Where's Mrs. Cordingley? I want the key to the Tower," he said.

"Oh, my gracious, this is hardly necessary," said Lord Carmine, trailing after him like a caught string.

Rufus found her in the laundry. "Mrs. Cordingley: the key to the Tower, if you please." He held out his hand.

Mrs. Cordingley's gaze went from Rufus, to Lord Carmine, and back again.

"I will not ask twice," said the knight. Though Mary Ann wondered what the threat was there; surely he had no plans of pulling a sword on her. Besides, the woman was made of iron through and through. The only real way to hurt her was by mocking her starching techniques.

But before he could deride her washing, Lord Carmine sighed and deflated on the spot. "Just give him the key, Mrs. Cordingley," he said, defeated. "Let the young man see for himself."

In a moment, it was done, and in another moment they were all standing at the top of the Tower stairs as Rufus fiddled with the lock. The door squeaked open. Sunlight streamed in through a barred window. The room was very conventional, with a simple, tidily-made bed, a kerosene lamp, a wooden chair and desk, a selection of non-fiction books and a spectacled man there of middle age and middle height, with a simple brown tweed suit.

He looked like a banker in a very simple, sane, straightforward bank. Or at least, that's what Mary Ann imagined they looked like. Turvy was not known for its simple, sane, straightforward banks—or bankers, for that matter. She was not sure where she even got the idea; perhaps she'd read about one in a poem once.

"Uncle Edmund!" Rufus said.

Uncle Edmund looked at him, blinked rapidly and pushed up his spectacles. "Rufus? Lad, I haven't seen you in a tove's age! My, you've become tall, haven't you? Hard to believe you're all grown up. Please tell me you're not a part of this scheme."

Rufus scanned the room. "Are you alone in here, sir?"

"Careful, son, don't get too close," warned Lord Carmine. "We're not certain how contagious he is. Besides, now that you've seen him and know I was telling the truth, it's time to return to our guests."

But Rufus was peering under the bed and looking behind the door.

Uncle Edmund turned to Lord Carmine. "What is this about?"

"Oh, nothing," said Carmine, grabbing Rufus by the arm and trying to drag him from the room, "the young man just got it in his head that it was someone else living up here. Didn't believe me it was you. But it's nothing." He waved it away and tried to put on a happy face. "Lady Carmine and I will be off on a little trip in the next day, but we'll make certain your food is still sent up on time and that you have everything you need." And Lord Carmine was now trying to shove everyone out of the room at once and close the door behind him.

But Rufus was tenacious. "Uncle, have you seen my sense of humor?" he called, blocking the door with his shoulder as it was about to close.

Edmund gasped. "Was that thing *yours*?" His eyes were filled with horror. "Great gryphons, lad, you must be as mad as your father!"

"Really should get back to our guests," persisted Lord Carmine.

Rufus glared at him and pushed the door wide. "So you *have* seen it!" he said to Edmund.

"Seen it?" The man wrung his hands. "They tried it out on me! Experimental procedure, you know. Diabolical thing! Lucky for me, my body completely rejected it."

By now Lord Carmine was as red as his name. "Oh, pay no attention to him. He's—"

"Sane?" suggested Uncle Edmund. "Sane enough to know I want no part of the nonsensical funny-business that bobbles about in that boy's head, that's for certain!"

The news lit Rufus' temper. "My father tried to give you *my* sense of humor?"

Edmund said, "First they forced it on me. Then they started plying me with the stuff to feed it, hoping it would sink in its hooks…grow…Like some poorly-punning parasite."

"Hear me out, son…" Lord Carmine was breathing heavily

now and Mary Ann was worried his heart might attack him. "I just gave him a small portion of your humor. Just enough so he'd start seeing the world a bit differently — jumpstart the creative madness in him, you know. And if it had worked, think of what a service you would have done for my brother, your own flesh and blood! He'd be able to rejoin society; his quality of life would have improved significantly. You'd have been a hero twice over!"

Rufus folded his arms and eyed his father coldly. "So I never did misplace it, did I? You stole it. You extracted it without my knowledge. I don't know when you did it but—" Except in that moment he did. The knowledge filled his face. "It was at my last Unbirthday party, wasn't it? You kept pushing the mushroom beer and I don't recall the rest. What kind of father are you?"

"You were always so merry and madcap," said Lord Carmine. "There was no way you could have focused properly on slaying the Jabberwock. And then the poem would never have come to fruition. So I had your humor removed. It was only supposed to be until you got through training and quested for the Vorpal sword. You would have gotten it back then. But once I learned your uncle was going sane ... talking sense, paying his taxes on time, and dressing in tasteful brown flannel, well…" he shuddered, "something had to be done. You would have done the same thing in my shoes."

"In your shoes, I would be completely unable to walk; they're the wrong size," Rufus said, clutching at his hair and pacing the room. "Honestly, Father, how could you do this to me? It was devastating! I looked all over for it. I gave myself hell about my absent-mindedness for weeks. 'How could you lose your humor, Rufus?' 'Think: where did you last see it, Rufus?'"

"An unfortunate side-effect of the endeavor," agreed Lord Carmine. "One sees these things in retrospect."

"So if you only gave him a portion of my humor and he rejected it," Rufus said, indicating his uncle, "where is the rest of it?"

"It's perfectly safe," said Lord Carmine. "It's being stored."

"Where?" Rufus growled. It was that Jabberwock-slayer tone again.

"Well," the Baron looked uncomfortable and sighed, "I suppose there's no keeping it from you now. It's being stored where one maintains humor when it's not in use but wishes to keep it fresh."

"And that is?"

Lord Carmine seemed surprised they hadn't guessed. "In the humordor, of course."

And closing and locking the door on his brother ("Wait! You mean no one's going to let me out after all?"), Lord Carmine led them down the Tower stairs to the kitchen, where a small wooden box sat, not unlike a tea caddy.

"It's been here? All this time?" Rufus buried his face in his hands.

Lord Carmine picked up the box and tapped its lid.

A tiny, sleepy voice said, "Knock, knock?"

"Who's there?" asked Lord Carmine.

"Riot," said the voice.

"Riot who?"

"Riot on time, here I am!" Peals of mad laughter rang out from the thing.

"Yeah, that's it, all right," said Rufus, sounding tired himself. "Give me that." And tucking the box under his arm, he left the room.

"You wanted to see me, My Lady?" Mary Ann asked from the door of Lady Carmine's quarters.

The woman was sitting at her vanity and dressed, winding curls into a pile on the top of her head. "Yes, dear, I do."

Her hands were still shaky, Mary Ann noticed. "Do you need some assistance?"

"Oh, I'd be very grateful," she said. And the lady gave her a handful of hairpins, which she began to secure into place.

"How are you feeling, My Lady? You look well. And the cloud is gone, I see." It would be nice to clean in the room without it being thoroughly rinsed first.

"That's what I wanted to speak to you about, child," said Lady Carmine. "Tomorrow we go to Queen Valentina's Unbirthday party in Neath."

"I understand so," said Mary Ann. "I hope you'll enjoy the journey and it won't tire you too much."

"My, you are thoughtful, aren't you?" Lady Carmine said reflectively, as if this one moment somehow brought it all home for her. "And that's why I would very much like it if you would make the journey with us."

"Me, My Lady?" Mary Ann's heart skipped a beat. "I very much doubt you'll need an extra housemaid with the Queen of Hearts' hospitality. Hearts Castle is supposed to be the finest of any land."

"You've been so helpful to me in such a rough time, my dear. And Celeste, well … One does not like to speak ill of others, but the girl just has so many other things on her mind. It's been hard for her to properly attend to the job. So I'm afraid I've had to dismiss her."

"Oh my…" Mary Ann understood why, of course, but she never liked to see it happen.

"That is why in her place," Lady Carmine continued, gently powdering her nose, "I would like you to accompany me to Neath. As my personal maid, you see."

"Oh, My Lady," Mary Ann had not been expecting this. "I only fluster the moldings. I don't know anything about all the details of assisting a fine lady such as yourself. You'd best find someone better-suited." Like someone who wasn't currently wanted in Neath.

"I feel certain you would learn and learn quickly," said Lady Carmine.

"But—"

"I would consider it a personal favor to me." There was a certain strength in her words now, which Mary Ann sensed required careful treading.

"Yes, My Lady," Mary Ann said. She would have to get out of it, of course. Perhaps she could steal away from the Manor in the middle of the night and hide in her father's cottage for a few days. It wasn't the safest of places, certainly, but if she remained on guard, and didn't burn a lamp, and kept the noise to a minimum, perhaps she wouldn't attract—

"Good." Lady Carmine rose and indicated several trunks by the door. "I am already packed, but you'll want to pack, as well."

"I've nothing," Mary Ann said, "so it won't take a moment."

"That's a girl. Always thinking ahead," said Lady Carmine, proudly. "Your new job starts tomorrow."

Mary Ann felt sick. How could she go to Neath? And not just Neath, but to Queen Valentina's Unbirthday party? Yes, there would be hundreds of people present, and there was perhaps some safety in that. But how could she ensure she remained out of the gaze of Jacob Morningstar? Would her invisibility be enough? Because it certainly seemed to be failing her lately.

And then there was the issue of those Wanted posters. The impostor Mary Ann had been running around Neath, wrecking homes and terrorizing courtrooms. Yes, True Mary Ann had Rufus as an alibi for at least one of the events. But logic was not a popular thing in either Neath or Turvy. She could not be certain that she would ever untangle herself from False Mary Ann's crimes. This was problematic.

On the other hand, if one ignored the deathly peril, this was precisely the sort of opportunity Mary Ann could have desired. Instead of sending Rufus on a mission to answer her questions, she could now gain information firsthand at the event. Why, if she and the knight worked together, they might just be able to solve the death of her father, expose the knave's motives, extract herself from danger and even, possibly, say "hi" to mum. It was these thoughts on which she tried to focus throughout the day, as she helped ensure the houseguests had all they needed for their visit. It was these thoughts that buoyed her into the evening as she watched Rufus looking more animated than ever, as he socialized with his royal guests. It was these thoughts that steeled her before bed, as Celeste knocked on their chamber door, tearful streaks down the powder on her face.

"Lady Carmine has gone to bed. I have a coach coming shortly. I'm going to my sister's family in Neath," she said. She turned to Mabel. "So those hair combs I lent you…I need them back. I need to *pack* them."

Mabel nodded, all eyes and open mouth, like a fish wondering what a dock was, and why it was suddenly flopping about on it. "Oh, yes, of course! Right away!" And Mabel swished off to get the items in question.

Now Celeste moved to Emmaline. "And you know that pin of mine you like?"

Emmaline nodded.

"Hold out your hand," she said. And Celeste dropped a little brooch made of tiny red glass flowers onto her palm. "You should keep it. It looks better on you. Matches your complexion."

"Oh my!" said Emmaline, wiping a tear and holding the brooch to her heart. "I—I couldn't."

But Celeste brushed away her protests. "It is done," she said. "And you…" Now Celeste turned to Mary Ann. "This is all your fault. Stepping on my toes with Lady Carmine…Trying to ingratiate yourself to take my position … I hope you're happy." She folded her arms. "Well? What do you have to say for yourself?"

But Mary Ann said nothing, for there was nothing to be said. It wasn't as if Celeste didn't know the truth of the matter. She merely needed to conjure herself a more soothing reason for her dismissal. Mary Ann always thought it remarkable, the sleight-of-hand one does to reinvent oneself, one's truths, while simultaneously never fixing a thing.

Mary Ann let her keep this illusion as a parting gift.

In an hour, Celeste was gone and the revelries downstairs continued, echoing into the night.

18

Mary Ann's day dawned early as usual, but the revelers had sunk into a deep stupor all across Carmine Manor, like a cursed household in a faerie story. As she descended the stairs, Mary Ann could hear snoring, as ferocious a snarling racket as any frumious beast could wish, and it seemed to be emanating from the hall in which King Garnet had been stowed. His snores were the stuff of legends.

Mary Ann found that Lady Carmine, who had only partaken of the evening's festivities briefly, was already awake.

"Are you feeling well enough to travel?" Mary Ann asked, after the woman consumed a hopeful quantity of breakfast.

"I am fit as a fiddle, in tune and ready to play," she chuckled, an impish smile crossing her face. "And I understand you helped Rufus locate his sense of humor again! Whoever would have guessed it ended up in a box in the kitchen? How delightfully improbable!"

Clearly, someone had given Lady Carmine a rather different impression of the events that had transpired. So Mary Ann simply said, "It was a joint effort, My Lady."

Like so many things, she imagined the truth would come out in time.

"My son was most beamish last evening with the guests," Lady Carmine went on. "I had quite forgotten what he was like before he misplaced his humor."

"He certainly seemed spirited," Mary Ann said, though she'd been too busy with her own duties to speak with him directly. "Now, what would you like to wear?" She held up two gowns. "The red? Or the red?"

They decided on the red, and Mary Ann began to assist the lady with the elaborate robing process. Mary Ann was quite pleased she managed to get through her preparatory tasks without accidentally collapsing her lungs by corset or smothering her in underskirts. And now, with that success under her cap, it sounded as if the Manor was starting to come to life. One of the valets had arrived for Lady Carmine's cases, and this gave Mary Ann a moment to get her own meager things from her quarters.

She laughed at the items she'd amassed: three housemaid uniforms (two Red Turivan one from Neath), one borrowed nightdress, one set of squire clothes (pinched from the line), and her father's account book. Having borrowed things from Emmaline such as a hairbrush, she wasn't sure how she would manage without. Of course, it helped to keep in mind that no one attending this party would be there to admire her.

She was about to exit the bedchamber, when she recalled her list—that little guide of questions she had compiled to give to Sir Rufus. While she no longer needed to tax him with it, she thought the list still might be useful. Surely, with so much activity at once, and a new job to boot, it would be nice to have something to ground her own actions. She would hate to miss an important opportunity to gather all the information she wanted, just because some critical point wasn't top-of-mind.

She slipped a hand under her pillow and...

"That's queer."

She pulled down the bedcover and lifted the pillow. Nothing. She patted the bedding. She lifted the dustruffle and peered under the bed. She peered behind the bedside table.

Gone.

When had she last seen it? She recalled it when she'd made the bed yesterday morning. As tired as she was, she had quite forgotten about it last night.

She took a few deep breaths to calm her pounding heart and told herself quite sensibly that there was no time to dwell upon it now. The shiver of anxiety was still there, though; it did not operate on things like sensibility. She hoped the missing item would not come back to bite.

Getting the group mobilized for the journey ahead proved to be something of monumental proportions. There were breakfasts to be had and children to attend, horses to rein and carriages to get into place. It took the entire household staff at full capacity, plus all the Red King's and Queen's servants to ensure everything went off with a hitch. (For the horses needed hitching; one couldn't go far without that.) Finally, once all pre-journey bodily fluids that needed expelling were expelled, the traveling party left Carmine Manor, a long line of red figures heading toward Neath.

Mary Ann had been given Lolly to ride alongside Lord and Lady Carmine's carriage. And it was from this placement, she could hear Queen Rosamund, a petite, no-nonsense woman with a big voice, shout, "All right, everyone! It is time to sing!"

Lady Carmine clapped her hands in the carriage. "Oh yes! A sing-a-long! How frabjous!"

Queen Rosamund said, "Remember, you must all sing as loudly as you possibly can. Because as we all know, the speed of sound travels at seven-hundred and sixty-one miles per hour. Whereas our horses, at a reasonable cantor, can only do ten to fifteen miles per hour. Which means, if we're very loud, our voices will reach our destination before us and have things set up properly by the time we arrive."

Mary Ann had never heard of that approach to travel, but then again, she tended not to be a part of groups.

The Queen began to sing, very loudly and quite off-key:

> A journeying we go
> A journey song we crow

We haven't a care if we ever get there
(Well, we do, but don't say so!)

And everyone joined in, though it seemed many didn't know the song and invented lyrics and melodies of their own. At least, they did all chime in for the chorus:

Clip-clop, slip-slop
The last one there is slow!

Which was very loud for certain, so it most definitely would reach Queen Valentina's castle in all swiftness.

By the time they stopped on the side of the road to take a break, Mary Ann's throat ached. She was pouring water for Lady Carmine from a corked bottle when Queen Rosamund herself passed by asking, "And did you enjoy the music, my dear?" She addressed this to Mary Ann.

"Why, yes, Your Majesty, very much," rasped Mary Ann, curtseying. "It helps pass the time so nicely. I apologize, though, I'm a bit hoarse."

"Of course you are," croaked the Queen. "We all are. That's how it's supposed to be. That's why these are called hoarse-drawn carriages, you know."

"I didn't realize that," said Mary Ann, always pleased to have learned something new. "Thank you, Majesty."

She winked. "That's why I'm Queen. It's my business to know these things." And she ran off to box the ear of one of the young pawns, who she'd spied shirking his singing duties along the way.

The Queen had only just left to do so when Sir Rufus came bounding over. Mary Ann almost didn't recognize him because never had she seen such a great grin on his face. "Hello, Mother! Hello ... you!" And he elbowed Mary Ann in a congenial way.

"So I understand your humor has been restored," said Mary Ann, rubbing her arm where a bruise would no doubt appear later. "How are you feeling, Sir?"

"I'm mainly feeling with my hands, of course!" he said and exploded in laughter. Or rather, exploded as well as one could who had been singing loudly for the better part of an hour.

The elbow had reminded her of something. "I have some items I'd like to discuss with you about your training," Mary Ann said, watching Lady Carmine's expression carefully out of the corner of her eye. "I was thinking when you're in the Jug Stance, you'll need to hold your elbow more perpendicular and—"

And this had the desired effect, for Lady Carmine said, "Oh, I'll let you two get on with that." And excused herself to the carriage.

"Training, eh?" said Rufus beaming. "What do you call a sword without a blade?"

"A hilt, I would guess," she said. "Er, look Rufus, I really didn't want to talk about training, anyway. I just wanted to speak with you alone for a moment. Now, with this Unbirthday party, we have an excellent opportunity to learn about Jacob Morningstar and his operations, as well as find out what possible motives there might have been to—"

"Pointless," he said, giggling.

"What?"

"The answer to my riddle," he replied. "'What do you call a sword without a blade?' 'Pointless.'"

"Ah, yes, very funny," she said, not finding it particularly funny at all. "Now, as I was saying, the motives behind—"

"What do you call a mad duck?"

She didn't even venture a guess on this one.

"Quackers," he said and started laughing again. "And did you hear the one about the Bandersnatch?"

"Er, I think everyone's getting ready to leave again," Mary Ann said, quickly. And they were, but that wasn't the reason for her haste. She hated to judge too soon, for he had been through so much of late and she had truly grown to care about him. But she feared that she greatly preferred Sir Rufus when he was humorless and depressed.

Quackers... *Really*... She grimaced and shook her head. The man had completely lost his focus. It appeared she would be on her own for any further investigation. A surprising sense of loss overcame her at this thought. Their solidarity had been so pleasant and all too brief.

By the time they reached Hearts Castle in Neath, no one in their traveling party had any voice left, but it didn't matter because no one could have heard them over the crowd already there. There were musicians tootling away, local jesters doing their famous hedgehog juggling, and the largest tea party Mary Ann had ever seen, with tables stretched across the lawn for a mile. There were Neathan courtiers of every suit and all the most elite citizens of Turvy. It appeared the party from White Turvy had already arrived, but perhaps only just, because Mary Ann overheard a few of them talking, sounding raw and dry.

Mary Ann scanned the crowd for familiar faces, the first of which was the Duchess of Additch, whose face was prominent on the best of days, there simply being more face per square inch than other people. At the moment, she was having it painted in portrait by an attending artist. It was a very good likeness so far, so Mary Ann imagined that artist would be run out of town shortly.

The group concluded their journey at the carriage house and stables. Both Goodspeed and Lolly seemed to find old friends right away. (It sounded as if the quality of oats was a prime discussion in their community.) Mary Ann followed Lady Carmine into the castle, and a well-dressed frog took them to her accommodations and sent a toad for their trunks. Those with high enough titles were given rooms, and the rest of the rabble had pitched tents on the expansive lawns. Mary Ann was assigned a sofa in a small sitting room off of Lady Carmine's quarters.

It took some time to get Lady Carmine settled and refreshed, and her belongings tidied, but that was fine with

Mary Ann. Ever since they set foot in Queen Valentina's castle, she had been overcome by unease. It wasn't so bad when she was with the group coming in, or even with Lady Carmine, for why would anyone look at a mere servant when such a fine lady was present? But inevitably, she would have to emerge into this society alone, and there were so many people from Neath she hoped to avoid. She would have to be as light-footed and unobtrusive as she knew how, on guard for every set of eyes.

Once Lady Carmine was ready, they left the room to explore the festivities outside.

Lady Carmine, it turned out, was a popular soul. It wasn't long before the woman had found companions and Mary Ann was left to her own devices. She screwed her Red Turvian maid's hat down as low as she could and moved smoothly, briskly, about the lawn assessing the area for anyone who might recognize her. Mr. Rabbit was fussing with the gift area, a pile of presents like Mary Ann had never before seen. She thought she spied a mirror-shaped present among them, wrapped in pretty paper and propped in a predominant spot.

Continuing to scan the crowd, she spied Mr. Milliner and his friends, who had taken over one of the longest tea tables for themselves and seemed determined to use as many different place settings on it as possible. (She felt very glad the job of cleanup was not hers this time.) The Duchess was still portrait-sitting, and Cookie Mills was over in a stall where meats were being grilled, giving tips to the chefs there on seasonings.

And that's when Mary Ann saw him: Jacob Morningstar, the Knave of Clubs. He was looking quite professional and grand, with his sweeping cape and square jaw. He stood chatting with the Knave of Hearts, a shorter blond man who was recounting his recent prison experience due to erroneous tart theft charges. It was at that moment that Mary Ann realized the ideal way to get information about Morningstar was to talk with a housemaid or chambermaid for Queen Valentina. There was no one so knowledgeable about the relationship dynamics of a household as the cleaning staff. And the opportunity presented itself when one such creature, the Six of Hearts by her dress, was working beside a stage, attempting a complicated initiative with hats, red ribbons and a flock of flamingos.

Mary Ann stood a moment to observe and realized the issue. Six was attempting to put these tied ribbons around the birds' necks, each one with a different letter on it. In theory, it seemed quite simple. In practice, it failed to take into the account that flamingo necks have their own agendas.

"May I help you?" Mary Ann asked after several minutes of tied and then lost bows.

"Oh, would you?" The maid's voice was all relief. "It's part of the surprise for Queen Valentina. And they're being dreadfully dodgy."

"I suspect flamingo wardrobe is a two maid job," Mary Ann reassured her.

And, indeed, it proved that when one person steadied the flamingo, while the other tied and hatted, things went along much more smoothly.

"There!" Mary Ann surveyed their work and dusted her hands. "See? Done in two nods of a dormouse's head."

"Only now comes the hard bit," said Six with a sigh.

"I've already been bitten hard twice," admitted Mary Ann.

Six pointed. "You see the letters on them, don't you?"

"Yes?"

"They're a message."

Mary Ann read the crowd of flamingos. "BUNNY RATHER INADEQUATELY VERMIN?" Oh, dear. Mr. Rabbit was not going to like this at all.

"No, no," said Six. "'It's supposed to read: MERRY UNBIRTHDAY QUEEN VALENTINA."

"Oh, that is an improvement," said Mary Ann.

"But they simply will not stand in the right order," said Six. "I ask them nicely, but they don't listen."

She was right. In the moment the maids had been talking, the birds had become a jumble of lettering, then: BURN ANY VAIN DEATHLY REQUIREMENT, then a jumble again in the blink of an eye.

Mary Ann said, "Perhaps we should remove the letters

altogether. They'd still be very pretty without them."

"Oh no!" Six's eyes were all fear. "We can't remove the letters. We have to have the letters. The Queen specifically asked for this."

Mary Ann raised an eyebrow. "An Unbirthday banner of well-wishes by hatted, beribboned flamingos?"

"Oh yes. Just that," said Six.

Mary Ann brushed a lock of hair from her forehead. "I thought you said this was a surprise."

"Yes, an Unbirthday surprise party. The Queen was very specific about that. She told everyone, then gave us lists with all the details she wanted."

"Well." Mary Ann sighed. "Do you not think she might be even more surprised with a banner reading: RUN NERVY HEART INEQUITABLY NAMED?" She indicated the flamingos' current configuration.

"Not in a way you would enjoy," said Six.

"Fair enough. Plan B." Mary Ann turned to the chorus of flamingos. "Could I get the M first?" she called. "The M? Please step forward."

But the V stepped forward, a hopeful expression on its face, followed by the Q who then got confused and turned its back to everyone.

"Not you, I want the M. Step back! M please…" She pointed to the bird in question. "You."

The M blinked and looked round, then nudged someone else forward.

"You see?" said Six. "It's useless!"

"I believe the trouble is, they do not know their alphabet," said Mary Ann. "I have an idea. I'll be back in a moment."

She searched the various tables of food, and sure enough, found precisely what she needed. She returned to the flamingos holding a silver tray of very large steamed prawns. From four of them, she formed an M shape. "This," she said, "is an M. You," she brought the labeled flamingo up. "Are wearing an M." The moment she showed it to the flamingo, the prawn letter was gobbled up.

"E," she said, taking two curved prawns to form the letter. She pulled a flamingo labeled E from the group and—gulp!— the flamingo ate the E. On and on this went, prawns into flamingos until all the letters were done.

"Right," she said. "Now: M-E-R—" And the flamingos began to line up in order. When the whole MERRY UNBIRTHDAY QUEEN VALENTINA was spelled out, she gave each flamingo an additional prawn and promised another at the end of the ceremony, if the job got results.

Six was standing mouth open so wide, Mary Ann almost tucked a prawn into it, as well, but they were running low and needed what they had for the finale. "My goodness, whatever gave you the idea?" breathed Six.

"Well," Mary Ann considered it, "I just remembered: you are what you eat."

The flamingo-wrangler held out her hand. "I'm Hexa Hearts, housemaid to Queen Valentina."

Mary Ann shook it. "Er, Tamsin Woods. I'm from Red Turvy, in Lord Carmine's household." She offered a shy smile. "I was wondering if you could tell me: who is that gentleman over there? He's very handsome."

"Oh, that's King Rudolf's valet, Jacob Morningstar. But I wouldn't bother with him, if I were you."

"Does he not socialize with other staff?" Mary Ann asked.

"Oh, he only has eyes for Queen Valentina. Everyone knows that."

Mary Ann laughed. "Except the King, I'd assume."

"Oh, I fear the King knows it better than anyone. It's just…" Hexa looked around nervously and leaned in to Mary Ann, whispering, "One likes that Queen Valentina is properly occupied. When not occupied, things can become—"

"I SPECIFICALLY ASKED TO BE SURPRISED WITH CRIMSON, HEART-SHAPED FLAMINGOS IN HATS WEARING A BANNER! THOSE BIRDS ARE NOT AT ALL HEART-SHAPED AND THEY ARE PINK AT BEST!" It was Queen Valentina, all right. She was possibly the most beautiful person Mary Ann had ever seen. Her rose-gold hair was swept up on top of her head in a cascade of curls, a crystal tiara encrusted with heart-shaped rubies reflecting light like a halo. Her collar was high and framed her flawless heart-shaped face. Her eyes were large and flashing. And her perfect red lips were twisted into a most lovely sneer.

Jacob Morningstar went rushing over to her. Mary Ann couldn't hear what he was saying, but the Queen did stop shouting.

"You see?" said Hexa.

Mary Ann assessed the fellow in disbelief. "Surely he cannot be the same Knave of Clubs who was known as the Bludgeon of Blackwater in the last game of War?"

Hexa nodded. "The same."

"Such a contrast, going from blood-thirsty soldier to obsequious servant," said Mary Ann, trying to picture it now in her mind. "I'm surprised he didn't join King Rudolf's Guard instead. What happened?"

"Queen Valentina happened," the maid told her. "As I said, he is here for her. He stays for her."

"Would he kill for her?" asked Mary Ann. The question just popped out and she feared it was not possible to put it back in its bottle.

"Anything," said Hexa, who didn't seem to find the question at all odd. "Anything for her."

And this was, perhaps, true because Queen Valentina was all smiles and coyness now, giggling behind her hand and saying, "Okay, nobody sees me! Don't look yet! I'll go and come back in!" And she ran off behind some red curtains on the stage.

19

Mr. Rabbit shouted, "Quiet, everyone! She's coming! Pretend like we're not here." And everyone stopped talking. The band stopped playing, and the only thing you could hear was the echoed snoring of that narcoleptic rodent friend of Mr. Milliner's, who'd fallen into the teapot again.

A sweet voice from behind the curtained stage said, "Why, I wonder what this stage is doing out here on my lawn?" And then Queen Valentina emerged, looked around, read the chorusline of not red-enough, not heart-shaped-enough flamingos, and gasped in surprise. "Why, is this Unbirthday party for *me*? You shouldn't have!"

"Presenting Queen Valentina of Neath!" shouted Warren Rabbit. And he blew his trumpet until he looked quite woozy from the effort.

"Recite something!" someone shouted from the audience. It appeared to be one of the Queen's own courtiers.

"Yes!" said someone else. "Do *My Heart Is in the Work*!"

"Do *Red Roses To Myself*!"

"Oh my goodness, well!" Queen Valentina blushed prettily, a fluttering hand going to her chest. "This is such a splendid surprise. But I fear I simply cannot recall anything appropriate to recite off the top of my head like this. If only I'd known to prepare something."

"Ohhhh," said the disappointed audience.

"Well…" she considered, "I suppose I do remember this *small* soliloquy that might be adequate for today …" She demonstrated the microscopicness of it between dainty thumb and forefinger. "From *Love and Axes*, Act One, Scene Four.' MUSIC! CUE THE MUSIC!"

A band was suddenly right there playing a moody background accompaniment. And the Queen began:

> Within my hands, the pretty, pretty rose,
> The sweetly fragrant token of my Love
> From tiny sprig was—boop! —awake and grows
> As soft and gentle as mock turtledove.
> But viny is the path of love once born
> And tangled grows the trail so love is lost.
> A touch! A kiss! The prick of bloody thorn
> Betrays the fickle heart. The love is tossed
> Into the garden, dry, the ground it cracks.
> The blossoms, once so perfect, come to stop.
> Wise gardener must seize the sharpened axe
> And with the swiftest blade give it the chop.
> But even underground the roots do lie
> From scorn and thorn, love shifts to dig and die.

People started to clap, and Mary Ann did, too, but all this trailed away as Queen Valentina launched into yet another verse. It seemed Her Majesty had a slightly different definition of "small." While Hexa took the opportunity to distribute the second round of payment prawns, Mary Ann decided there would be no better time than now, while everyone was transfixed, to do a little investigation on her own. She slinked off across the lawn to Hearts Castle.

There were so many rooms, Mary Ann almost forgot that she was on a mission and not a pleasure tour. There were sitting rooms and standing rooms, a greenhouse where everything was red, an indoor theater, and a portrait gallery of portraits all painted of Queen Valentina in her various stage performances. There was a memorabilia room which contained posters and review clippings of Queen Valentina's shows, as well as news articles about the last War, which led to the Hearts family's rule of Neath. The two topics were treated as logical extensions of each other. There was a library, filled with history books about the Hearts family, but also a surprisingly large collection of contemporary romance novels. The most startling room was the collection of death masks, presumably of people who had displeased the Queen during the course of her illustrious career. Drama critics sat on one side, former political enemies on the other. Mary Ann shuddered at the plaster casts, for they looked altogether too much like the original severed heads for Mary Ann's taste. She made a quick exit and that's when she found the Armory.

The weaponry was floor to ceiling and included everything from the tiniest dagger to a massive cannon. Mary Ann scanned the room for the axe and momentarily spied it, about halfway up the wall, hung across two pegs. It would be a stretch for her to reach, but not much work for a strapping fellow like Jacob Morningstar. Indeed, anyone with access to the castle and a chair, or a bite of Burgeonboosh, could take it with ease.

"What engages you here, my old friend?" came a voice.

Mary Ann whirled to see Chester, the Duchess' cat, perched on the back of a chair.

"Oh, Chester! Lovely to see you!" The cat's bright eyes looked at her sharply, suspiciously. "Er, I'm working for Lady Carmine of Turvy these days. She thought she might have left something in here," Mary Ann said. "Her … handkerchief. Perhaps it's over here." She made a point of peering at the items on a table. It was a stack of large cards, each with a word printed on it. One said, "LAZY," another "HIDEOUS." There was "LIAR," "CHEAT," "CORPULENT," "SCOUNDREL," "VAIN," "SNEAKY," "THIEF," "SMELLY," "TRAITOR," and many more. "That's curious. I wonder what these are doing in the weapons room."

"You know as well I do that words are sometimes the worst weapons of all," purred the cat.

He was not wrong.

"And which of those describes you today?" Chester asked and hopped up onto the table. "I would suggest this one…" He pushed the LIAR to her. "And possibly this." Here SNEAKY was the choice. Then he smiled.

Mary Ann sighed. Of all the people to find her, it had to be this cat. He was generally a lovely fellow, but often too insightful for comfort.

She decided the direct route was the way to go here. "What can you tell me about that?" Mary Ann said and pointed to the axe.

A crease formed between the cat's eyes as he stared at her. "Your finger?"

"No, not my finger." Because apparently even insightful, magical cats who smile and can disappear-at-will have some issues with how pointing operates. She instead walked over, grabbed a chair, hopped onto it and tapped the wall underneath the weapon in question. "This axe."

"Ah," said Chester, the smile growing broader, "then you heard the news."

"What news?"

"That the axe, too, can come and go unseen," said Chester, licking a paw.

"Actually, I did," she said. "And I'd like to know what prompted its disappearance."

"Then you have your first thing in common with Queen Valentina," said the cat.

"What?" Mary Ann blinked. "She didn't know?"

"She was…" The cat pushed a word to her. The card read: VICIOUS. "And…" He pushed a second card: WHINY. "She accused everyone and anyone she could think of, but then, the item in question was back the next day. After that, some jam tarts went missing. She still hasn't recovered those, though, despite the trial."

"She didn't know who took the axe…" Mary Ann muttered,

the truth of it sinking in. "It wasn't on her orders…"

"'Epiphany' is a good word," said Chester. "You look as though you're enjoying it now."

"You wouldn't know where Jacob Morningstar's quarters are?" Mary Ann asked.

"I'm afraid," said the cat stretching, "that I am not invited into the castle often. But to be honest, I was not invited today, either." And the cat smiled. "Frabjous seeing you again. Just make certain no one else does. I hear your name has been rather sullied here in Neath. A shame …" And the cat disappeared. She thought she heard his voice say, "She didn't look a bit like you." But then the sound was gone, too.

Mary Ann decided to seize her chance—while everyone was occupied at the Unbirthday festivities—to search the castle for the valet's room, as well. The wonderful thing about castles, thought Mary Ann, was their tendency toward tradition. And tradition meant that the lord and lady of a house would have chambers on the uppermost floor and their closest servants nearby. It narrowed down things considerably.

With the castle empty, this gave Mary Ann the opportunity to stroll the halls unhindered. So it wasn't long before she was upon the third floor, inside the chamber of King Rudolf. She had grown used to a certain amount of red in the décor from her time in Lord Carmine's manor, and it appeared King Rudolf used the same decorator. The difference was the repetitive hearts motif, and on that, it was wall-to-wall streamlined representations of the interior organ.

The valet had a small room off of this and like those of most servants, there were not many personal possessions to assess. A small chest of drawers had been provided, and a careful search of that revealed only some very well-cared-for clothes in fine fabrics.

Next she searched a trunk at the foot of the bed, containing blankets, but underneath she found a few books (nothing dear tucked between their covers), an old cutlass and some maps. She looked under the pillow: nothing. She felt around under the bed mattress: empty. She peered under the small table: clean.

She glanced around the room. There simply was nowhere else to search. She caught her own face in the mirror, looking even more deeply disappointed than she thought she felt. The act somehow aligned the mood to the expression. What a fruitless trip it had been! Then she noticed the shadow that the mirror made on the wall. Odd ... It looked deeper than the frame itself would suggest. She peered along the mirror and— yes! The backing seemed to be slightly too thick. She struggled to unhook the mirror from the wall and now there was no doubt. Something had been fixed to the back. A small stack of paper, tied in string, dangling from a nail.

She moved to sit on the bed and then unwrapped the package. In it were several notes in red ink and a wide, loopy, almost childlike handwriting. She unfolded the first one:

> Blood is red
> Love is to cherish
> Blood loss, love lost,
> Two reasons to perish

Mary Ann made a face. Was it a love poem or threat? She supposed it was up to the recipient to decide. She moved on to the next one. It was an accordion-folded piece of heavy paper in the shape of a heart. On it was printed:

> To My Number One Fan.
> From the Heart,
> Tina

They're not getting any better, are they? Mary Ann thought. Then she opened the last one:

> How do I love you?
> I count the reasons here
> Your chiseled jaw,
> The way you tuck your hair behind your ear
> You understand my beauty,

You love to see me shine
You're my morning star, you are!
So glad to know you're mine

Mary Ann put it down and considered that, perhaps, it was just as well that the Queen had gone into acting and not writing. After that last poem, she wasn't sure she wanted to even know what the rest of it was. But for the sake of thoroughness, she pressed on.

The next item in the bundle was a small, watercolor portrait of Queen Valentina. There was also a red handkerchief and several yellowed slips of paper. They were receipts. One for a ruby brooch, one for ruby earrings, and the last one ... The handwriting was instantly familiar. It was a receipt from J. Sanford Banks to one Jack Clover, in regards to a carved chaise longue with a heart motif. It was on her father's and Banks' stationery and Banks' address was circled on it.

Jack Clover ... Mary Ann remembered that name from the books. As far as she could recall, the project had been paid and delivered some time ago.

"Jack Clover." She said it aloud. She hadn't picked up on it at the time, but it certainly appeared to be a pseudonym for the Knave of Clubs. So he had purchased furniture directly from Mr. Banks, thereby creating a connection between the valet, Banks and Rowan Carpenter ...

But it was so long ago. What could have gone wrong with the deal? And was this the only entry under Clover's name?

She took a desperate moment to think but simply couldn't recall. A chaise, though ... Finding the item couldn't be too difficult, could it? Her father's work was distinctive.

Mary Ann tucked all the items back together and bound them up as they had been, then hung them on the nail. In a moment she had replaced the mirror, wiped a few smudges and straightened the coverlet where she'd sat down. Then she moved back into the King's quarters.

It was no surprise that the chaise was not there. She moved to a more likely spot, the Queen's abode. This was an adjoining space and so lush and lavish, scented and gilded, Mary Ann found it almost nauseating in its Muchness. Why, it was precisely the décor version of the woman's love poetry. There was so much desperately begging for attention, it was almost hard to even see if the chaise were there.

She thought she had it for a moment, tucked in the corner and covered in blankets. But upon closer inspection, she discovered it was several dresses, carelessly tossed, covering a large bronze of a peacock, its tail extending behind it in closed, hand-painted splendor. That was when she heard a noise in the hall, and a second later, she had ducked behind a curtain.

"Oh dear!" an elderly female voice said. "Why are those still out?"

There was a rustling of skirts. A second, younger voice said, "She was in such a tizzy, ma'am, I didn't get round to putting them away. It was labor enough getting her dressed and out the door, it was."

"Well, do it now. We can't have her see them like that. Double-quick!"

Mary Ann didn't dare breathe as the lady's maid bustled around the chamber. She prayed that the red of her own skirts was enough to blend into the red draperies. She prayed the red of her shoes couldn't be discerned from the red rugs.

And after what seemed like a very long moment, the Queen's maid sighed and left. Mary Ann peeked out from her spot and darted to the door, then checked the hall and made her escape. Her uniform wasn't particularly helpful for running, unless the skirts were hiked up. It seemed that Mary Ann could have speed or modesty but not both. And in a flash, and flashing her legs to half the castle, she was back outside, deep into the Unbirthday crowd. Queen Valentina was wrapping up her short soliloquy.

The audience applauded with an enthusiasm that seemed genuine.

"Thank you, my dear hearts," said the Queen. "Thank you all!" And she blew kisses to the crowd and someone handed her a bouquet of roses. Red ones, of course.

Mr. Rabbit was on stage now and followed a short blast of his trumpet with, "Next, in honor of Queen Valentina's late spring Unbirthday, we shall have a croquet match in the garden. Anyone wishing to participate, please report to the garden now."

The crowd began to disperse, leaving Mary Ann ill-at ease about being out in the open and recognized. So she scanned for Lady Carmine and when she found her, she stopped short and froze.

Lady Carmine was talking to Mary Ann's mother.

There was no doubt about it. For years, Mary Ann had struggled to picture the woman who had left her and her father when Mary Ann was a small child. She had retained only the vaguest images in her mind—a gesture, a turn of the head, a smile, a scent. But now the haze had cleared and the image crystallized before her eyes. And Mary Ann had no sooner taken it in, than Lady Carmine waved her over, calling, "Tamsin, there you are! Let me introduce you to Clarissa Snow."

Mary Ann stood rooted to the spot. If there were a thousand possible ways to blow one's cover before cake, this scene surely ranked in the top five.

"Oh, it's all right. Come, dear," cooed Lady Carmine, waving the maid forward like she might coax a timid puppy. She turned to Clarissa Snow. "My new lady's maid. Lovely girl. She's been a great help to our household. Very skilled in healthcare and meteorology, as well as Jabberwock fighting. But somewhat nervous in the interpersonal skills."

Mary Ann saw now that dodging the encounter would be far more obvious than simply joining them, so she thawed her legs and moved to the group. She curtseyed and bowed her head. "Madam Snow."

"Tamsin, a pleasure," Clarissa Snow said. Her hair, Mary Ann noticed, was the same dark blonde of her own but with more of a wave to it. It had been arranged with some care and topped with the white, knobbed cap of a White Turvian pawn. She wore it far back on her head, framed by an array of coordinated plaits, the rest hanging loose. "You know, I once lived in Red Turvy for a time. Some beautiful scenery there."

Lady Carmine said, "Oh yes? And what brought you there? I thought you were White Turvian from birth?"

"I am." She smiled, a wistful one, fragile like spring flowers. Mary Ann had not gotten those genes. "I had fallen for a Red Turvian artisan," the lady in white explained. "Or I should say, I fell for art. Sadly, I learned that art may be nourishment for the soul, but it is not a fine conversationalist on a winter's night, or a loving hand upon one's face. The art is sometimes the best part of the artist."

"And that's why you left?" Mary Ann jarred as she heard her own voice.

But Clarissa Snow did not bat an eye. "Oh, I was young, and the battle drums of my homeland called, and I became swept up in this idea of changing the world. Or at least my circumstance within it."

"It must have been quite easy to do," said Mary Ann, "if there were nothing to detain you." She cast it out there, a vague hope tied to the end. It was a question she'd contemplated in some form or another for most of her life.

"Oh," said the woman, with a wave of her gloved hand, "we all have our minor bumps in the road. Yet we roll past—do we not? —by giving it greater drive and retaining a sharp eye on the horizon."

"It depends," said Mary Ann, "whether one is the carriage driver or the bump."

Clarissa Snow's expression was blank for a moment, then she let out a tittering laugh clearly designed to cover up any lack of understanding. "Well, I am so glad of the peace between Red and White Turvy," she continued. "Long may it prosper! I believe events such as this prove our collective dedication to continued unification."

"Agreed!" said Lady Carmine, who looked like she thought something had happened between them but couldn't say just what. "How fortunate we are for these years of reconciliation."

"Yet…" began the Snow, "I meant to ask." She leaned in

conspiratorially. "What is going on in your part of the realm? First, I'd heard something about a mass tove suicide and then a questionable boating accident of that door-to-door walrus fellow."

"Oh, that." Lady Carmine looked embarrassed. "Well, yes, that's something of a muddle at the moment. But it's being handled by the best investigators in the land."

Mary Ann turned her laugh into a discreet cough.

"I'm sure you'll sort it all out," said the Snow, not sounding sure of it at all. "I only ask because I knew the gentleman peripherally. Sandy Banks, I mean."

"Oh, did you?"

She nodded. "Business partner of the artisan I'd mentioned. I cannot imagine he is taking this well."

"As I understand, he's not taking it at all," said Lady Carmine. "He's passed."

At this, Clarissa Snow's eyes went wide. "Passed? Rowan Carpenter? When?"

"Quite recently, it would seem."

"Madness!" Her eyes seemed to be retaining an excess amount of moisture. "It wasn't also in the boating incident, was it?"

"I'm not really able to share information at this time," said Lady Carmine.

Especially since no one's been briefing her, Mary Ann thought.

"Well," Clarissa Snow dabbed at her eye with a handkerchief, "that's sad news about Rowan. We were a poor match, but I certainly didn't wish him ill." And a light crossed her face. "His daughter. She lives here in Neath, I believe. Someone should tell her."

"I'm sure they've taken care of that very thing," said Lady Carmine.

His daughter. Mary Ann looked at the ground.

Trumpets sounded in the distance.

"That'll be the croquet match!" said Clarissa Snow. "I do love a good game. Will you come?"

"I'd love to," said Lady Carmine and they started off

together. Lady Carmine turned, seeing Mary Ann had not moved from the spot. "Tamsin, dear—are you joining us?"

"I'm not feeling very well," Mary Ann said. "If you could spare me for an hour, I might spend some time out of the sun."

"Of course, dear." Lady Carmine's face was all sympathy. "I'll see you after the game."

"Thank you, My Lady."

And Mary Ann watched them, Red and White, take the path to the Queen's croquet garden.

20

Truthfully, Mary Ann *was* feeling a bit tired and queasy. It's all very well to go through life with the sense that you're unwanted and completely alone in the world. It was another thing altogether to hear it confirmed firsthand. She was heading for a cup of tea from the now-vacant tea tables — it appeared Mr. Milliner and his friends had taken their cups and a pot with them to the match, since that table had been picked clean — when a voice said, "There you are! I've been looking all over for you! Guess who I just spoke with?"

Mary Ann didn't need to look up. "I'm sorry, Sir Rufus, I'm not really feeling up to more jokes. May I pour you a cup?" She raised the pot.

"Yes, please. And it's no joke. Guess!" He pulled up a chair.

Mary Ann sighed as she grabbed him a clean cup. "Amos Quito? Nana Yourbusiness? Mikey Doesntfitinthekeyhole?"

"I said it wasn't a joke." This was a tone she recognized. The petulant one from his Depression days. "Oh, I see," he said. "You're still upset about our little interaction on the way here, eh? Yes, I'm sorry about that."

"You are?" She thought this might be the first apology she'd ever received in her life. It was certainly her first from him.

"Yes, getting my sense of humor back was a bit of a shock

to the ol' system. You know, the humors need to adjust in the body. It was too much at once there at the beginning, but it feels like it's evening out now."

"Aren't you going to say it's not evening at all, it's daytime?" She dropped three sugar cubes into the cup.

"No." He slid the cup before him. "Though I wish I'd thought of it." He grinned. "But since you won't guess, I'll tell you who I spoke with. I had a chat with Jacob Morningstar."

She almost spilled the cream. "When was this?"

"Before the Queen's surprise performance kicked off. You were probably unpacking Mother at the time."

"And?" She hopped into the chair next to him.

"And he was terribly worried about the stage management aspect of things. Had he gotten enough roses? Did they need more candles? Where was the girl with the flamingo chorusline? That sort of thing."

"I see," she said. The tea was strong but cold.

"He doesn't seem to have the axe on him. That I can tell you," Rufus said.

"No, it's hanging in the Armory just like Ace said it would be."

Rufus blinked. "You were in the Armory?"

"Just go on." She waved a hand. "You spoke to Morningstar?"

"Yes. So I cleverly managed to bring up the topic of mystical weaponry. I started with how the Vorpal sword had just shown up before I needed it, but then it vanished again— "

"It did?"

"Oh, hadn't I mentioned?" He scratched his head. "Yes, right after our last training session."

"So that must mean your training with it is complete," she said.

He considered it. "Why, yes. I suppose so! Seems curiously quick, though."

It did and she felt sorry for this. They had been good times.

He said, "Anyway, so I told him how I'd need to quest for the Vorpal sword to finish the job."

"And…?"

"And I said, 'In the final War, you were that fellow with the club, eh? The one they used to call Bludgeon of Something-or-Other, due to your fine walloping skills.' And he said, 'Yes, but that was a long time ago.' And I said, 'You mean you never want to get out-and-about these days with a good blade or brain-whacker in your hand? Just for old times' sake?' And he laughed and said, 'Why, I suppose I might, if the right opportunity came along.' How about that?"

"Well, I talked to one of the maids here," Mary Ann said, "and she confirms what we've all been hearing, that Jacob Morningstar is madly in love with the Queen. And that King Rudolf knows about it and is okay with it because it keeps her busy."

"That I could understand."

"Now, when I searched his room—"

Rufus frowned. "Whose room?"

"Morningstar's."

The eyes went wide and the ginger eyebrows shot skyward. "Well, rook me! You've been productive!"

Mary Ann smiled. "In Morningstar's room I found a bunch of old papers. In addition to a lot of truly awful poetry from the Queen, there was an invoice from J. Sanford Banks for a chaise longue, covered in hearts, made out to and paid for by one Jack Clover."

"And who's that then?" He grabbed a biscuit.

"Jack…*Clover*…" She waited for it to sink in.

"Oh," he said, through the crunch of biscuit. "So Morningstar secretly commissioned a prezzie for the Queen…"

"And as far as I know, it was delivered, too. There were a few unpaid balances listed in my father's accounting book, but I'm quite sure that wasn't one of them. So the piece is around here somewhere. It's not in Queen Valentina's chambers, though."

"Strange motive for revenge," he said, wiping his mouth. "Unless your father didn't have a proper return policy?" He winked.

"I'd like to find the chaise," said Mary Ann.

"What will you learn from that?"

"Haven't a clue," she said.

"Frabjous!" he said, leaping from the chair and slinging his cup onto the table. It clattered in its saucer. "Then let's go."

With the croquet match going on in full-swing and everyone either playing or cheering on their favorite player (read: Queen Valentina), Mary Ann and Rufus were free to search where they pleased. They hit every room on the ground floor and ultimately found the chaise in the Conservatory, along the window next to a harpsichord that had been gold-leafed and painted in scenes of Queen Valentina's plays. At a quick glance, Mary Ann could see the chaise was some of her father's best work, the intricate carving as fine and precise as ever, and featuring enough hearts and fat winged archer babies to make even the moodiest queen sufficiently impressed.

"Huzzah!" cheered the voices outside, and Mary Ann could see a hedgehog careen across the field and crash through the topiaries, then scramble into the safety of the shrubbery. She hardly blamed it. Sport was hell.

"Anything out of the ordinary about the piece?" Rufus asked. "Anything that would make your father's business a target?"

Mary Ann was searching the design for a cleverly-hidden message and feeling in the upholstery seams for some secreted item. She came away with crumbs and a bit of quill feather. She climbed under the piece and extended a hand. "Pass me that letter opener I saw?"

Rufus glanced around and grabbed the object from the top of a small painted writing desk, handing it to her. "What are you up to?"

"Nothing that will matter to anyone, if I do it properly." She pried off a few of the underlying nails.

"So tacks-ing," he said and laughed wildly.

"Please stop."

"Sorry." He tried to assemble himself into a mood more appropriate for the occasion and crouched down beside her. "Humors are so hard to regulate. Perhaps I need a good leeching. Spy anything?"

"Not so as I can tell." She felt around within the seat, hoping to unearth something, anything worth the price of a man and/or walrus' life. But horsehair was her sole reward, which was to say: none. She pushed the tacks back into the netting and then the wood. She dusted off her hands and rose. "I find it interesting that Morningstar commissioned a sofa for the Queen and here it is, straight out in the open."

"Sounds to me like it's all been out in the open, from what you say," said Rufus. "But do you think he could have commissioned the thing on behalf of the King? He is the fellow's servant."

"Then why hide the receipt?" Mary Ann asked. "Why put it with other receipts that clearly appeared to be personal gifts?"

"You've stymied me," said Rufus. He glanced at the harpsichord. "I wonder if the fellow's musical." He leafed through the stack of sheet music on top of the instrument. "There are all love songs here. Gooey stuff, too, if you're into that."

"I wouldn't know. I've never had the luxury of goo," said Mary Ann.

"Well, someone uses the room. These are recent newspapers." He indicated the copies of *Neath Undercover* and *The Turvy Mirror* on a table.

Mary Ann's eyes settled on the paper from Turvy. The headline read: "Carpenter Dead. Manhunt On for Woman." Mary Ann snatched up the paper. "Listen to this: 'Rowan Carpenter was found dead, buried in a shallow grave late last Punday'—It was not shallow! Douglas did a cracking job on it and—"

Rufus pointed to the paper and cleared his throat.

"Right, yes. '— Shallow grave late last Punday, and Turvy

Square Four investigators also discovered a floor stain upon the scene that they believe to be blood. The grave was marked with what appears to be a feminine hand.' Curse my penmanship! Why did I have to get all fancy? … Oh, yes, yes, I *know*…" She told Rufus and went back to the paper.

"'Carpenter was survived by one child, a Mary Ann Carpenter who is now wanted for questioning. Sources indicate Miss Carpenter may also be wanted in association with the destruction of personal property and the public disruption of a trial in Neath. She may currently be going under the name of Alice.' Which is ironic," Mary Ann said, turning to Rufus, "because Alice is the one name your father hadn't tried out on me." She returned to the paper. "'If you see Miss Carpenter, send a rocking horsefly to Red Turvy Square Four guards immediately.'"

And there was the finished drawing that Pat the handyman had done of the intruder at Mr. Rabbit's. This person. This possible Alice. This fake Mary Ann.

Mary Ann wiped her brow with a handkerchief, sneering, "Tweedles. If only they'd stuck to rattle collecting and bickering and skipped the day jobs, the world would be a better place."

A cheer emanated from outside the window, and they could see the crowd was dispersing. Based on the way Queen Valentina was being hoisted above their heads in a golden chair, and the way a number of the guests were being led off in shackles, it seemed the Queen's team had won.

Rufus tugged at her sleeve. "We'd best not be found wandering around in here. Better to melt into the crowd, eh, 'Alice'?" He grinned but it vanished quickly when he saw her expression. "You were a lot more fun when I was depressed."

"I was not so many other people then," she said.

They moved down the hall and spied a shadow at the entrance, so they ducked into the first room they could.

A high, melodic voice said, "Herald, tell them I am going to change my clothes, and then I shall be down to open my Unbirthday gifts. I expect that they will all be precisely what I didn't know I always wanted."

"Yes, Your Majesty," said Warren Rabbit, for Mary Ann knew that quavering voice so well.

A figure swept down the hall, past the door, and they heard footsteps click-clicking up the stairs. Mary Ann and Rufus took this moment to make a break for it.

Outside, Mr. Rabbit was relaying the Queen's message, while the remaining unshackled guests enjoyed another round of tea, cakes and sandwiches.

Various performers had started up again, practicing their stilt-walking, comedy or testing out poetry dedicated to the Queen. It was difficult to keep an eye out for all the people Mary Ann was hoping to avoid, and she thought it rather helped that Rufus was tall, flame-haired and dressed in his courtly best. It kept the focus away from her. Her invisibility powers were not what they once were.

Mr. Rabbit signified the gift-giving portion of the event by another blast of his horn and Queen Valentina glided forward in another elegant gown, this one covered in live rosebuds. As she moved to the center of the stage, all of them bloomed at once and the crowd oohed and clapped.

"Now, the moment you've all been waiting for," Valentina said. "You may watch me open my prezzies! Gather round, everyone! Gather round." She sat in a throne to one end of the present table, while some low-level members in her court brought a gift forward. Mr. Rabbit read off the tag. "From King Rudolf, Your Majesty."

She didn't actually tear off the paper herself, she had the Three and Four of Hearts do it. Her rosebud lips pursed and moved a bit off-center as she evaluated the item. "Oh. Another tiara." Her tone was flat and bored. "Thanks ever so, Rudy."

"Rudy," a distinguished-looking man who was sitting at the opposite end of the table said in a hopeful tone, "It's got an engraving."

She took the tiara and read along the inner rim. "'My Dearest Valentina, love is our crowing achievement.' Charming…NEXT!"

It seemed the gifts were part of a never-ending sea. She

received cloaks and gowns of the finest fabrics, jewels of unimagined value, flamingos dyed a deep red (that one was quite a hit, since Mary Ann knew she was in the market for better brand-cohesive flamingos), and a set of romantic adventures featuring her as the lead character. She received sets of rose gold dinnerware, life-sized portraits of herself, a lake (not in a box; that wouldn't transport well), and a voucher from someone promising to name their first-born child after her. Mr. Milliner gave her a hat so large and magnificent, it was designed to ride along on a wheeled framework around her. The Duchess (who Mary Ann knew never particularly liked Queen Valentina) gave her a gift certificate to the Pepper of the Month Club, and Jacob Morningstar, gave her a beautifully-painted clock where a mechanical figure lopped off another mechanical figure's head at the stroke of the hour.

She clapped her dainty hands at that and laughed. "Just my sense of humor! Oh Jacky, you know me so well!"

When she got to the package that Mary Ann was quite sure was the looking-glass, Mary Ann noted Mr. Rabbit's face was particularly drawn, his eyes fearful and darting.

"A mirror," she said, as it was revealed to her. "Very pretty. What does it do?"

"Do, Your Majesty?" asked the Rabbit, and Mary Ann could see him quaking in his courtly robes. "Why…it…it…"

She looked at him narrowly.

And Mary Ann watched as the answer came to him. "… It showcases your unmatched beauty, my dear Queen." And he bowed so low the tips of his ears touched the ground.

"Oh." She smiled and peered into the mirror. "It does, doesn't it? Aces!" She pushed it aside. "Next!"

Mr. Rabbit mopped his forehead and Mary Ann sighed with relief. They never had found out how to make the mirror work as a portal. It seemed destined to spend its life as mere artistic furniture now. But that was probably just as well; Mary Ann had carefully watched Morningstar when the mirror was brought forward. There was no sign whatsoever of concern on his part; his interest appeared to be the same as with any gift that hadn't been his. It was all very curious.

Two hours later, the presents were finally all received and acknowledged and, as no one had been sent to the dungeons for it, Mary Ann considered it a success. Half of the party-goers, however, were wilted or asleep and all of them leapt a bit when the Queen stood suddenly and shouted, "Entertainment! It's entertainment time now. I performed for you, so it's only right that you perform for me. What songs and poems about my greatness will you be surprising me with today?"

Naturally, this was not something anyone wanted to be the first to attempt. But the guests did have various tributes prepared and after some arguing, they sorted themselves into a lineup. There were musical compositions written for her, as played on mandolin, flute and Jubjub bird. There was an on-land Lobster Quadrille featuring lobsters in water-filled helmets. There was a great heaping of poetry and song of varying skill levels.

And then the Two of Clubs stepped onto the stage. He was a mild-mannered fellow of sturdy build and middle age who looked as if all the hair that had been on his head had decided to relocate to his upper lip and side-whiskers for a better view of things.

"Ahem," he said, "today I shall aspire to delight you with my comedy stylings. I shall start with my impression of someone I believe we all might recognize." And in a second, the man's form changed entirely. He stood there before them the perfect likeness of King Rudolf, from the very top of his crown to the curly toes of his shoes.

"Greetings, my loyal subjects! King Rudolf here. Anyone know where I might find some jam tarts? We seem to be down a few!"

And the crowd laughed.

"Or how about…" The King shrunk to two-thirds size and became white, fluffy and twitchy. "… Harold here?" And he looked precisely like Mr. Rabbit, who stood only a few feet away. "They call me Harold because I'm a Herald, but my real name's Warren because my mum thought it sounded homey."

By now people in the crowd were shouting, "Do me! Do me!"

The Two of Clubs took the trumpet from the real Mr. Rabbit and tried blowing into it. It made an awful, airy blat, and he playfully looked into the bell of the instrument, as if something were wrong with it. He then thrust it back into Mr. Rabbit's paws. "Or why not … this fellow?" And the faux Rabbit grew quite tall indeed and was suddenly the very likeness of Jacob Morningstar. He saluted the crowd crisply. "Anyone care to hear me talk about my heroics in the final War? I have twelve hours to spare."

And the crowd laughed again.

But Mary Ann Carpenter was not laughing. She was gaping. She stopped gaping long enough to look at Sir Rufus, who was also gaping. He gaped her direction now and they pulled each other aside from the crowd, to gape together in a small cluster of trees.

"What's this fellow's name?" Mary Ann asked.

"Twain Morningstar, I believe," said Rufus.

"Morningstar! Any relation to the valet?"

"No idea."

"How does he do it? That changing?" She eyed the impressionist again, awestruck. "I didn't know anyone could do that."

"Well, 'anyone' can't. It looks like deuces are wild."

"The Deuce you say!" gasped Mary Ann. "Do you know anything about this fellow?"

"Not really. I keep telling you, it's not like I've socialized with Neath's lower deck much. Perhaps we could find someone to—"

But Mary Ann was already on it, dragging him by the wrist to Hexa Hearts, who was leading the banner of flamingos back to the garden lagoon. "Hexa," she called, "what do you know about that fellow on the stage just now?"

"Oh, Twain Morningstar?" A flamingo was nibbling on her hat. "He's so funny and talented, isn't he? Such a card!"

"A wild card?" asked Mary Ann.

"Yes, the only decent one we've got these days. I'm afraid my nephew, Dewey Hearts, has never been very good with impressions," she said, with a sad shake of her head. "Does all right with the voices, but the faces are a horror. And as for the other Twos, they were, um…cut…in the final War."

Rufus asked, "But did Twain Morningstar fight in the War?"

"Of course, Sir," she said, sounding surprised. "Quite well, as I understand. Then he went with Jacob Morningstar to Queen Valentina's side when the King of Clubs was killed. He's Jacob Morningstar's cousin, I think."

"And he lives here at court?" Mary Ann asked.

"Yes, he's got a two-room cottage out back by the hedge maze. He does landscaping now." Hexa squinted. "Why?"

"Thanks," said Mary Ann. And she and Rufus started out in a brisk stride that broke into a full-fledged run that led around the castle and into the back gardens.

Unlike Turvy, in Neath, you could actually get where you were going by running with intent.

"I think the hedge maze is this way," Mary Ann said as they ran. She'd seen it from the window of the Queen's room. "So just to be sure we're on the same page here—"

"He's not a page, he's a gardener," snickered Rufus. At her pointed look, he said, "It just slips out."

"But you are thinking what I'm thinking, aren't you?" she asked. "That the person I saw kill my father was not actually Jacob Morningstar at all. It's Twain Morningstar, in full-on wild card mode."

"It would explain a lot, wouldn't it?" said Rufus. "To dress as your cousin who has influence with the Royal Family, in case anyone saw you? You commit a murder as a simple gardener in the Royal house, your accusers have somewhere to go. They can take it all the way to the Queen and it might just be listened to. You might just become a marked card. But if you commit a murder as the King's valet—and the Queen's beloved—then bringing it to the Queen's attention becomes highly sticky."

"But motive," said Mary Ann. "What's the motive here? I didn't see any business dealings with him in the books at all.

And unfortunately, I wasn't watching him when Queen Valentina opened the mirror, were you?"

"No, I had my eyes locked on Jacob Morningstar and your furry former employer," said Rufus.

"And did you notice? Morningstar the Valet didn't seem bothered by the gift or even especially curious about it."

"I noticed his lack of noticing." They arrived at the cottage clearly labeled, "Two."

Mary Ann tried the front door, and it was not locked.

"So what are we looking for?" Rufus asked. "I personally would like a nice confession letter and some bloody clothes, but I recognize I tend to dream big these days."

"You take this room," Mary Ann said, indicating the parlor. "I'll take the bedchamber."

"Right," said Rufus. "I'll shout when I find whatever it is."

"Please do," she said.

She heard him thumping around in the other room while she began on the sleeping quarters. It was a small room with lots of natural light streaming through the drapes. It looked like it had been decorated at the same time as the castle, with the same red print textiles bearing the Hearts' family pattern. She started with the side table and the dresser, then peered up into the fireplace, looked under the bed (so dusty! the man needed a good housemaid), then the wardrobe closet. Most of it was clothes—gardening clothes, royal event clothes, as well as extra blankets.

She grabbed a chair and climbed upon it to investigate the items on the upper shelf. She moved several blankets and an extra pillow, and that's when she saw something at the very back of the upper wardrobe. It appeared to be a small, weathered wooden box. She strained and teetered on the chair to reach, but her fingertips only just brushed it.

"Rufus?" she called, realizing somewhere along the way she'd dropped the "Sir" altogether, and that was not the least bit proper.

But in a flash, he was beside her. "Found something?"

"Can you grab that?"

He traded places with her and had the box down in a moment. He handed it to her. "You have the honors."

"It's probably nothing," she said, not believing it was nothing for even a second. The box seemed to be made of driftwood.

She swung the lid and inside the box was a small ocean's worth of pearls.

"My, my, my!" said Rufus with a smile. "Perhaps he's planning a fancy new outfit for the Queen's next Unbirthday."

But Mary Ann had lost her breath.

"Are you quite all right? You're very pale. You've gone all White Turvian on me." He fanned her with a hand.

"Son of a Bandersnatch, I get it now," she said and her voice sounded very distant in her ears. "It all makes sense."

"Sense? Here in Neath? Why, that's quite an achievement. How'd we do it?" He dug into the box and let a handful of pearls run through his fingers. Some sand also sifted down into the bottom of the box. "Was I right about the party outfit?"

"Sorry, no." She smiled. "But I think I know where these came from."

"Well, if you want to be literal," he said, "so do I: oysters."

"Exactly!" she said.

"Oh." He scratched his head and looked surprised. "So you do actually want to be literal?"

Her smile grew broader. "Yes."

"Didn't see that coming," he said. "Explain?"

"These pearls," she said, "are the motive, the evidence, and also reveal the identity of the real murderer."

"Hold on." He leaned on the chair. "Real murderer? But you saw Jacob Morningstar — or rather Twain Morningstar impersonating Jacob Morningstar — kill your father with an axe."

"I did. And he was hired by the ones who paid him with these pearls."

Rufus sized up the treasure before them. "But only a queen would have access to that amount of pearls. Or a jeweler."

"Or an oyster," said Mary Ann.

"We're back at that literal thing again," he said. "An oyster?"

"Not just one oyster. Based on the quantity, color and shape of these pearls, many oysters. I'd say all the remaining oysters along the river worked for quite a bit of time to make this box of pearls."

"The oysters paid a hired killer in pearls to off your father?"

"My father and Mr. Banks. And—" Mary Ann's mind was swimming now, practically surrounded by a sea of ideas. "And the raths! Of course! It's so obvious!"

"The raths, too?" Lines creased Rufus' forehead. "But why?"

"Why did Twain Morningstar and his uncle bow down to Queen Valentina when their suit lost the final War? Why is Mr. Rabbit so servile? Why did I lie before I knew I could trust you? Survival! Plain and simple. It makes people do mad things."

Rufus raised an eyebrow. "Your father was a big seafood fan, then, was he?"

"Huge!" Mary Ann shouted gleefully. "Things to know about my father: he was a fine woodworker, a beautiful whistler, mediocre in the dad department, and ridiculously fond of seafood. Especially oysters."

He grinned. "And not in the taking it on long walks in the moonlight way, I'm guessing."

"Actually, there was this one time," she said.

He looked uncomfortable. "I believe I'd rather not know."

"Well, it was no happy ending for the oysters, that I can assure you," Mary Ann told him. "Yes, indeed, getting rid of my father, Mr. Banks and those raths was absolutely vital to the Turvy oyster populations' continued survival."

"But wait," said Rufus, who was just about caught up now, "the raths died because they ate poisoned shellfish. So are you saying—?"

"Sometimes sacrifices must be made for the greater good," Mary Ann said, her smile falling away. "I suspect that was what happened there."

"What a way to go," sighed Rufus. "Poisoned themselves

only to have their corpses devoured. Dear me, I shall never eat oysters again."

"I believe that was the point," she said. "Oh, yes, this was a forwards murder plot, all right. Thoroughly pre-planned. There'll be no undoing this one."

Rufus nodded, looking grave. "I'm very sorry," he said.

"At least now I know," she said. "And, frankly, I should have figured it out sooner. My father's raven neighbor loves to decorate her nest with found objects. When I visited, I noticed she had all these tiny shoes. They reminded me of my childhood, so I assumed they were doll shoes. But now I see: it was from meals with Father. He'd separate out the oyster shells for mosaic projects and then toss the little shoes in the bin. Shoes from the oysters' tiny feet..."

Suddenly, Mary Ann recalled the glimmering tracks around the servants' bedchamber in Carmine Manor ... and the tiny footprints that were gone by morning. The oyster's wet shoeprints had dried in the fireplace heat. That oyster had tried to save her life.

"I didn't even know oysters had feet," said Rufus now.

"Looking at it from their perspective, it's tragic," said Mary Ann, the magnitude of it all overcoming her. "The hundreds and hundreds of oysters Father led from their beds. He chatted with them and gained their trust, only to devour them all with a nice vinegar and pepper."

"But, Mr. Banks," said Rufus, "surely he wasn't all that bad?"

"As bad or worse!" said Mary Ann. "A terrible glutton, he was! But yes, I'm certain if we spoke to my father's neighbor she would say she got those shoes from my father's rubbish."

"Unless, of course," said a voice from the door, "no one gets the chance to ask her." Mary Ann and Rufus turned. It was Twain Morningstar, and he had the axe.

21

"Nobody ever makes things easy, do they?" asked Twain Morningstar as he stood in the bedchamber doorway, axe at the ready. "You were given ample opportunity to put this all behind you. I understand you were even warned. *Nicely*. But did you let it go? You did not. You dragged..." his eyes flicked to Rufus, "... *friends* into it."

"So where does this leave us?" asked Mary Ann, as she scanned the room for something, anything, to become a makeshift weapon. "You plan to kill us, as well? You might be able to off me without anyone blinking an eye, but Sir Rufus is a knight of Turvy. He will be missed."

Rufus turned to her, looking concerned. "You would be missed."

The sincerity in his tone was startling, disarming, even if she had been armed at all. Which she wasn't. "Would I?"

"Of course!" He seemed surprised she'd even mentioned it. "You've been indispensible, both to my family and me. Why, I would have been but gristle stuck to the Jabberwock's toothpick, if not for you. My humor would have been locked away in a humordor forever to gather dust and historic disconnect. You, Mary Ann, have made all the difference."

"How very kind," she managed.

"How very true," he insisted.

"Oh, for the love of Neath," Twain Morningstar growled, and it broke the spell in an instant. "That's the trouble with being menacing in a land where everyone's off their tea kettle. No one has a proper sense of danger."

"Well," Mary Ann thought quickly now, "the axe *is* very scary. And you do wield it in such an ominous way."

"Yes, very!" agreed Rufus, taking the cue.

"And Rufus is free to correct me, of course," Mary Ann continued, "but I think we'd both feel considerably more terrified right now, if we hadn't just seen you do such an inspired comedy set back there."

"Indeed, your King Rudolf was spot on," said Rufus. "Huzzah you. Ovations all round."

Twain's face broke into a shocked smile. "Was it? Thanks very much. You know, I was a little concerned about it because it's hard to balance the funny in a Queen's Unbirthday crowd situation, without getting too politi—hey!"

And that's when Mary Ann grabbed up the fire poker and pointed it at him.

"You're coming with us," she said.

"Where?" He was backing up towards the front door.

"You're going to tell Queen Valentina all about how you got these pearls," said Mary Ann.

"I'll do no such thing," Twain snapped. "Those pearls are my ticket out of here. Do you think I want to be a gardener all my life? Do you think I bowed and scraped and mowed and 'scaped all these years for nothing? I want my own theater where I'm the headliner every night and…and…" he searched for the words, "… box seats with those marvelous little gas lamps all round them. And I'm going to get them." He motioned to the wooden container. "Give the pearls to me."

"No-how," said Mary Ann.

"All right, then. Go to Queen Valentina with them. See if I care," he said, stepping aside from the front door and lowering the axe. "And then what? So? I have a box of pearls. They could be from anywhere. You can't prove anything. The oysters won't be so shellfish as to whelk on the deal. They'll clam up. So all the mussel's behind me. It'll be your word against mine."

"And mine," said Rufus.

"Ah, yes: the Turvian Jabberwock slayer and Lord Carmine's son..." Twain considered this. "You have some clout certainly. But remember: I am the Queen's husband's valet's second cousin," he proclaimed, "and —" He stroked his chin. "Actually, it doesn't sound as grand when you put it that way, does it?"

They shook their heads.

"Right, once more from the top." He cleared his throat. "I am the favorite cousin of the Queen's favorite personal confidant and as such, I have the Queen's ear."

Rufus burst out laughing.

Morningstar's face went red with anger. "I do! It's the Queen of Diamonds'— a War souvenir. Valentina let me keep it after her enemy's execution. It's in a very pretty jar." He pointed to a bookshelf with the non-axe-holding hand.

It appeared the man was right. In a very pretty jar, there was definitely something floating that looked ear-ily ear-shaped. Mary Ann was glad they hadn't noticed that sooner in their search. It might have hung them up for the rest of it.

"So go on," pressed Twain. "Go talk to Queen Valentina. See where that gets you." Twain stood back from the door and waved them onward. Mary Ann and Rufus backed out past him, a careful eye on his hatchet. Rufus went first and Mary Ann followed, the poker keeping a safe distance between them.

They made it outside, slamming the door on their assailant, and together they dragged a wrought iron garden bench before it to buy them some time. As they ran back toward the Unbirthday festivities, Mary Ann could hear glass shatter, an ornamental shrubbery curse someone, and the thump of something heavy clattering to the cobbled path, more glass tinkling.

"There went the front window," called Rufus as they fled. "I suggest picking up our pace."

It was hard to keep one's head in a chase situation such as this, thought Mary Ann. More so, when your pursuer had a hatchet and might separate head from neck at any time.

They reached the Unbirthday crowd again. The group was in the middle of a rather chaotic water ballet presentation involving dodos, ducks and other waterfowl in a Royal pool. The music wasn't quite timed to the movement, and none of it was timed to anyone else, so the twanging instruments and infernal squawking made concentration impossible. Mary Ann scanned for the Queen in the audience and spotted her forthwith. That lady had a bird's eye view of the entertainment from a high throne-like chair.

Mary Ann and Rufus were pushing through the onlookers, toward the Queen, when Twain shouted: "Look! There! It's that Mary-Ann-Alice person! Isn't she the one wanted for causing a mistrial in the stolen tarts case?"

And at a wave of his finger, everyone looked from him to the direction he pointed. Everyone around Mary Ann and Rufus stepped back six feet.

"It is!" cried Mr. Rabbit, for the first time ever recognizing his housemaid immediately. "She made an awful mess of our trial! And she wrecked my home!"

"And assaulted me!" shouted Bill Leafliver, the lizard handyman who still bore the slings and bandages of his outrageous misfortune.

"And got me sacked!" said a voice, and Mary Ann realized, it was *Celeste*, of all people. She was standing there with a woman who must have been her sister, for the resemblance was profound, and three small children, all like DwindleAde copies. And at this moment, the former lady's maid pulled a slip of paper from her pocket, holding it aloft. "And I have a list of her nefarious plans and nasty spying right here!"

Mary Ann cringed. So that's where her checklist had gone.

"You think that's bad," Mr. Milliner spoke up now, "she abandoned my friends and me right in the middle of our tea with… *no clean cups!*"

This was the offense that made the crowd cry out in horror.

The Duchess wasn't able to top any of that with her own story of abandonment. So instead she proclaimed, "And the moral of this is: not every servant is maid-to-order. Or a housemaid in hand is worth two in the bush."

And everyone agreed quite powerfully at this wisdom.

"Your Majesty," began Mary Ann, hoping to hasten things. She curtseyed before Queen Valentina. "I have important news to share with you about one of your court. We believe that Twain Morningstar is responsible for—"

But the crowd was already hastening in a different direction. "Grab her! Take her to the dungeon!" someone said.

"Take her to the gallows!" someone else shouted.

"Take her to the nearest wash basin! The teacups need scrubbing!" said Mr. Milliner.

"Son of a Bandersnatch," muttered Mary Ann for the second time today, and she thrust the box of pearls at Rufus. "Tell them everything," she said to him. "Explain as best you can."

And since she still had the poker, she batted her way through the crowd and took off running. She wasn't precisely sure where to go and it was hard to make sensible decisions about it when you had the population of two realms chasing you, demanding your skull and/or scullery skills.

She could make a break for Turvy, but that was unlikely to help. The whole Red Turvian guard wanted her for questioning in several murders. Was there enough value in turning herself in to them and telling them the whole story? Possibly, but it was hard to imagine D.I. and D.M. Tweedle ever being her saving grace. Things simply did not go that way in Turvy. The most she could do, she thought, was lose the crowd, find a good hiding place and stall long enough that Rufus had time to persuade Queen Valentina of the situation. That was her best option, and there were no guarantees there, either.

So she headed for the Queen's gardens. There were enough structures and topographical elements to make direct visibility hard for her pursuers, but less chance of being trapped somewhere with no way out. She ran past the croquet garden, over the ruts and furrows that made the game a challenge. She dodged through a rose garden, the roses all in varying shades of red, and twisted her foot a bit in one of two holes, where it looked like rose bushes had been removed rather hastily. She regained her bearings and was soon right back where it all began, Twain Morningstar's cottage. There was no back door there, so hiding in his home was hardly an option. Then she looked right, to the hedge maze.

She'd never done this maze and now was not the time to try it. Instead, she took several steps inside, removed her Turvian housemaid's cap and tossed it over her shoulder to the entrance. It rolled and settled believably in the threshold. Then she left the maze and headed into the vegetable garden.

It had been a good year for broccoli, for it stood twenty feet high and the florets, ten beyond that. The thicket stank a bit, though, and Mary Ann wondered if that alone would prevent her pursuers from poking about, should she choose to hide there. But it was too close to the castle, so she moved on. The cabbage yawned and stretched its leaves as she ran by. The corn asked why she was running and promised an ear to the ground. Some baby peas cried at being awakened so abruptly and Mary Ann paused to cradle and shush them before someone heard. Fortunately, they fell back asleep in but a moment.

By now, she'd reached the Queen's flower garden and it being a warm day, the flowers were all nodding their heads. Mary Ann was careful to slip through as quietly as she knew how. She came to a garden wall with a door, just her size, and she tried the knob, surprised to find it open. It led to a long hallway with a very tall, glass, three-legged table. Along the wall were doors…so many doors.

This, Mary Ann thought, *should make it hard for anyone following me this far. I'll choose a door at random and go in and hide for a spell. Then I'll pop out, find Rufus, and reevaluate.* So she closed her eyes, spun around and pointed. It seemed she'd chosen the third door from the end of the left side. It was a very large door, indeed. To reach the knob, she would need to be taller. Much taller.

But, being Turvian by birth and of Neath by trade, she knew well to keep a bite of Burgeonboosh with her whenever possible. And without pockets, she'd had to get creative about how that was done. She looked around modestly, fished down the neck of her dress, into her corset, and withdrew a handkerchief with a small, rather smashed quantity of the cake. Then, she thought, *Even if they find me momentarily and I'm extraordinarily large, they'll have to at least listen to what I say. Let's see them try to behead me if I'm twice their size. The most they'd manage is a good be-ankling.*

So she took the bite—it was warm—grew to a manageable size for door-opening and did so.

To her surprise, it proved to be a small room with stacked cases across the floor and garments on a rail hanging above her head. She took one look at one single garment of heavy velvet material, covered in hearts and encrusted with jewels, and it told Mary Ann precisely where she was.

I'm in some kind of storage for Queen Valentina! Heart racing, she started to return to the hall, planning to choose another door, but the hallway door booted her back inside and slammed shut behind her. It was perfectly dark in the room now and there was a grinding sound, the room vibrating. In a moment, the ceiling was starting to lower and the back wall pressed in. There was quickly becoming nowhere to go and so Mary Ann climbed onto trunks and ducked her head between clothes just to stay upright at all.

Finally, the movement stopped, and her fingers frantically searched for the doorknob to the hallway.

She was not entirely surprised that at some point, the knob had excused itself and vanished. She tried pressing on the wall, hoping it would give. It did not. She tried prying it open with the fire poker that, by now, was bruised into her hand. No, Neath construction was made most sound. Besides, even if she did get it open, she very much doubted it would lead to that same hallway. There wasn't much you could count on in this place. She thought it had made her a bit jaded.

All right, she thought, determined to cheer herself. *This is as good of a hiding place as any. Certainly no one would think to search the Queen's storage for me, since I would never think to hide here. All I need now is to lie low and see how the landscape has changed.*

So she sat on a trunk resting her head on a fur coat and thought about her next steps. If Queen Valentina believed Rufus' accusations, it would likely go to trial—ideal because it would at least confine Twain for a while. Mary Ann knew what the legal system was like in Neath. It was knee-jerk and easily distracted. So it would be very important to get out the points against Twain Morningstar as quickly and clearly as possible.

While the current evidence against Twain was largely circumstantial, it surely was enough to launch an investigation. The pearls, she thought, were compelling enough to prompt some very serious questions. Not to mention, Mary Ann and Rufus could both testify to Twain's motives firsthand, as he'd explained them. Mary Ann wasn't even the only one to see the figure who looked like Jacob Morningstar at Rowan Carpenter's home at the time of the murder. The trees saw him there, in pursuit of her with the murder weapon.

The oysters, too, should be brought in for questioning, Mary Ann thought. They shouldn't be allowed to shuck responsibility for their crimes. And with a little persuading, Mary Ann suspected at least some of them would crack under the pressure and confess.

She adjusted her head. The fur coat, she noticed, was soothingly warm and suddenly purry.

The coat said: "You do get invited into all the most interesting places, don't you?"

"Chester?" Mary Ann sat up. She couldn't see the eyes and smile in the dark, but she was sure the cat saw her.

"You've made this a very memorable Unbirthday party, that is for certain," he said. "I haven't had this much fun in ages. It's good to liven these things up from the usual obsequious tributes, don't you agree? It keeps Her Royal Wonderfulness from becoming complacent."

"Did you come from the party just now?" Mary Ann asked. "What's going on out there?"

"Oh, I don't think you'll like it," said the cat.

"Tell me, anyway."

The cat sighed. "They're still looking for you, you know, and Sir Rufus has been sent to the dungeon, in preparation of being beheaded. The gardener has convinced the Queen that you and the knight were in allegiance to rob him."

"Rob him! What would your average landscaper be doing with a huge box of loose pearls?"

"He said he was gardening and he found them growing in the field where the wild pigs dig for truffles."

"That's absurd! Why would pearls grow in a truffle field?"

"He claims it's a simple case of pearls before swine."

Mary Ann gritted her teeth and growled. "And the morel of this is, never trust a wild card."

"So what do you plan to do about it?" asked Chester.

"Free Rufus, of course," said Mary Ann. "I'm just not sure how to get down to the dungeon without being seen."

"You have your invisibility, do you not?"

"I'm not so sure I do any longer, Chester," she explained. "It's been spotty, of late. Everyone seems to be noticing me like mad these days."

"Ah yes," said the cat. "You've discovered your You. It happens to the best of us. And it's very hard to go back on one's own. You'll need a You suppressant to get you through, I fancy."

Mary Ann was only half-listening. "If I use DwindleAde, I can become so small perhaps no one will see me. But it'll take me forever to reach the dungeon. Each foot will feel like a mile. I'll never get there in time."

"The suppressant is nothing you eat or drink, my dear," said the cat. "It is what you feel about yourself. How did you feel when you first went invisible?"

Mary Ann considered this. It was never that she'd felt small or low. Mostly, she'd felt nothing. Like nothing she did to keep the household running was visible or that it couldn't be swapped out for the work of someone else equally transparent. That she was disconnected from everything that mattered, on a different plane of existence while life all moved around her. That her world was all Do and yet never Be. It was all Between. And that gave her an idea.

In a moment, she pressed on the wall opposite the one she'd entered, a door popped open and she saw she hadn't been hiding in a room at all; it was a standing wardrobe. She had also been in there so long, she must have shrunk back to her regular size, for everything outside the wardrobe appeared in reasonable proportion. She stepped from it and scanned the Queen's quarters. The King's chamber was to the left and the valet's leftward beyond that, so the maid's quarters were most likely to the right. In a moment she had gotten her hands on an extra maid's uniform from the court of Neath. She stripped off her Turvy clothes and put the new clothes on. They fit her illy.

They were perfect.

"I told you," said the cat, who was silently watching all this, "the suppressant is not a thing that can be eaten or worn. It—"

"Oh, I know. But this helps get me into the mindset." And she closed her eyes and thought back. Back to that first time in the Duchess' home with the sun streaming through the window and the Duchess' gaze streaming through Mary Ann. She thought about how she felt in that moment, that first time she faded away into the background.

"Oh, say, that is very good," said Chester. "You'll go far with that."

I only need to get as far as the dungeon, she thought, but did not say so. She didn't want to break the spell. She grabbed up her fire poker. And like a warm, spring breeze, she left the Queen's quarters.

The mindset got easier with every floor. As she passed the occasional guest returning to their chambers or servant running an errand, Mary Ann simply was not there. She was not there on the stairs down to the second floor, and she was nowhere down the steps to the first.

By the time she reached the corridor leading down to the dungeon, it was as if she had never been. So she was somewhat taken aback when she had almost completely walked past the two guards at the dungeon entrance, when out of the corner of her eye she saw one guard do a double take.

"Oy! Hold on a mo," said the guard, a mustachioed fellow with four clubs etched into his armor.

Mary Ann stopped and turned. She was nothing... Of no consequence... She was the cracks in the sidewalk... The space between the strings of a badminton racquet ... The mist at dawn...

He gestured. "What's that you got in your hand, girl?"

"Only a fire poker," she heard herself say.

"Oh." He gave her an unfocused look. "A fire poker." He turned to the other guard, a fellow in armor etched with eight clubs. "Can we let her in with a fire poker, Otto?"

Otto looked on the chart in his hands. "Knife ... cosh ... sword... mace..." He scratched his head. "It don't say nuffin' here about no fire pokers, Faw. On account of it not being a weapon. It's—what do you call it? —one of them household implements."

"Oh," said Faw again, considering the point and finding it quite reasonable. "Right. Okay, then."

Mary Ann gave him a smile, a nothingy smile, one he would forget the moment she was gone, and he smiled back.

Then she struck him on the head with the fire poker.

In a second, Otto was right there with the kind of incisive retort that befit his elite training in the Queen's Royal Guard. "Hey! You can't—"

She struck him, too. She took the key ring off of his unconscious form (and his belt), and rushed past the cells, peering into each one. There were a sizable number of people from the croquet game, several sadly raking their mallets along the bars. There was an assortment of waterfowl, who presumably hadn't impressed the Queen with their water ballet. There were mimes...

And there was Sir Rufus, who saw the housemaid, stood up and ran to the bars. "Mary Ann! How did you know I was here?"

"An old friend told me," she said. She began trying the keys.

"And do you know I'm now charged with robbing Twain Morningstar?" Rufus asked.

"I do." Key two was no good. She moved on to the third one.

"And did you know you're wanted for robbery, as well? So it's best you just leave now and forget all about me. My mother and father are aware of the situation—I told them everything—and they're appealing to Queen Rosamund to use her pull with Valentina to—"

"No good."

"You won't hear me out?"

"The key: it's no good," she said and tried the fourth one.

"I'm supposed to get a trial," he said hopefully.

"Oh yes, I've heard these trials are very efficient. Sentencing first, verdict afterwards," said Mary Ann. She heard a groan out of one of the guards, so she tried to speed things up a bit on the locksmith side of things.

"I did like my head," Rufus was saying now, wistfully touching his freckled face. "The way my chin was at just the right spot for propping it after a tiring day. And the way my hair showed an independence of spirit despite the will of a comb. Jolly self-possessed, it was. So brave."

Fifth key: no good.

"I liked my neck, too," he said, patting all around it. "It did such a cracking job holding up my head and nodding at things. It never let me down."

The guard was twitching awake now, so Mary Ann rushed over and gave the fellow a quick touch-up in the fire poker department, and his partner one for good measure, then it was back to the keys.

"It's a shame I'll never get to quest for the Vorpal sword now," Rufus mused. "If only that infernal faerie had let me pick it up when we were there. But that's epics for y—"

"Ah!" said Mary Ann, and the cell door swung open. "You can stop writing yourself off now. Come along."

They headed toward the door and all of the prisoners began shouting, "Free me!"

"And me!"

"I didn't do nuffin' wrong!"

"Nor I!"

"I did," said someone Mary Ann couldn't make out in the darkness of the cell. "I did right turrible things. But I'll say I didn't, if you'll let me out."

Mary Ann looked at the enormous ring of keys. "No time," she said, and tossed the ring their direction. It skidded to a stop outside of the first cell and the croquet players grabbed for it. "Sort it among yourselves!"

Mary Ann and Rufus stepped over the guards and dashed up the dungeon stairs. She was clearly not invisible now and unlikely to return to that state any time soon.

"My parents were meeting the Red Queen in the rose garden to discuss the issue," said Rufus, as they ran down the hall to the back door. "If we could get to them and plead our case to her, perhaps—"

From where they were, it sounded like much of the search party was in the hedge maze. Mary Ann suspected this based on the shouting and thumping coming from that direction. And it didn't sound like they were entirely sure how to get out.

"It's this way, I know it!" came one voice.

"No, that way! I thought I saw a sign," said another.

"My sense of direction is impeccable and it's upways. We'll just get a ladder and climb over the hedge."

"And where do you keep your ladder? In your waistcoat pocket?"

Rufus laughed but Mary Ann was more interested in reaching the rose garden. Fortunately, Lord and Lady Carmine were there with Queen Rosamund, as planned.

"Your Majesty," said Mary Ann, stopping short in a breathless curtsey that almost sent Rufus crashing into her. "If you have a moment…Sir Rufus and I have information that's vital to solving the crimes that have recently swept Red Turvy. And the accusations against us have been levied by one of the very parties responsible. We have learned that—"

"Queen Rosamund may feel she has a moment," said a high,

chilly voice, "but you two do not!" Queen Valentina stood at the garden entrance, chin up and pointing at the two fugitives. "Off with their heads!" she screamed.

The problem with this plan was that the bulk of her guard, including her executioner, was in the hedge maze.

A voice said, "Er, soon as we can, Your Majesty."

"On our way. Maybe," said another.

"Well, fine," snapped Valentina, "I shall take care of this myself." And from behind her back, she drew the magic axe.

"Your Majesty," said Rufus, as quickly as he could, "please let us explain. Mary Ann saw someone who looked like your valet, Jacob Morningstar, behead her father, Rowan Carpenter, a craftsman of Turvy and notorious shellfish-lover. Since then, Carpenter's business partner and thirty raths — all renowned oyster fanciers — each died recently under suspicious circumstances. The Two of Clubs, Twain Morningstar, as you know, has wild card capabilities and does the perfect impression of his second cousin; we saw it today. We also found in his possession a large number of pearls. We believe these were given to him by the oysters of Turvy, as payment for the murder of their greatest enemies." He took a deep breath to replenish all that had been lost, and he looked to Mary Ann. "Did I miss anything?"

"Yes," said Mary Ann. "That is Twain Morningstar."

22

The person who looked like Queen Valentina rushed at them, axe swinging. Mary Ann tried to block the first strike with the fire poker, but the axe ripped right through it with a zingy, metallic sound. Mary Ann dodged out of the way. Lord and Lady Carmine screamed and hid behind a trellis. Queen Rosamund was completely unruffled. She remained stiffly seated, a look of distaste on her face. "Valentina, dear, this behavior does not become you!"

"Any ideas?" asked Mary Ann of the knight.

"What I wouldn't do for a Vorpal sword right about now," said Rufus.

Mary Ann spied a number of stones in a flowerbed and gathered two of the largest, pitching them at the heart-clad figure. The first rock missed, but the second struck the Queen's shoulder. Valentina let out a yelp, but didn't drop the axe. Rufus saw Mary Ann was onto a good thing and followed suit, gathering what rocks he could and pitching them in a bruising shower.

"How dare you assault a Queen!" said the impostor, trying to shield his face from the rain of rocks. Hitting them with the axe reduced them to a cloud of dust and pebbles. "Now come here and present your heads like proper subjects."

By now a group of Unbirthday revelers had arrived to see the source of the commotion. "Seize them!" said the fake Queen, and Mary Ann was grabbed by Mr. Milliner, his knobby hands firmly planted on her shoulders. He smelled like over-steeped tea and felt stiffener.

He said, "You slipped away once, didn't you, girl? But it won't happen again."

She saw Rufus had been seized by a gryphon, its talons screeching against the knight's metal shoulder plates.

"Very nice!" said the fake Queen. "And now, we will be done with this charade once and for all."

She stepped forward with the axe.

"Charades? Ooh, I do love a good game of charades! Count me in…" came a high, buoyant voice. Then, in a heartbeat, the voice had grown cold and suspicious. "Hold one moment…" And on to angry, "Who is this?!" The speaker was, in fact, Queen Valentina.

The false queen turned. "Why, I'm…" Morningstar certainly did think fast, "you, of course."

"Impossible!" Queen Valentina said. "I'm me. I've been quite myself all day. Also, I've had rave reviews to the effect that I am 'incomparable,' the 'one and only.' So what is this about?"

"Haven't you heard of someone being beside themselves?" Twain Morningstar asked.

"Well…" the Queen considered this, "yes…"

"This is what it looks like."

"Don't believe him! That is Twain Morningstar," shouted Mary Ann, "imitating you and trying to kill us because I saw him murder my father, Rowan Carpenter."

"He also killed a prominent Turvy business man and a neighborhood of raths," said Rufus.

"Nonsense," said Queen Valentina, though she didn't sound entirely sure.

"I did hear their story," said Queen Rosamund rising and stepping forward, "and it would go a long way toward explaining some little death issues we've had in our realm lately."

"Oh, we're not going to let these thieves and prevaricators distract us with lies, are we?" asked Morningstar. "We're far too intelligent to fall for that."

"We are very bright," agreed Queen Valentina.

"We should just execute them," Morningstar said. "We've spent too much of our valuable time on this already."

"We are quite busy," said Queen Valentina. "And I hear there's a game of charades going on somewhere. I'm splendid at charades. I win every game."

"Exactly. We have better things to do. And they've put a gorrible damper on our Unbirthday festivities. This is our day and they're making it all about themselves. It's so selfish! We only get five or six of these major Unbirthday bashes a year."

"Too true," said Valentina. "I hate it when things are supposed to be about me and other people insist on stepping into the spotlight with murder accusations and things."

"Your Majesty," Mary Ann said, "Twain Morningstar is posing as you and trying to manipulate you. If it's not him, then where is he? Shouldn't he be here somewhere?"

But Morningstar had an answer for that, too. He turned to the Queen. "We thought we heard him say he was very tired after that frabjous Unbirthday performance of his and he went inside to have a little nap."

"Quite understandable," said Valentina. "I once napped for three days after I performed in the play *Absinthe and Obsession*. Though that might have been because we used real absinthe on stage."

"If he's you," pressed Mary Ann, "then have him prove it. Ask him something only you would know."

"We hardly see a need for that," said Morningstar, tightening his grip on the axe. "It's just another distraction to steal our attention."

"Please, Your Majesty! Who knows you better than you?" Mary Ann said.

"Oh, very well," sighed Queen Valentina. "Something

personal…Something only I would know…" She thought very hard for a moment, then beamed. "Yes, I've got it!" She turned to Twain Morningstar. "What is our favorite color?"

Mary Ann winced.

"Uh…" Morningstar looked at the roses, at the castle, at Queen Valentina's gown. "Red?"

Queen Valentina gasped and stepped back. "It's crimson! Crimson is our favorite color! How could you not know that?"

"But … but … they're the same thing!" said Morningstar. "They're syno—"

"Red is lowbrow, boorish and pedestrian!" shouted Queen Valentina. "Crimson is tasteful, elegant and sumptuous! They're miles apart!"

The Red Queen, Rosamund, gave a sour twist of her mouth.

But Valentina was pointing and shrieking. "Betrayer! Impersonator! OFF WITH HIS HEAD!"

It was at this moment that a few of the guards had finally stumbled out of the hedge maze and leapt into action. Though the leap was short because they saw two Queen Valentinas standing before them and they were fairly sure that was one surplus to requirement.

"Seize him!" shouted Queen Valentina, pointing, thus helping them along in their thought processes.

Morningstar realized the impersonation wasn't doing him any good now, anyway, and he changed back to his Deuce image. "It was just a bit of fun, Your Majesty," cried Twain frantically, as the guards surrounded him. "Some lighthearted tomfoolery for your Unbirthday."

"Executioner!" Valentina shouted.

But before the executioner could lumber over, Twain Morningstar had swung the axe at the guards, slicing the hand off one fellow and the tip of the nose off another. Indeed, the deck had been cut and the wild card disappeared into the crowd.

"After him!" Valentina shouted.

"How will we know him?" one of the guards asked. "He could be anyone."

"He'll always be the one with the axe," said Mary Ann.

And the uninjured guards recognized the truth of this and went in pursuit.

"And as for you two," said Queen Valentina to Mary Ann and Rufus. "You have pursued justice against the odds. You have been resourceful and clever. Those are qualities I prefer having attributed to me. So as of now, our history books regarding this incident will say I'm the one who solved this whole thing. And what I'll need from you is a sworn statement to the details I learned and how I went about it all."

"Well, you see, Your Majesty," began Mary Ann, "It's like this—"

"No, no. Don't tell me." She put up a hand. "I can't be bothered with all that, I'm very busy. Tell it to my historian," she gestured to an owl that stepped forward with a quill and paper. "I'll read about all the wonderful things I did later."

An unnervingly short moment had passed before the guards came running back, one of them carrying a rather bloody magic axe.

"Well?" asked Queen Valentina. "Where is he? Did you find him? You're not him, are you?" She indicated the one with the axe. "Repetitive gags are boring, you know."

"Found, Your Majesty," said the guard, poking awkwardly at the ground with his boot. "And then, er, subsequently lost. On account of, there was a bit of an accident..."

"Am I going to be happy?" asked Queen Valentina, her rosy lips a tight, irritated bud. "I don't like not being happy."

"Er..."

"And I can't say most others like it when I'm not happy, either," she said. "It's a point we share."

"... Or rather, to say, there was a bit of an axe ident," continued that guard slowly, "as the fellow was running with the axe, and he tripped into a hole where one them white rosebushes once was, that we ripped out, that nobody got round to replacing yet, and what I'm trying to say is... Twain Morningstar dented himself quite thoroughly with the magical weapon in question."

Valentina peered at the guard over folded arms. "Are you saying he's dead?"

"I am saying he is not of the existentially present," said the guard.

"All right then," she said. "Bring me the body!"

"Can do," said the guard. "Which parts would you like, Your Majesty?"

She blinked. "Parts?"

"George," he turned to another guard, "we're going to need a burlap sack. Or three. Four."

"Um," said the Queen. "Okay, hold just a moment there, George. I have quite changed my mind. The Royal Mind has been changed! Do not bring me the body. Here is what you shall do."

"Yes, Your Majesty?"

"He's already in a hole, is he not?"

"Yes, Mum."

"Then leave him there and shovel the thing in." As the guards scrambled off to do as ordered, she noticed Jacob Morningstar's anguished expression and she went to him, arms extended. "Oooh," she cooed, "I am sorry about your cousin, Jacky." She patted his face. "But these things happen. Who hasn't lost a beloved relative to the odd self-axing?"

The valet nodded but he didn't look very bucked-up by it.

"Now," Valentina said, turning back to the group, "once my historian gets down the tale of my heroic detective work in solving the Turvy murders, I shall need my playwright to whip me up a nice performance piece about it—a simple three acts will do prettily. I'll need that jar of pearls of Twain Morningstar's brought to me as a necklace — er, evidence. Evidence. And I'll need this Alice-Mary-Ann person here—" she gestured to the housemaid, "beheaded for the damages to Harold's house—"

"Herald," mumbled Warren Rabbit.

"— And also for enbiggening in the middle of my tarts trial, then vanishing before telling us anything of use. I daresay that threw off my whole week!"

"But that wasn't me at all!" said Mary Ann.

"That's right," said Rufus. "I was with her when the trial was going on, so it couldn't be her."

At this, the Queen's expression softened. "Is that true? Oh, my goodness ..." She rested a hand on his arm, a sweet, surprised smile on her lips. "You were with her, were you, dear?"

Rufus nodded. "Yes, Your Majesty. For some hours."

"Well, now, I'm so glad you mentioned it," she said warmly. "Thank you ever so much, Sir Rufus. You're a dear fellow for speaking up like that. For that changes my view of things significantly."

Mary Ann felt her shoulders start to relax.

"Accomplices so rarely confess. This was really quite refreshing. Still—" she shrugged, "—your head goes, too. Seize them! Make them comfy! Get my story out of them! Then behead them!"

Mary Ann was very tired of running. It was, perhaps, too much of a good thing, she thought, as she and Rufus fled the scene. She could hear Lord and Lady Carmine making another plea on their behalf, but there was no reason to stick around to learn the results. Especially when beheadings were distributed like show leaflets. It was a wonder there was anyone left in the land to behead.

"Come along," shouted Rufus, motioning, with a glance at the dimming sky. "This way!"

Mary Ann said, "But where are we going?"

"The stables!" he said and they tore across the field. "We'll get the horses and go to Turvy. It will be dark in an hour. We can lose them there."

"Lolly's no match for the guards' horses," called Mary Ann. "You go. Take Goodspeed. I'll figure out something."

"Then we'll steal a second horse," he told her. "Or you can ride with me."

"You won't make good time with both of us riding Goodspeed," yelled Mary Ann.

And a moment later, they burst through the stable doors.

Mary Ann slammed them shut again and barred the entrance while Rufus scanned the horses.

"You," he said to a horse breathlessly. It was a beautiful chestnut creature with a black tail and mane. "How would you like a new employer?"

"Well, I don't know, do I?" said the horse. "What are the benefits? What are the hours? Is it farm work or carriage-pulling? Are saddles involved or is it bareback? How many times a week will there be sugar? I'll need to see this in writing and have my solicitor—"

"All right. How about you then?" Rufus asked a white stallion.

"I work for the White Knight, Sir Albin," it said. "I couldn't betray him like that, poor fellow. He needs me."

"You?" Rufus asked a sleek black horse.

"I only just got here," sighed the horse, looking tired. "I've been running all day."

Mary Ann said, "Rufus, please... Just go saddle Goodspeed. I'll deal with this."

Someone was banging on the stable doors now. A voice said, "It's locked somehow! They've locked us out!"

"Well, break it down!" came the Queen's voice.

"What with?"

"You fools!" screamed the Queen. "We have a magic axe, you know!"

"Hey, yeah!" someone said, like this was a novel idea. "We do have that magic axe, don't we? ...Only, where's it got to?"

"I dunno," said someone else. "Otto had it last. Otto: where'd you put that magic axe Twain Morningstar had?"

"Haste, haste," Mary Ann demanded, feeling like Rufus' horse-saddling business was happening in slow motion. "They're looking for the axe."

"I heard them. Hasty is my middle name," said Rufus, gathering the saddle and bridle. "I'm kidding, though. It's Clancy."

But Mary Ann wasn't in the mood to joke; she was busy thinking of next steps. She realized that while the pack of the

Queen's Guards was shuffling all around them wanting their heads, it was probably not the ideal time be in uffish thought about one's career goals. But such were the questions twirling about in Mary Ann's head now.

She was a liability if she stayed with Lord and Lady Carmine as a maid. And she'd burned so many bridges in terms of her employability today. She was by no means artistically talented like her father. And sales from his remaining stock wouldn't last for long. Aside from being a housemaid, she was good at but one thing. One thing that hadn't happened yet—her formal sword training. She remembered the trainer's name: Cornelius Clashammer.

She recalled where the other Red Knight had said he lived: in Thither.

And Mary Ann could think of one innovative way someone could get to Thither very, very quickly.

Sort of.

"All right," said Rufus, mounting Goodspeed. "Let's go. Where's your horse?" He looked around.

"I'm not taking one," she said.

"Well, you don't think I'm going to let you run along behind me? That's just...rude."

"I'm not going with you to Turvy," she said. "I'm going to finish my training. In Thither. If I don't complete it, it's highly possible your whole Jabberwock epic will be undone. I can't let that happen. Besides," she tugged at her collar, "I really could use a career change."

"Even so," he persisted, "you'll still need a horse. So get a move on."

She remained planted. "There is an alternative way to Thither, you know."

For a split second, his face was all confusion. Then he groaned. "Oh, not that bloody mirror again! It's as much as useless, remember? We don't know how to activate it."

The voices outside: "Did Otto find it? He did? ...What do you mean, he put it in the toolshed?...Yes, I know it is, but..."

"I was thinking about it," Mary Ann continued, "and I was

trying to recall exactly what the glazier said when I asked how the mirror worked."

"You'd said there was some right word you utter and it lets you go through... I *know* ... We've been over this. Can we just get out of here? There's no —"

"Exactly," said Mary Ann. "That's exactly what the glazier said. But I think now that it's not what she meant ... Maybe."

Rufus hissed, "Mary Ann Carpenter, are you willing to risk your neck on Maybe?"

"Worlds have been built on maybes," said Mary Ann.

Rufus looked from her, to the rattling door, and sighed. "Last I saw the mirror, it was propped against the gifts table with the rest of Queen Valentina's Unbirthday loot. You do realize that once you get there, you're going to have mere minutes to say this mysterious right word and to go through. If you're wrong, there is no room for error."

"I know," she said.

"All right," he said.

She blinked. "You're not going to talk me out of it?"

He smiled. "Has that ever worked?"

And she realized at that moment, he really did see her.

"Right," he said, slinging on his helmet and taking the reins. "Goodspeed and I will help you get to the mirror. After that, it's all up to you."

She nodded. "When you get to Turvy, tell Douglas Divot he can have anything in my father's workshop. Whatever he wants."

"The excitement might kill him."

Mary Ann moved to the door. "And when your parents return, please tell them I'm so sorry. About everything. Explain to your mother. They were very kind to me." She quietly removed the bar across the door handles, then ran back and joined Rufus on Goodspeed.

"One..." said Rufus.

"I hope you know what you're doing, Sir," said Goodspeed, eyeing the doors.

"Two ..."

Cheers came from outside. "Yay, Otto's got the axe! Now come here and put some muscle into it!"

"Three!" Mary Ann, Rufus and Goodspeed all shouted.

The axe made its first contact with the unbarred door. And to the surprise of everyone outside the stable — including and especially Otto — the stable doors burst wide open, a horse with two riders blasting through like a leggy cannonball.

It was instant mayhem. Guards went flying backwards. Mr. Rabbit let out a high-pitched scream. Mr. Milliner lost his hat.

Mary Ann found it all strangely satisfying.

The trio rounded up to the festival area at a full gallop, tearing across the long field before Goodspeed finally slowed alongside the gift table. The mirror, given its size and color, was easy enough to spot.

Jumping down from the horse, Mary Ann peered over her shoulder and saw the crowd far across the field, barreling toward them.

"Now it's your turn to be hasty," said Rufus, flipping up his visor, worry spilled across his face.

"Hasty is my middle name," she said, flashing him a nervous smile. "Actually, you know it already. It's Ann." She took a deep breath and approached the mirror.

Meanwhile, Goodspeed was raring to go. "Please, Sir," he begged. "We've no time."

"In a minute," snapped Rufus.

"Think of my mare and foals back home, Sir."

"You haven't got a mare and foals," said the knight.

"True, but I'm a planner," insisted the horse.

Mary Ann grabbed onto the mirror frame. Oh yes, this was the moment. And if her intuitions were right, it was all absurd. And completely mad. And a bit stupid. So, it was unquestionably the very best shot she had.

In a clear, bold voice, Mary Ann Carpenter — housemaid, current fugitive and, with any luck, future swordfighter — announced to the realm: "The Right Word."

Rufus and Goodspeed both groaned, with Rufus giving her an additional: "Great gryphons, woman! That was your Maybe?

If I'd known that, I would never, ever, not for one single, solitary moment have —"

But his words fell away, for the mirror surface was growing wavy and a new landscape was forming within it. This was one of sharp mountain peaks and trees with leaves of orange, purple and gold.

"Goodbye, Rufus," she said, for the angry mob was closing in now. And what they may have lacked in smarts, or good sense, or physical coordination, they more than made up for in drive and determination. She reached out and squeezed his hand. "Be well."

"And you." For a man with a freshly-found sense of humor, his face was all seriousness. "Will I see you again?"

"Quest for your Vorpal sword," she told him. "And after — if you should wonder and dither whether to wander yet further ... to Thither ...?" She smiled and left it at that.

Thither awaited. And it was a whole new world of Maybes.

ABOUT THE AUTHOR

Jenn Thorson is a marketing writer by day and an author by night — so sort of like Batgirl, but with less crime fighting and more carpal tunnel. She lives in Pittsburgh, PA, with two curious cats, one of whom smiles but is not from Cheshire. Her stories have been published in the *Humor Press*, the journal for the *Lewis Carroll Society of North America*, *The Timber Creek Review* and *Romantic Homes* magazine. Her humorous sci-fi book trilogy is called *There Goes the Galaxy* and is available at Amazon.

IF YOU ENJOYED THIS BOOK...

The Curious Case of Mary Ann is an independently published novel. So if you enjoyed this book, the author would be frabjously excited if you'd tell your own mad crew about it.

One way to help is by reviewing the book on **Amazon.com**. Amazon ranks its books, in part, by the number of customer reviews a book receives. So you can help *The Curious Case of Mary Ann* reach *even more* eyeballs by going to Amazon online, searching for the book and creating your own review.

You can also:

- "Like" the Jenn Thorson author page on **Facebook**, for regular book news and author updates at: **Facebook.com/jennthorsonauthor**

- Visit **jennthorson.com** to check out news articles and goodies related to her books

- Follow the author, Jenn Thorson, on **Twitter** at **Twitter.com/Jenn_Thorson**

22487121R00137

Printed in Great Britain
by Amazon